PALETTE OF BLOOD

The Basilica Diaries
Book Two

Richard Kurti

SAPERE
BOOKS

PALETTE OF BLOOD

Published by Sapere Books.

24 Trafalgar Road, Ilkley, LS29 8HH

saperebooks.com

ISBN: 978-1-80055-945-5

PART ONE

1: BLOOD

Rome, 1503

The painting astonished Rome from the moment it was unveiled; perhaps that's why the murderer selected it.

Salvator Mundi was enormous: twelve feet high and eight wide, it had filled the entire west wall of lawyer Antonio Ricardo's Grand Salon, dominating the space. As you creaked open the carved mahogany doors and entered, the spiritual impact was immense: Christ emerging from the darkness, his right hand raised in benediction, his left holding a celestial orb, his mournful eyes looking at you with enigmatic sorrow.

Divine Forgiveness seemed to emanate from the painting and touch all who gazed upon it.

The chattering classes agreed that with this one work, Vito Visconti had finally proved himself to be a Great Artist. Ricardo, the patron who commissioned the masterpiece, couldn't have been more delighted. Like a peacock strutting his feathers, the lawyer had demonstrated his worth and status to the whole of Rome; he was a man of importance.

Until the killer struck.

The first week of Advent had brought some welcome relief to the onerous daily routines of the housemaid Rosetta. She still had to get up at dawn to clean and relight all the fires in the great townhouse, but because Padrone Ricardo was making a big display of piety in the run-up to Christmas, there were no overnight guests or supper parties to worry about. Of course, that would all change on the 24th, when three weeks of fasting and prayer would give way to decadence and wanton indulgence with no expense spared; Padrone Ricardo wanted his parties to be the most talked about in Rome.

Best not worry about that now, Rosetta thought as she trudged up the stairs carrying a heavy bucket of kindling in one hand and an iron ash box in the other; *just enjoy the calm while it lasts*. If she was lucky, she might even be able to grab a little time off to visit her mother before the social frenzy began.

As she reached the main landing, Rosetta put down her load and paused for a moment to rub the pins and needles from her fingers. She watched her breath condense in the feeble dawn light that dribbled through the high windows.

Six fires lit, four to go, she thought. She hoped there was enough kindling to go round, or it would mean another trip to the cellars, and she really didn't fancy that.

But as Rosetta bent down to pick up the buckets, she noticed a red stain seeping out from under the doors of the Grand Salon. It looked like spilled wine, maybe from the night before. She sighed and shook her head; Padrone Ricardo must have snuck down to the pantry in the night when all the servants were asleep, and drunk himself into a stupor. He was probably fast asleep in the leather armchair right now, bottles of spilled wine at his feet.

So much for piety.

The housemaid reached out to the door handles, then hesitated. What if the master wasn't alone? What if he'd woken in the night overcome with lust, and summoned one of his favourite courtesans? The last thing Rosetta wanted to see at this time in the morning was her master's scrawny white arse, but if she missed out the fires in the Grand Salon, the house would never warm up and she'd earn a beating from the Head Steward.

What to do?

She looked at the trickle of red wine under the door … and felt a shiver of dread. Wasn't the stain too thick for wine?

Rosetta bent down and touched the fluid with her fingers; it felt warm and slippery. She sniffed it … and recognised the metallic tang.

This wasn't wine, it was blood.

What had happened on the other side of those doors?

Quickly she yanked the handles down, pushed the doors open … and froze.

Rosetta's mind struggled to understand what her eyes were seeing. Nothing made sense. Familiar things were scattered across the floor, but everything was in the wrong place.

A hand.

A foot.

A head.

An arm.

Bits of the master's favourite painting.

All jumbled up.

And why was there so much blood?

Rosetta screwed her eyes shut, then snapped them open again.

And suddenly she understood what she was looking at.

Her master's body had been hacked to pieces: feet, hands and intestines were strewn across the polished marble floor; swirls of blood were daubed around the body parts, framing them with colour the way a child smears paint across a page.

Interspersed with the body parts were fragments of the vandalised *Salvator Mundi*: Christ's hand had been wedged between Ricardo's bloodstained buttocks, the ragged piece of canvas containing the celestial orb had been placed in the middle of the chaos and stuck to the floor with blood; shards of the heavy gilt frame were repurposed as stakes and driven into what was left of the lawyer's torso.

The only things that seemed to make any sense were the heads. The painted face of Our Lord had been cut from the canvas and tied around Ricardo's face like a bloody mask. Tied with strips of the lawyer's own skin.

It was an atrocity. A desecration. A blasphemy.

Rosetta's stomach retched and she vomited in the doorway, adding the stench of sour milk and half-digested bread to the chaos.

2: TIME

Cristina Falchoni held her breath to steady her fingers as she delicately oiled the verge-and-foliot clock in her library. Using a long needle, she dropped a single tear of lubricant (distilled from boiled whale blubber) into each of the oil-sinks, then watched the mechanism draw the fluid into its beating metal heart. "That should keep you running smoothly for the rest of winter," she whispered.

As Cristina closed the cabinet that protected the clock from dust, she caught her reflection in the glass door: unruly black hair framed her pale, finely sculpted face. She was thirty-one and had waited six long years for a second chance; now the moment had arrived.

Her focus shifted from her reflection to the ticking mechanism, and Cristina wondered what had aged better: her, or the clock?

The previous summer she had replaced the escape wheel because the teeth had started to wear, causing the pallet to slip, mistiming the seconds, but ever since the timepiece had been as good as new. Could the same be said of her?

Cristina had been braced for grey hairs when she turned thirty, and she'd even bought a special pair of tweezers to manage the situation, but so far they had remained in their leather case. Many young women in Rome fretted about getting older, and the anxiety often drove them to plaster their faces in Venetian ceruse, inadvertently making them look older still as well as deathly pale. Cristina refused to indulge in such vanities. Cleopatra had bathed in sour milk, Cristina bathed in the river of knowledge; perhaps both approaches could be effective in staying young.

There was a knock at the library doors and Isra entered. "Professor De Luca is here, mistress."

Cristina smiled; it still jarred to hear Isra address her so formally. Their friendship had deepened over the years but both women agreed that in public it was important to keep up the pretence of mistress and housekeeper. The deception had proved useful on numerous occasions, from catching out dishonest tradesmen, to negotiating a better price with suppliers, to being alerted to scandals before they broke; and with the 'Great Project' now resurrected, Cristina knew it was vital to have ears everywhere. "Thank you, Isra. Show him in."

"Very good, mistress."

As usual, the professor bowled into the room in a chaotic flurry of books, plans and lists. "Clear a space, Cristina!" he exclaimed, hurrying towards the large table that ran the length of the library. "I nearly dropped this lot halfway across the Piazza!"

Hurriedly, Cristina moved a pile of books, and De Luca plonked all his papers down. "Basta!" he gasped, and started mopping the sweat from his brow. All those years of exquisite dining at Sapienza University had given the professor a distinctive paunch, but he was probably the least vain man in Rome, and whenever Cristina had suggested a diet, he would reply, "What's the point of being at the finest university in Europe if you don't dine like a king?" His logic was hard to dispute.

"I'm astonished the Pope has acted so quickly," De Luca said as he stuffed the handkerchief back into his robe and made himself comfortable at the table. "Thirty-seven days.

That's how long he's sat on the Papal throne, and already we're making huge progress."

"I think Pope Julius II is going to be the answer to our prayers," Cristina replied, pouring De Luca a large sherry.

"What's he like? As a man?"

Cristina reflected on the few occasions she had come across Julius when he was a cardinal. "I've not seen it, but they say he has a violent temper."

"Well, that could help us," De Luca shrugged. "Those are precisely the sort of men who get things done."

"He is also fiercely ambitious. Pope Julius is determined that the authority of the Holy See will be displayed in majestic buildings."

"Perfect," De Luca smiled. "My type of Pontiff."

"And he is clearly impatient," Cristina added.

No-one could deny that; on the first day of his election Julius had issued a challenge to leading artists to design a new St Peter's Basilica, barely a month later he published the shortlist.

"A period of greatness is coming, Cristina. I can feel it. And you and I will be part of it."

"So, what have you discovered about the competing designs?"

"Nothing." The professor rummaged in his documents and retrieved a leather folio. "They're all being very secretive. But I have put together some notes about the artists."

Cristina sat next to De Luca as he laid out the pages neatly.

"Now, the Medici family are championing Sangallo. He is a strong candidate. He's built everything from villas to monasteries, and he was Lorenzo de' Medici's favourite architect."

Cristina's eyes scanned the list of buildings designed by Sangallo. "These are good."

"The Sforzas are throwing their weight behind Bramante. He's not nearly as prolific, and he's the oldest of the artists, but he did design the Tempietto, which they say the new Pope loves."

"And I know for a fact that Cardinal Riario is allied to the Sforza family," Cristina noted, "so that gives them influence inside the Vatican."

Professor De Luca picked up the next sheet of paper. "This one is something of a dark horse. Vito Visconti is being championed by the Colonna family."

"I thought Visconti was primarily a painter?"

"He is. But he's a painter everyone wants to commission. His admirers believe there is nothing Visconti cannot do, that he has been touched with genius."

"If genius is required, why isn't Leonardo da Vinci's name on the list?"

"He is the Orsini family's favourite. But Da Vinci's a risk. He has a worrying habit of leaving things half finished, which raises the question, does he have the staying power to build a great basilica?"

"Surely, Professor, there is no finer engineer in Europe?"

"Only if he turns up."

Cristina studied the sheets of paper. "Just these four?"

"That is the list from which the architect will be chosen, and I really think any of these artists would create a striking St Peter's."

But trusting to chance was not something Cristina believed in. "Professor, we must make it our urgent mission to ensure that only the most brilliant design wins."

De Luca blinked. "Surely that is in the Pope's hands now?"

"That is certainly what he believes. But I don't think it has to be that simple."

There was an urgent knock at the door and Isra entered the library. "Sorry to interrupt, mistress, but a letter's been delivered."

"We're a little busy. I'll deal with it later."

"It's from Signor Sabbia."

Immediately Cristina looked up. "What did you say?"

"Signor Sabbia has delivered a letter."

"Sabbia? You're sure?" Cristina could see the alarm in Isra's eyes.

"He said it was important, mistress."

Cristina understood the coded message and stood up. "I'm sorry, Professor, can we resume tomorrow?"

"But, but … we've only just begun."

"You can leave all your papers here. They'll be quite safe."

"Perhaps I could wait?"

But Cristina was already at the doors. "Isra will show you out. Forgive me, but this must be attended to."

"Why? What's happened? Can I help?" he called after her, but there was no reply.

Cristina hurried down the stairs, through the front doors and was gone.

Time was of the essence, because 'Signor Sabbia' was the trigger phrase signalling that the most shocking of crimes had just taken place.

3: JURISDICTION

"I hope you're braced for an argument!" Domenico Falchoni called over his shoulder as the two men rode north along the right bank of the Tiber, heading towards the Piazza del Popolo.

"Argument about what, sir?" Deputato Tomasso replied.

"Protocols. Jurisdiction. Anything the City Watch can think of."

"They're going to be disappointed. We answer to the Holy Father. No-one outranks him in Rome."

"Except God."

"But He doesn't really intervene in criminal investigations, does He, sir."

"Not yet, Tomasso. But we live in hope."

Tomasso didn't know quite how to reply. Tuning in to his boss's dry sense of humour had been one of the many challenges Tomasso faced after being promoted to Deputy of the Apostolic Guard. Before then, he had only seen the disciplinarian side of Domenico, a man who took leading the Vatican's security force very seriously. Yet the moment he became Deputato, Tomasso found himself treated more as a confidante than a subordinate. It was a delicate friendship and he was careful to avoid overfamiliarity.

They dismounted in Via dell'Oca, tied their horses to a railing, and looked up at Ricardo's grand townhouse. Five storeys high, nine windows wide, the terracotta façade adorned with elegantly carved porticos and balustrades, this was a residence that demanded respect.

"There's no such thing as a poor lawyer, is there Tomasso?"

"No, sir. They're either rich, or hacked to death."

"What a choice."

Domenico led the way through the arched entrance and into a cobbled courtyard, where the servants were huddled together, shivering in the drizzle. A few were worried about their murdered master, most were wondering how they would find another job so close to Christmas.

"Get inside!" Domenico instructed. "Warm yourselves up."

"They told us to wait here, sir," Rosetta replied. "And not to touch anything."

"'They' being the City Watch, I assume?"

"Yes, sir."

"Well, I'm in charge now. And I don't want you freezing to death."

The servants exchanged wary glances, unsure who to believe.

"Off you go!" Tomasso commanded. "If we need you, we'll find you."

The servants shuffled uneasily towards the warmth of the kitchens, while Domenico and Tomasso headed in the opposite direction, up three flights of white marble steps, until they came to the mahogany doors leading to the Grand Salon. Immediately the guard saw them, he called back into the room, "Sir! They're here!"

Moments later the sergeant of the Watch appeared, his jowls quivering defiantly. "Turn around and go home!"

"Not exactly a warm welcome," Domenico smiled.

"This is none of your business."

"I wouldn't be so sure."

"City murder. City Watch. End of discussion."

"And yet…" Domenico reached into his jacket and pulled out a legal document. "The Holy Father bought *Salvator Mundi* from Antonio Ricardo just three days ago. So it is very much a Vatican affair."

The sergeant snatched the bill of sale from Domenico's hand and studied it, desperately hunting for a reason to find it invalid.

"It bears the Holy Father's seal," Tomasso said. "In case you were wondering."

The sergeant glared at Tomasso.

"With the painting destroyed, and no chance of a refund from a dead man, Pope Julius is understandably anxious," Domenico explained. "So if you don't want to experience the Holy Father's notorious wrath at close quarters, I suggest you withdraw your men and hand this matter over to us."

"*Vaffanculo!*" The sergeant thrust the bill of sale at Domenico, then returned to the Grand Salon and started to round up his men.

Ten minutes later, Domenico and Tomasso had the crime scene to themselves. Yet the moment they entered the room, Domenico felt a twinge of regret about having fought so hard to take control of the case. This was a crime scene of demonic violence.

Domenico noticed that his deputy had gone very pale, and knew he had to get him out of the room before he fainted. "Seal off this entire wing of the house."

"Yes, sir."

"No-one is to come in without my express permission. And that includes the servants."

"Understood." Tomasso hurried away, grateful for the excuse to get some fresh air.

Slowly, Domenico turned in a circle, taking in the full madness of the killing … and his mind flashed back…

To Sorano, on the borders of the Papal States and the Republic of Siena…

To the sixty days his battalion had laid siege to the ancient hill town…

To the relentless artillery bombardment designed to break the will of everyone inside the walls…

To the chaotic horror the 'conquering heroes' found when the town finally surrendered.

Body parts.

Rubble.

Bloodstains.

Grief.

Incomprehension.

Artillery deconstructs reality with savage indifference … and the same was true of this room.

Domenico crouched down to study the lawyer's severed head, sickened by the care with which the murderer had cut long strips of skin from the victim's legs to create ribbons of flesh that now tied Christ's face to Ricardo's.

He heard footsteps returning. "Make sure this is kept in a very tight circle, Tomasso. I don't want details of this butchery spreading. Least of all to my sister. Who knows how she'd react?"

"She'd be alarmed. And rightly so."

Domenico spun round and saw Cristina standing in the doorway. "How did you find out so quickly?"

"Is that really the question to ask? When faced with this?" Her eyes darted across the madness of the killing floor.

"We shouldn't jump to conclusions, Cristina."

"Too late. And you know it." She picked her way across the floor, trying to make sense of the fragments of canvas and flesh. "This is no coincidence, Domenico."

"There are hundreds of reasons why someone would want to murder a lawyer."

"Not like this. Enemies kill lawyers in dark alleys, not by desecrating paintings of Christ."

"It still doesn't mean —"

"Open your eyes! A new Pope resurrects the plan to build a new St Peter's, then a few days later this happens! If this isn't a warning, then what is?" Cristina didn't mean to snap at her brother, but her guts were screaming at her that this atrocity was just the beginning, that things were going to spiral out of control, that the twin monsters of fear and unreason were going to devour them again, just as they had six years ago.

Domenico heard Cristina's breathing become shallow with anxiety. He crossed the room and stood directly in front of her. "We have to break this down and keep a clear head."

Cristina nodded, but her eyes were locked on the bloody remains.

Domenico took his sister's face in his hands and forced her to look at him. "Let's focus on the basics. Find out everything we can about the victim. Who were his enemies? Who stands to gain from killing him? And why do it like this? What does it symbolise?"

"I can work on those."

Domenico looked past Cristina to Tomasso who had just returned. "Get reinforcements here straight away. Look for signs of forced entry, question all the servants."

"Understood, sir."

"Has anything been stolen? Who had access to these rooms? What were the victim's movements leading up to his death? You know what needs to be done, Tomasso."

"Yes, sir." The Deputato hurried down the stairs to get the investigation moving.

Domenico looked at his sister. "Will you be all right?"

"Only when I have some answers."

"Then let's get to work."

4: AMERIGO

The Apostolic Guards had been well trained. They surged through the house with professional calm, each man knew exactly what he had to do and how his work fitted into the murder investigation.

With so many eyes focussed on the Grand Salon, Cristina decided to look in the opposite direction, and started wandering through the house on her own, trying to get a better sense of the victim.

Fine art hung everywhere. Newly commissioned and extravagantly displayed, Ricardo favoured painters from the Florentine school, but also owned a collection of Dürers that had been shipped from Nuremberg, as well as a disturbing depiction of Hell by Hieronymus Bosch. In pride of place were three paintings by Visconti that hung in the master bedroom, depicting the ancient Greek Muses; the lawyer was clearly a discerning follower of artistic fashion.

But there were no signs of family life anywhere in the house, no dressing rooms for women, no nurseries for children, and no parlours or music rooms for aunts. Everything in this building was dedicated to projecting an image of wealth and masculinity: huge terrestrial globes were positioned on each of the landings, *kilij* scimitars captured from Ottoman armies hung above the doors, and one salon had even been devoted to a display of embalmed animals. How ironic that the curator of all this violence should have suffered such a macabre death.

Three short blasts of a whistle echoed through the house, signalling the Apostolic Guards to return to the Grand Salon and report their findings. The central staircase immediately filled with the clatter of hobnailed boots, so Cristina used the quieter servants' stairs instead, which brought her out by one of the water closets. As she made her way along the hall, she stopped suddenly and gazed at one of the display niches. A set of six battle maces had been mounted in a semicircle, but one of them was missing. Cristina peered closer and ran her fingers over the empty space; there was a faint dust outline, indicating that a mace had hung there until very recently.

Where had it gone? Who had taken it?

Cristina's eyes darted round the landing, searching for the missing weapon; she dropped down on all fours to look underneath the furniture, and finally caught a glint of metal behind one of the wall tapestries. She reached into the gloom and retrieved a battle mace.

Two feet long, it was heavy and cold, with eight vicious spikes emerging from a cylindrical iron head … spikes which were now covered in blood and fragments of torn flesh.

Cristina arrived back in the Grand Salon just as Deputato Tomasso was finishing the unenviable task of reassembling Ricardo's fragmented body. He retrieved the left hand from where it had fallen and placed it at the end of the victim's arm as if he was playing a macabre children's game. Everyone stared at the gruesome exhibit.

"The murder weapon was most likely an axe," Tomasso explained. "Look at the hack wounds, here … and here. Around the neck it took a number of blows to cut through the spine. Same with the legs."

"Have you recovered the weapon?" Cristina asked.

"Not yet."

"At least the body is complete," Domenico muttered. "The killer didn't take any trophies. Once we've finished here, take it to the city morgue. We'll have to make a detailed record of the wounds."

"Er, how do I move him, sir?" Tomasso asked.

"Carefully?"

"Someone will have to sew him back together," Cristina explained. "They can't bury him like that."

"Be thankful you don't work in the morgue, Tomasso." Domenico opened his notebook. "Listen up, everyone. From questioning the Chief Steward and the housekeepers, this is what we know about the victim." He started reading from his notes. "Antonio Ricardo, thirty-one years old. Not from Rome originally. Born in Florence. Was a friend of Amerigo Vespucci, navigator on the Columbus voyages to the New World."

"That was how he made his money?" Cristina guessed.

"Exactly so. He was part of the consortium that backed Coelho's expedition. Became very rich, very quickly, and wanted to convert that wealth into status. Hence all the art. And his love of throwing spectacular parties."

"Seems he was trying to make himself the most eligible man in Rome. Maybe to marry into one of the great families," Cristina mused as she looked at the savaged corpse. "Didn't quite work out as expected."

"So, possible motives?" Domenico challenged the group.

"Theft?" one of the guards suggested. "A burglary gone wrong?"

"The chief steward said nothing's missing. Silver plate, jewellery … it's all accounted for."

"A jealous rival?" Tomasso said.

"Possibly," Domenico replied. "But the doors and windows are undamaged. No-one heard any strange sounds like forced entry or breaking glass. And there were no house guests."

A stumped silence descended on the group.

"Could a wild animal have got in?" one of the younger guards asked.

Two of his colleagues stifled a giggle. "Like a wolf with a carving knife?"

But Domenico considered the idea carefully. "We need to keep an open mind. But there would be paw prints in the blood, teeth marks on the body. A wild animal wouldn't be careful."

All eyes scanned the floor — amidst the blood, it was clear there were no animal marks.

"I found this," Cristina held up the battle mace. "Hidden behind one of the wall tapestries. It belonged to the victim."

Domenico took the mace and studied the metal spikes. "I thought the murder weapon was an axe?"

"Maybe the killer had both," Tomasso suggested.

"Or maybe it unfolded something like this." Cristina started pacing around the body. "The killer got into the house. Somehow. Or he was already inside when the house was locked up for the night. Either way, when everyone was asleep, he didn't make his way up to the bedrooms to murder Ricardo, instead he came here, to this room, specifically to find this painting."

"To steal it?" Domenico asked.

"No. To destroy it."

Tomasso frowned. "I don't understand."

"Perhaps the murderer didn't intend to kill. Perhaps what he really wanted was to destroy this celebrated work of art," Cristina explained. "So he started hacking it to pieces with an axe, first the frame, then moving on to the canvas. At some point, he made a noise which disturbed Ricardo, who came downstairs to investigate. As he approached the Grand Salon,

Ricardo grabbed a mace from the wall outside to use as a weapon. He came in, disturbed the intruder, they fought. The intruder grabbed the battle mace and turned it on the lawyer." Cristina knelt down next to the corpse and pointed to some puncture holes on the side of the head. "Here, see? These wounds match exactly."

"Why didn't the intruder run away after he'd killed?" Domenico asked. "Why stay and mutilate the body?"

"I don't know. Not yet," Cristina replied.

"And why would anyone want to attack a painting?" Tomasso added. "And arrange everything in such a bizarre pattern. It doesn't make sense."

Cristina nodded grimly. "Perhaps because the world is full of madmen and fanatics."

"No," Domenico was adamant. "This is not the Evangelicals of Light."

"How can you be so sure?"

"We've spent the last six years hunting down every lead and eradicating them. The Evangelicals are not responsible for this atrocity, I'd stake my life on it."

Cristina looked from her brother back to the savaged body of Ricardo. "Then we are facing a new and deranged enemy. I don't know who they are, but I am convinced their target was that work of art."

"It still doesn't answer the question of why," Tomasso said. "Why attack a painting with such hatred?"

Cristina picked up the fragment of canvas containing Christ's right hand. "*Salvator Mundi* was painted by Vito Visconti. Visconti is on the shortlist to design the new St Peter's. I fear someone is trying to disrupt the creation of a new basilica. Again." She turned to her brother. "We must alert the Holy Father immediately."

5: ADMONISH

Pope Julius II summoned them all to the Sistine Chapel for the sole purpose of intimidation. He immediately grasped the significance of Ricardo's murder, and knew that he had to act swiftly to prevent plans for the new St Peter's foundering on the rocks of Rome's dynastic rivalries.

"Don't say anything," Domenico urged as he snuck his sister into the Chapel through one of the doors in the east wall.

"I've already said I'll behave."

"Promise me."

"How many times do I have to repeat myself?" Cristina replied testily.

The Sistine was already buzzing with anticipation as Rome's powerbrokers filed in, sizing up their opponents and jockeying for position. Instinctively, Cristina's gaze went to the Chapel walls, where the lives of Moses and Christ were depicted in a series of huge, brilliantly coloured frescos by Botticelli and other Florentine masters. This glorious art had made the Chapel famous across Europe, but the haunting figure of the Devil, disguised as a hermit tempting Christ to throw himself to his death, sent a chill across Cristina's heart; perhaps the harrowing images of Ricardo's violent death were still too fresh in her mind.

She craned her neck back further and gazed up at the vaulted ceiling. Painted a tranquil blue and studded with hundreds of gilt stars in concentric circles, the celestial depiction created a perfect atmosphere for meditation, and Cristina was grateful that the artists hadn't been tempted to cover the ceiling with Biblical scenes as well.

Outside, the clock in the old basilica started to toll four, and an expectant buzz galvanised the Sistine Chapel as everyone braced for the Pope's arrival.

Cristina studied each of the factions in turn…

The Medici clan were gathered around their favoured architect, Giuliana da Sangallo. Prominent cheekbones and hooded eyes gave Sangallo the appearance of a wealthy merchant rather than an artist. Yet if you were judging by looks alone, Donato Bramante was an even less likely candidate: the top of his large, domed head was completely bald, but the man had tried to compensate by growing a lush mop of curls around the sides. He had an intelligent face which bore the permanent hint of condescension, yet his patrons, the Sforza family, didn't seem to mind.

Panic had descended on the Orsini clan as their chosen artist, Leonardo Da Vinci, had failed to turn up. Urgently they despatched messengers, but it was too late, the cardinals had already started to file into the room, heralding the imminent arrival of the Holy Father.

The Chapel fell silent.

The cardinals took their places.

Then suddenly a voice whispered in Cristina's ear, "I've always wanted to keep a Pope waiting."

She spun round and saw a striking man in his late fifties standing close to her, an Ottoman bandana wrapped around his long, dark hair.

"But alas, I hear the punishment is excommunication." As he smiled, the man's pencil moustache gave an irreverent twitch. "What do you think?"

"I … I think you're about to find out," Cristina replied.

"Should I be scared?" The man's eyes glinted with mock horror.

Yet from the way he spoke, Cristina sensed there was little that would scare this man. "You could always escape to Constantinople." She recovered, glancing at his bandana. "As you've already dressed the part."

The man laughed and leant forward in a dignified bow. "Maestro Visconti. But a woman of your beauty can call me Vito."

Cristina was taken aback. "Oh. I'm so sorry."

"To have met me?" Visconti looked offended.

"No. But I saw your painting this morning. What was left of it. *Salvator Mundi*. You must be devastated."

"Aah, that." Visconti gave a thoughtful sigh. "Such is life."

"But it was a masterpiece. The loss is immense."

"There are no depths to which jealousy will not stoop."

"You believe that was the reason? Jealousy?"

"I try not to concern myself with the struggles of men. My only concern is for art. And beauty." His eyes ran over Cristina as if she was a model about to be painted. "Nothing else matters."

"But you have also lost a generous patron."

"Indeed." Only now did Visconti's face fill with genuine sadness. "Ricardo was that rarest of beasts: a man of great wealth and great taste. And yet … an even greater prize awaits." He looked over and saw that Pope Julius II was now entering the Sistine Chapel.

"Forgive me," Visconti whispered to Cristina, then slipped into the crowd and made his way to his patrons.

An altar boy robed in a white surplice walked in front of the Holy Father, striking a small handbell to announce the presence of God's voice on Earth, yet Julius II was clearly impatient with the stately progress, and nearly clipped the boy's heels as they processed. When they finally arrived at the dais and Cardinal Riario began the lengthy ceremonial introduction, Pope Julius's patience snapped.

"Enough! They know who I am. And more to the point, I know who they are." His eyes ran over the assembled nobles, lighting on each face just long enough to ensure that everyone knew they were being scrutinised. "You are here because you have the privilege of being involved in one of the greatest projects of the age. I am not a modest man. I have ambition. Soaring ambition. Not for myself, but for the glory of the Church. I believe the authority of the Holy See *must* be expressed in majestic buildings that will stand until the Last Judgement. These edifices must be so wonderous that it will seem as if they have been created by the hand of God himself. Only then will belief strengthen from one generation to another. Only then will all the world accept and revere the Holy Church. Only then will dissenters be forever silenced."

Pope Julius let the echo of his words decay, enjoying the moment of absolute power. "And you … this select band of nobles and artists stood before me, you have been chosen to create one of these miracles in stone: a new St Peter's Basilica that will embody the greatness of the present and the future."

The dynastic families murmured with pride, enjoying a moment of self-congratulation.

"And yet…" Pope Julius pronounced ominously. "I find myself forced to summon you here to admonish you. The sole purpose of holding a competition was to find the most brilliant design for the basilica. To avoid corruption and cronyism. Yet now, my great project is embroiled in sordid murder. Let me be clear: this will not be tolerated. Anyone who tries to throw the process into confusion will have to deal with my wrath. And trust me, that will not lead to forgiveness, but to the most severe of punishments."

Many in the Chapel felt uneasy, yet the principals of the great families took the reprimand in their stride. As dynasties, they had seen popes come and go, this 'theatre of anger' was all part of the game.

"The timetable is running and it will not be stopped," Pope Julius continued. "You will be expected to present your designs in ten days' time so that we may tighten the shortlist further. I do not want any more atrocities to compromise God's will. This contest must proceed in peace. Have I made myself clear?"

Julius' gaze studied the nobles. He did not expect anyone to speak ... but the Medici were not just anyone.

Giovanni di Lorenzo de' Medici, newly turned twenty-eight and eager to flex his muscles, cleared his throat. "Holy Father, with the greatest respect, many of us here find this 'competition' a rather demeaning affair. Previous Popes have been more amenable to negotiation, and I wonder if that might not be a better way to proceed?"

Bribery. He was talking about bribery, and effectively praising the last Borgia Pope for his corruption.

The barb was not lost on Pope Julius. "I will not live by the morality of the Borgias!" His voice trembled. "The monster Alexander desecrated this Holy Church as none before. He usurped papal power by embracing Satan! I forbid, under pain of excommunication, anyone to speak or think of Borgia again."

The most powerful families in Italy lowered their heads, pretending to be cowed like chastised school children. But this was all part of the game.

6: BANDANA

As everyone filed out of the Sistine Chapel, Cristina slid discreetly into the shadows behind one of the pillars in the adjoining corridor. People often gave their most unguarded reactions in the moments immediately after a meeting when they thought no-one was looking; behind this pillar Cristina was unseen yet still within earshot, so perfectly positioned to catch any careless comments. It was a technique Isra had taught her while explaining how domestic staff kept abreast of what was really going on inside a grand house. A particular favourite was the 'false climb', where a servant would leave a room then repeatedly walk left-right-left-right on the *same* step, giving the impression of going upstairs whilst actually going nowhere; from there they could eavesdrop on the room they had just left, then silently creep away when they were done.

As she listened now, Cristina heard many of the younger nobles complain about the Pope's high-handed behaviour and authoritarian manner, but the more seasoned members of the dynastic families remained resolutely silent as they walked away, keenly aware that privacy could never be taken for granted in someone else's quarter.

Suddenly a voice whispered in Cristina's ear, "I see you know that trick as well."

She spun round and once again found herself face to face with Visconti. "I … I was just waiting for my brother."

"Of course you were," he smiled. "A perfectly innocent explanation. Which is why it is so effective."

"I really don't know what you're implying."

"It is a trick I use all the time in my workshop," Visconti went on. "How does one know what a patron is really thinking? By positioning apprentices and servants, 'the invisibles' who no-one notices, in precise locations where they can eavesdrop on conversations."

Cristina studied Visconti's mischievous face and realised that denials were futile, he had seen through her. "So, how did you read the room this afternoon?" she asked, hoping to move the conversation onto safer ground. "Who is the favoured artist?"

"Why, me of course!" Visconti beamed.

"No. Seriously. Tell me."

"Very well. I shall." For a few moments, Visconti allowed his calculating soul into the open. "Bramante is a mediocrity."

"Harsh."

"But true. Look at the man, he has bureaucrat written all over him. The Pope will love the fact that he can be controlled, but when did Bramante ever create anything to excite the spirit or inspire the soul?"

"The Tempietto?"

"Please. The man's a one-trick pony."

"Yet you can hardly say that about Da Vinci."

"A no-show. He may as well have farted in the Pope's face!" Visconti laughed at his own joke.

"You really think crude humour qualifies you to design St Peter's?"

"No. But my genius does."

"Sangallo could say the same thing."

"Sangallo's a *puttano*." Visconti shrugged. "His nose is so far up the Medici buttocks, it's a wonder he can build anything straight."

Cristina studied the man, wanting to condemn his arrogance, yet strangely blindsided by his earthy charm. "That appears to narrow the field to you, Maestro Visconti."

"From your mouth to God's ears." Then with a swift movement of his hand, Visconti whipped off the Ottoman bandana, letting his long black hair tumble down his shoulders, and placed the cloth in Cristina's hands. "A gift from the soon-to-be Chief Architect of St Peter's Basilica."

"No, thank you." Cristina tried to hand the bandana back, but Visconti closed her fingers around it.

"Do not break an artist's heart with rejection, Cristina."

"How do you know my name?" She suddenly had an uneasy feeling that she was getting caught up in a game whose rules she did not understand.

"Genius knows. It always knows." Visconti smiled.

Cristina studied his dark brown eyes. Who was this man? He talked like a braggard in a gaming salon, yet his paintings… Cristina had seen the genius in them. The intensity, the depth of emotion. How could such profound work be produced by such a childish man? Perhaps vanity was the secret of his genius.

"Signorina Falchoni!"

The abrupt voice startled Cristina, pulling her from her thoughts. She turned and saw Deputato Tomasso approaching. "Your brother needs to see you."

"Are you blind, soldier?" Visconti objected. "Can't you see we are talking?"

"I wasn't addressing you," Tomasso replied.

"I believe you mean, 'I wasn't addressing you, *maestro*.'"

"If you insist, 'maestro'."

"I do."

Tomasso tried to ignore the barb. "Your brother said it was urgent, Signorina."

"And I say it will have to wait." Visconti edged round to put himself between Tomasso and Cristina, but Tomasso pushed him to one side impatiently.

"Do not touch me, grunt!"

"It's official business, 'maestro'."

Cristina could feel the hostility crackling between these two men and was anxious to avoid a fight in the corridors of the Vatican. "If you'll excuse me, I'd better be going," she said.

"You can bear to be parted from me?" Visconti lamented.

"Duty beckons."

"Then adieu, Signorina." The maestro gave a theatrical bow. "Keep the bandana close."

Cristina followed Tomasso down the corridor and made a point of not looking back.

"That was not empty rhetoric. The Holy Father meant every word." Domenico looked intently at Cristina, Tomasso, and two lieutenants who were gathered round the long table in his office in the Vatican barracks. "If the dynastic families get locked in a destructive vendetta out of their eagerness to win the design, there is a real risk that Pope Julius will scrap all plans for a new St Peter's."

"But he is the first Pope to understand the full significance of this," Cristina interjected. "'God's creation on Earth to silence dissent.' Those were his words."

"Do you know why the Holy Father chose Julius as his papal name?" Domenico replied. "In honour of Julius Caesar. He intends to be a warrior pope. A feared pope. As we speak, he is drawing up plans to wage war in the peninsula to enlarge the Papal States and consolidate his power. Compared to that, a new basilica is froth to dazzle the masses. And if it turns into a series of distracting scandals, the Pope will not fight to save it. Believe me."

Cristina felt her heart tighten. She had waited six long years for this, nothing must be allowed to snatch it away. "Then we must catch the murderer and unravel whatever dark conspiracy is growing."

"Exactly."

"So we're working on the assumption that one of the dynastic families is behind this?" Tomasso asked.

"It's as good a premise as any," Cristina replied. "At least it explains motive."

"It also puts us at a disadvantage," Tomasso admitted. "We have only managed to infiltrate one of the families with a covert operative, the Orsini."

"Then get a message to him this evening. Arrange a meeting. Let's see if he knows anything," Domenico instructed.

"Yes, sir."

"I can talk to Cardinal Riario about the Sforza dynasty, as he is championing their interests."

"Realistically, would he speak against his allies?" Cristina asked.

"That depends if he is a cardinal first, or a politician," Domenico replied.

"I think we can rule out the Colonna family," Cristina offered. "They are backing Visconti, and they wouldn't destroy their own man."

"Which leaves the Medici," Tomasso concluded. "They are very secretive, and very mistrustful of Vatican officials."

Domenico turned to his sister. "Could you take care of that, Cristina? Can you find a way of infiltrating the Medici palace?"

"I think so."

"Then we all have our assignments. We'll gather back here at the same time tomorrow to review what we've found."

But just as everyone started to leave... "I need to see the murder scene one more time," Cristina announced.

"It's too late," Domenico replied. "The body's being removed this evening."

"Then I must get straight back there."

"We've done everything we can —"

"I think we may have missed something," Cristina insisted.

"We just agreed a plan, Cristina. You're to infiltrate the Medici."

"The murder scene may yet eliminate one of the dynasties. Or incriminate one. Either way, it would be stupid and negligent to ignore potential leads."

Domenico recognised that awkward tone in his sister's voice. When she was in one of her stubborn moods, arguing was pointless.

7: COLLAGE

Why wouldn't they just let her get on with it? Why did Tomasso insist on accompanying her to the murder scene? Did he think her stomach wasn't strong enough? That she was going to faint? It irritated Cristina, for if she was going to think, *really* think, she needed peace and quiet, not an over-eager Apostolic Guard hovering close by.

As they entered the Grand Salon, Cristina was relieved to find everything just as they had left it: Ricardo's temporarily reassembled body had been covered with a shroud, but all the blood smears and fragments of vandalised painting were exactly where the killer had placed them. The servants had been given strict instructions to touch nothing, and they had stayed well away.

The pungent smell of death caught the back of Tomasso's throat. "They could've opened the windows," he muttered.

"And risk letting crows fly in to peck at the body?" Cristina replied.

"We can't work in this stink."

But Cristina was already tying a sandalwood-scented handkerchief around her nose and mouth. "If you want to make yourself useful, why don't you check the house for any signs of forced entry?"

Tomasso was puzzled. "We've already done that."

"Then double check. Something may have been missed."

"But —"

"Inspect every window and door closely, look for scratches on the locks, cracks in the wood, broken windowpanes. One can never be too thorough."

Realising that Cristina wanted to be rid of him, Tomasso wisely decided not to argue, and sloped off to start work.

Cristina pulled the shroud away and stared at Ricardo's desecrated, grey body.

She bent down and using a magnifying lens, examined the two gold signet rings on the lawyer's left hand. One bore a miniature engraving of the points of the compass, the other had an image of Ursa Major, the navigator's favourite constellation. Presumably, Ricardo wore them as a daily reminder of how he had acquired his wealth, and that much more was still to come.

Constellations. Patterns. Shapes in the random…

Cristina looked across the huge floor at the chaos: bits of painting, pools of congealed blood, shards of gilt frame surrounded by arcs smeared in blood. Did the pattern mean something? Was it hiding a message, or was it random?

She picked up each of the cold, waxy body parts in turn and studied the wounds. Yes, the gross cutting had been done with an axe, but there were different marks as well, fine scores in the flesh as if the murderer had cut grooves in the body before wielding the axe to sever the bones. She studied the lacerations through her lens; they had been cut with a blade that was exceptionally fine and very sharp. Much sharper than a kitchen knife.

Suddenly, Cristina had an intuition that reassembling Ricardo's body so hastily could have been a mistake, and she decided to reconstruct the crime scene exactly as it had first been found. She closed her eyes, trying to recall that first ghastly impression, visualising which piece of severed flesh had been placed where.

Guided by her memory and the pools of dried blood on the polished floor, Cristina tiptoed through the carnage, returning each body part to its original position.

As she worked, she discovered that the copious blood smears were not accidental; they had been formed deliberately, with brushstrokes, as if painted, and different sizes of brush had been used on different patches of blood. Crawling around the stains on her hands and knees, she eventually found a single bristle in one of the smears, then using a pair of tweezers, she plucked it from the blood and held it up to the light. It was definitely the bristle from a paintbrush.

Strange. And perhaps significant.

Cristina paced slowly round the Grand Salon, studying the scattered pieces from different angles, trying to understand the philosophy of this murder.

The rattle of a door opening jolted her from her thoughts. Cristina looked up and saw Tomasso enter the Grand Salon. "I thought you were checking windows and doors?"

"I did."

"Already?"

Tomasso looked confused. "That was two hours ago."

"Oh." It was interesting how quickly time passed when you were absorbed in a problem, Cristina mused.

"Have you discovered anything new?" Tomasso asked.

The tick of a clock seemed so absolute, yet the experience of time was very subjective. Perhaps time was relative to each individual and their own unique perspective.

Perspective.

Cristina tilted her head to one side and gazed deeper at the chaos on the floor. "Deputato Tomasso, would you fetch me a stepladder. There must be one in the house. The tallest they have."

Tomasso hurried off. When he returned, he was carrying a ten-foot stepladder that he'd found in the cellars. "Where shall I place it?"

"There." Cristina pointed to the centre of the room, right in the middle of the tangle of remains.

Tomasso picked his way across the floor, then carefully set out the ladder so that it would not disturb the evidence. He shook it to make sure it was stable. "And now?"

Cristina climbed to the top of the ladder, then looked down at the debris of human flesh and painted canvas. She narrowed her eyes to defocus them. And glimpsed it.

"Dear God," she whispered.

"What is it?"

Cristina didn't reply, she just stared in consternation at the pattern laid out beneath her. There was nothing random about this carnage, it had been carefully arranged to create a giant collage of a ghastly image.

Once you'd seen it, it was impossible to unsee...

It depicted Antonio Ricardo being torn apart by two giant hands; it captured the precise moment of his destruction. The ten long smears of blood were fingers gripping various parts of the victim's body. The shards of gilt frame represented pieces of the figure's bones fragmenting as they were broken. The ragged bits of torn canvas had been positioned to give an impression of the giant blood-hands bursting through the floor, shattering the very surface of this room.

"Are you all right?" Tomasso asked.

Cristina shook her head. "This isn't just a murder scene, it's a picture."

"What?"

She climbed down. "See for yourself."

Tomasso hurried up the steps and defocussed his eyes. "I don't see it. What am I looking for?"

"Don't try to see it. Let the image come to you."

Tomasso blinked, tried to relax, and suddenly saw it. He jolted backwards. "Dear God! It's obscene."

"And yet … strangely brilliant."

"That's not really the word I'd choose."

She shook her head. "How could I have missed that? It was staring at me the whole time."

"Sometimes the hardest thing to see, is what is right in front of you," Tomasso ventured.

But Cristina was no longer listening to him.

8: VAULT

"Are you seriously asking me that question?" Cardinal Riario's tone was uncharacteristically cold, all the diplomatic charm discarded in a moment.

"We are making the same enquiries of all the dynastic families, Your Eminence," Domenico explained.

"I am not one of them!" Riario snapped back. "I am a cardinal. My first duty is to the Church and the Holy Father."

"I appreciate that, Your Eminence. I meant no offence, but…" Domenico tried to think of the best way of phrasing the question.

"But?" Riario demanded.

Domenico's eyes fixed on a solitary bee that was hovering around the grapevines. He had hoped that Riario would be in a more relaxed mood, as tending plants in the Vatican Garden was one of his favourite pastimes, but it was clear that Cardinal Riario never relaxed. Perhaps that's why he had climbed so high, so quickly; at just forty-two, no-one doubted that he would one day sit on the Papal throne. The best approach was to keep this calm and professional.

"Your Eminence knows all too well the significance of the competition to design a new St Peter's. The winning architect will find themselves in charge of the most expensive building project ever undertaken. Vast and lucrative contracts will be put out for tender. It will dominate the business of Rome for years if not decades."

"Grandmother. Eggs. Enough," Riario said sharply, clipping one of the vines with his pruning shears.

"Forgive me, Your Eminence, but in that context, it would not be surprising if the dynastic families went to extreme lengths to eliminate their rivals."

"Such as butchering wealthy lawyers?"

"Perhaps."

"You want to be careful who you accuse," Riario warned. "That is a dangerous game."

"I'm not accusing anyone."

"Then why are you interrupting my gardening?"

"I am asking questions to eliminate rather than accuse. And as you have such close links with the Sforza family, and they are championing Bramante, I thought you might…"

"Might?" Riario really wanted Domenico to damn himself with his own words.

"Have a particularly insightful opinion to share," Domenico replied.

Riario snipped a rogue stalk from the vine and sniffed the leaves. "As it happens, a delegation from the Sforza family did visit me."

"When was this, Your Eminence?"

"Shortly after news of the murder broke. They asked for a favour."

"Did they threaten you?"

"Not at all."

"Did they threaten anyone else?"

"Quite the opposite." Riario hung the pruning shears back on his belt. "Come with me."

Domenico thought Vatican City held no secrets for him. After all, it was his job to know every inch of the vast complex of buildings inside the walled enclave, so he was surprised when Cardinal Riario led him towards a humble gardener's lodge in the centre of the grounds and swung open the doors to reveal a group of seven Cistercian monks.

"Where are the groundsmen?" Domenico asked.

"There's no point questioning these monks." Riario smiled. "They have taken a vow of silence."

As Domenico's eyes adjusted to the gloom, he realised that there was no gardening equipment in here; instead, the room was filled with dozens of large, slim wooden crates. "I … I don't understand."

"These are some of the Sforza family's most treasured art works. The moment they heard news of the destruction of *Salvator Mundi*, the head of the family ordered his carpenters to pack all their paintings securely for transportation."

Domenico looked at the stacks of wooden crates, imagining all the saints and Virgin Marys cowering inside, fearing for their lives.

"The favour they asked of me," Riario continued, "was to arrange for this precious art collection to be stored in the Vatican's Deep Vaults, the most secure place in Christendom."

"We have Deep Vaults?" Domenico's mind was racing to keep up.

"The fact that even you didn't know is a sign of just how secure they are," Riario replied. "But as you are the Head of the Apostolic Guard, I believe I can let you in on the secret."

One of the monks unlocked a heavy bronze door and hauled it open, revealing a ramp spiralling down into the gloom. Domenico walked to the doorway — flaming wall-torches were dotted at various intervals, but the bottom of the ramp vanished in darkness. "How long has this been here?"

"A thousand years. They were originally the catacombs where the early Christians hid to avoid persecution. Over the centuries they have been extended and reinforced with brick retaining walls." Riario turned to the monks. "Shall we?"

Gently the Cistercians picked up a large, flat crate, a man at each corner, and carried it through the bronze doorway. Riario and Domenico followed them down the ramp and into the earthy smell drifting up from the Deep Vault.

"How many paintings have they asked you to store?" Domenico asked.

"One hundred and ninety-one."

Domenico gave a sharp intake of breath. "That's going to take a long time."

"Which is why they have started immediately."

Eventually the ramp levelled and opened out into a vast chamber, subdivided into a honeycomb of small brick-built rooms, each with its own set of secure oak doors. The sheer scale of the place took Domenico's breath away, yet the Cistercians knew exactly what they were doing, and calmly carried the boxed painting along the main corridor towards a chamber whose doors were already unlocked.

"What else is down here?" Domenico whispered.

"The true treasures of the Church," Riario replied.

"So all the gold and silver, the artwork that is on display in the Vatican … that isn't everything?"

"I am speaking of a different kind of treasure, Domenico. Down here are the intellectual and spiritual foundations of the Church. The original manuscripts of Thomas Aquinas. Ancient Christian scrolls recovered from Jerusalem during the First Crusade. Solomon's letters directing the construction of the Temple. Fragments of papyrus text written by the Apostles Matthew and John. And that is just in the first two chambers."

Domenico was speechless. What could anyone say in the presence of such venerated objects?

"So you will understand," Riario explained, "that the Sforza asking for their paintings to be stored with these treasures, demonstrates how seriously they take the attack on *Salvator Mundi*."

"We were all shocked, Your Eminence."

"The Sforza wept at the destruction of such a masterpiece. And they were filled with dread lest their own collection should suffer a similar attack."

Domenico watched the monks carefully lay the wooden crate in one of the chambers. "This certainly is not the behaviour of guilty men," he agreed. "Unless the Sforzas are making a great display of concern precisely to deflect suspicion away from themselves."

The cardinal scoffed. "Now you are talking with the paranoid intelligence of your sister."

"And yet," Domenico persisted, "the prize of winning St Peter's is so great, it could surely tempt the saints."

Riario turned on Domenico, his eyes glistening with indignation. "In Italy, the truly great families are not defined by money alone. They are not arrivistes who got lucky with trade. They are great because a deep love of culture and scholarship defines who they are. Shame on you for not understanding that. But then, you are merely an overpromoted soldier." He pointed to the ramp. "Now leave."

9: FLOWERS

Cristina pushed open the front doors and immediately started sneezing. No wonder, the entrance hall of her house was packed with freshly cut flowers. Great bunches of orchids, tulips and lilies lay like a carpet of soft colour across the stone floor; jars of bluebells, sunflowers and daffodils had been positioned on every piece of furniture and shelf, and standing in the middle of it all, trying to squeeze a bouquet of purple roses into a vase, was Isra.

For a moment, Cristina thought her housekeeper had gone mad. Perhaps a seizure had gripped the young woman's mind, and in some delusional state she had descended on the flower market at Campo de' Fiori and purchased everything in sight.

And then Isra spoke. "Any man that does this is not to be trusted."

Cristina gave a small sigh of relief, Isra was still very much Isra. "Who on earth sent them?"

"Even worse, they didn't arrive at once. Deliveries have been coming all evening. Every time I tried to get on with my work, another knock on the door. Another interruption."

Delicately, Cristina ran her fingers over the blooms, admiring the richness of the colours. "You didn't answer my question. Who sent them?"

Isra rummaged in her pocket, pulled out a small scroll tied with a red ribbon, and handed it to Cristina. "This was the only clue."

Cristina broke the medallion of sealing wax, released the ribbon and unfurled the scroll. It was a beautifully drawn silverpoint sketch on ochre paper … a picture of herself in the Sistine Chapel, listening with a look of intense concentration.

Isra peered over Cristina's shoulder. "He's caught you well. Did he sign it?"

"He didn't have to. This was drawn by Vito Visconti."

"*The* Visconti?"

"He was there this afternoon when the Pope issued his warning. We exchanged a few words."

"It looks to me as if you exchanged far more than that," Isra observed.

"Don't be ridiculous." Cristina rolled the paper up again, trying not to blush.

"One chance meeting, and he does a sketch like that? Sends a boatload of flowers?"

"He is part of the investigation. That is all." Cristina tried to pick her way through the flowers towards the stairs.

Isra reached out and caught her arm. "I know men."

"What are you talking about?"

"I know men in a way that you do not. You must be careful."

"He's just trying to be charming," Cristina shrugged. "It's a harmless flirtation."

"Trust me, men who do things like this —" Isra pointed to the deluge of flowers — "who promise you the world, they're the ones to avoid."

"I'm not a young girl, Isra. Don't talk to me like one."

"You're the most intelligent person I know. But that's what makes you vulnerable to men like Visconti."

"He's an artist. They are extravagant people."

"Bombarding you with thousands of flowers isn't extravagant, it's childish. Immature. Unstable."

"It makes no difference to me." Cristina started climbing the stairs. "Come along, we have work to do."

"You're not keeping the flowers, are you?"

"Leave them for now."

"Shall I send them to the Hospital for the Incurables?"

"Isra, we have more important things to worry about." Cristina ushered her housekeeper into the library. "Look." She laid out a large sheet of paper on the table, dipped a quill into one of the ink pots and started drawing a diagram. "This is what the murder scene looked like from above…"

Cristina sketched quickly, marking the position of each body part, every piece of the painting, every smear of blood. The moment she had first seen it, the image made such perfect sense, it burned itself onto her mind, making recall easy. When she'd finished, Cristina wiped the ink from her fingers and stood back from the desk. "You see? The murderer drew us a picture in blood: a pair of demonic hands bursting through the floor and tearing both Ricardo and *Salvator Mundi* to pieces."

Isra's body jolted as she saw it. "That's appalling."

"And fascinating."

"Why would anyone do such a thing?"

"I think the 'why' is clear. It's an attempt to throw the design competition into confusion. The question we need to focus on, is *who*? Who is capable of creating such a disturbing scene?"

"Someone who is talented as well as evil," Isra said grimly.

"Agreed. But if you have that much talent, why would you turn to evil?"

"And how did they get access to the house without breaking in?"

"There is so much that is baffling about this case." Cristina's brow furrowed.

"Could someone inside the lawyer's household be involved? Could they have let the killer in?"

"It's possible. But none of the servants have a motive. Ricardo was a fair employer; he didn't beat or abuse his staff."

"Money is always a motive," Isra replied. "A fat bribe opens all doors."

"Perhaps. I'll get my brother to assign guards to watch the house, see if any of the servants suddenly change their behaviour."

Isra picked up the diagram of the murder scene and studied it. "This wouldn't have been easy. Cutting flesh needs surgical techniques."

Cristina's eyes glinted with an idea. "Many students dissect cadavers to help them understand anatomy. First thing tomorrow, visit all the morgues and hospitals in Rome to compile a list of people who have acquired dead bodies for study."

"That could be a long list."

"Not if we cross reference it."

"With what?"

"The killer didn't just wield an axe, Isra. He used proper brushes of different widths to paint in blood, and fine scalpels to score the flesh ... he used art supplies which he may well have bought specially to commit this crime, so that he could destroy them afterwards."

"There can't be many merchants supplying artists' tools."

"If I follow that lead, we might find an interesting overlap with the cadaver list."

With the plan for the next day agreed, Isra went downstairs to the kitchens to prepare supper. Cristina waited until she heard the clatter of pans coming from the courtyard, then she took the small scroll from her pocket and unfurled it.

She gazed at the sketch of herself, unnerved by the portrait's accuracy; it wasn't just a physical likeness, it was as if Visconti had looked into her mind and caught the intensity of her thoughts.

Cristina was so used to being invisible, she'd assumed that no-one had really noticed her presence in the Sistine Chapel. Yet this great artist had turned his gaze on her and seen who she really was.

10: INFORMANT

Where would Rome have been without its scaffolder-monks?

As Europe tumbled into the Dark Ages, devouring itself in warfare, and the Goths, Vandals and Alani tribes swept across the continent picking over the remains of the Roman Empire, the religious orders knew that if their precious abbeys and cathedrals were to survive, the monks would have to rebuild using their own hands. Intrepid orders set about training themselves in the stonemasons' crafts, and it wasn't long before monks became the most skilled scaffolders on the Italian peninsula. So when the city authorities finally approved the current renovations of the Pantheon, it was monks they commissioned to construct the complex scaffold around the ancient building.

Everyone loved the Pantheon with its striking simplicity and great dome, but it was a difficult structure to maintain. The huge oculus in the roof that let in shafts of sunlight also let in birds, damp fogs and the occasional snowstorm; now, after standing for a millennium and a half, the repairs were urgent.

Yet it wasn't the architecture that attracted Domenico to the Pantheon, it was the ability to hide in plain sight. He knew that the frenzy of activity made this a perfect location for secret meetings with his network of informants embedded in Rome's chattering classes. Throughout the day, a stream of carts delivered hundreds of wooden poles and fastenings, while mule trains fed steadily growing mountains of bricks, cement and plaster. A sound-cloud of chisels, hammers and crude laughter engulfed the building site, making eavesdropping impossible; hawkers roamed freely, selling food and drink to the monks, while curious onlookers added to the chaotic atmosphere. It all meant that no-one paid the slightest attention to Domenico as he made his way between great piles of cement sacks to meet Capello, his eyes in the Orsini household.

"There's always money for churches," Domenico said casually.

"Churches and bribes," Capello replied, indicating that he had not been followed, and they were free to talk. Had he replied, "They're going to need a bigger collection plate," Domenico would have walked straight past, pretending that he didn't know Capello, and was merely exchanging pleasantries.

Domenico stopped next to his informant and the two men shook hands. Capello had a strong grip, and with his square jaw and stocky, muscular build, Domenico was glad they were on the same side.

"Are the Orsini behind the lawyer's murder?" Domenico asked, keen to keep the rendezvous as brief as possible. "Are they trying to intimidate the other families to withdraw?"

"If that was their plan, it's been a spectacular failure," Capello replied. He had a way of speaking that made everything seem like unwelcome news. "Leonardo Da Vinci was so shocked by the murder and the desecration of the painting, he has fled the city and returned to Florence."

"He's scared?"

"Appalled. He thinks Rome is a barbaric city run by philistines. He said you wouldn't get this kind of vandalism in Florence. That even butchers value art there."

Domenico frowned. "It sounds to me as if he is just using this as an excuse to leave."

"I heard the argument." Capello shrugged. "The whole house heard the argument — it was heated. Da Vinci was screaming at the duca, 'Barbarians! Animals! Culture is wasted on this city!' The duchessa started crying, begging him to stay. It was a mess."

"What did they say to try and persuade him?"

"A man like Da Vinci isn't easy to talk down from a rage."

"Did they offer him more money?"

Capello sucked air through his teeth. "That would've just made it worse. It's all about the principle for him. Respect for art."

"So what are the Orsini going to do now? Withdraw?"

"I'm not sure."

"How can they compete without an artist?"

"They're pretty gloomy. They know their chances of getting the job are slipping away fast. That's one huge money pot they won't be able to dip their fingers in."

Suddenly a site foreman appeared, he was counting the sacks of cement. "Did you deliver this lot?" he demanded.

"Nothing to do with us," Domenico replied.

"Where did the driver go? It was supposed to be checked before he left."

"Have you tried the other side? Next to the stables?" Capello suggested. "Maybe he's watering his mules."

The impatient foreman walked away, muttering to himself.

"Sorry I can't be more helpful," Capello said when they were alone again.

"No, no. At this stage ruling someone out is valuable," Domenico insisted. "It means we can focus our efforts better."

But Capello could see that Domenico was frustrated by the lack of leads. "There was one idea that came up, might be interesting to follow through," he ventured. "As I was serving supper, I heard the duca discussing it with his eldest son. He wondered if Da Vinci was secretly working for the Borgia."

Domenico's mind quickened. "Da Vinci did a lot of work for Cesare Borgia when his father was Pope, but Julius II hates the Borgias with a vengeance."

"And hasn't he banished them from Rome?"

"Their palace will be empty by Christmas. But … it's not empty yet."

"Could this murder be one last *vaffanculo* from the Borgias?" Capello asked. "A final chance to stop the new basilica from being built?"

"Leaving murder and destruction in their wake is a Borgia speciality," Domenico said grimly. "Murdering a lawyer and destroying a masterpiece is exactly the sort of the thing they would do to spite someone."

"Or maybe just for pleasure," Capello added.

11: SCALPELS

"Huh." Padrino Coda studied the single bristle through a magnifying glass. "Interesting. Where did you say you retrieved it?"

Cristina hesitated. Should she come clean and tell him it wasn't red paint that had stained the bristle, but the blood of a lawyer hacked to death the previous morning? "It was … on the surface of a picture. In a friend's collection."

"Oh? Who was the artist?"

"I can't remember. Some Flemish painter, I think."

"And what was the subject?"

"A market scene. In Leiden."

"Huh. Strange." Padrino Coda studied the bristle again. "This is not the sort of brush they normally use in the Low Countries."

Cristina scratched her ear nervously. Why hadn't she just told the truth from the start? Padrino Coda wasn't suspicious, simply curious, *very* curious, and now she risked alienating the one man in Rome whose help she needed.

No-one quite knew why he was called Padrino; godfather to whom? Every genius in Rome? There were no formal qualifications for merchants selling supplies to artists, and their guild didn't have craft status. Perhaps 'Padrino' was an affectionate label he'd earned because he was so good at his trade; all the renowned artists came to him, and it was widely known that if you couldn't get it from Coda, you couldn't get it from anywhere.

"I need a more powerful magnifying lens,' the Padrino muttered, disappearing into the back office to start rummaging.

Left alone in the shop, Cristina gazed in awe at the towering shelves and vast cupboards overflowing with supplies. The pigment racks held hundreds of glass jars containing all the exotica of colour: beetles and dried berries, cochineal, malachite, azurite and lapis lazuli ready for grinding and mixing with walnut or linseed oil; canvases of all different textures and grades were draped over rails suspended from the ceiling; there was wood for making frames and wood for painting on, easels, drawing mannequins, fabric samplers, and an entire wall of brushes. And that was before you even went upstairs.

The bead curtain clattered as Padrino Coda returned carrying the biggest magnifying lens Cristina had ever seen. "This should do the trick." He sat on a tall stool, used a mirror to deflect a shaft of sunlight onto the workbench, then studied the solitary hair.

Cristina listened to his breathing as he concentrated. Finally, he put the lens down.

"Huh. This from a sable brush. Each bristle plucked from the creature's tail. It is one of the finest paintbrushes ducats can buy."

This was exactly what Cristina wanted to hear; the field was narrowing. "Do you sell many?"

"There is not a huge demand. Too expensive. The last one I sold was back in the spring."

"Do you know who bought it? Do you keep records?"

"Do I keep records?" Coda seemed offended. "Huh!"

He grabbed a ladder and scrambled up the treads with the vigour of a man thirty years younger. Retrieving a heavy ledger, he slid back down, plonked the volume on the workbench and rifled through the pages.

Cristina peered over his shoulder and saw the names of just about every famous artist on the Italian peninsula listed next to their purchased supplies.

"Here." Padrino Coda's finger stopped at a slightly smudged entry dated 4th May 1503. "Items sold: Sable hair for bristles, beech slivers for the handles, ferrules and crimps…" He hesitated.

"What have you found?"

"That's interesting. The purchaser, whose name is now smudged into oblivion, also bought a set of Negroli blades."

"He bought knives?"

"Scalpels, to be precise."

"What for?"

The Padrino shrugged. "Artists' apprentices use them all the time. Cutting canvasses, slicing pigment ingredients, trimming brushes. But these…" Coda pointed to the ledger entry. "The Negroli blades are particularly fine. Tempered steel, like the best swords. They hold their sharpness better than any other blade."

"Could you cut flesh with them?"

Coda looked up from the ledger and scrutinised her. "Why would an artist want to cut flesh?"

"They can be strange people." Cristina tried to shrug it off, but the Padrino's hackles were up.

"What are you really searching for, signorina? Because you have done nothing but lie to me from the moment you entered my shop."

Cristina attempted a coy smile to defuse the tension. It didn't work. "You're right, Padrino Coda. And I apologise."

"Words are cheap. If you are truly sorry, then start being honest."

"I do not want to put you in any danger, and that is the truth. But I can tell you that I am asking with the full authority of the Apostolic Guard."

"Huh." The old man ran his bony fingers through the thinning hair on his head.

"Are you sure you cannot make out the name of the man who purchased the scalpels?" Cristina asked.

"See for yourself." Coda spun the ledger round, but the name was illegible. Had it been smudged deliberately? Was someone going to great lengths to cover their tracks?

"Has anyone else bought these Negroli blades in the last few months?"

Coda's eyes scanned the ledger lines. "Last month … a set of six blades were put on the Medici account."

"For their artist? For Sangallo?" Cristina said.

Coda shook his head. "Sangallo buys all his own supplies. Very fussy. Checks everything himself. Doesn't even trust his apprentices. No, these blades were for the Medici family. On their personal account."

"Buy why?"

Coda slammed the ledger shut. "That is of no concern to me."

Connections fired in Cristina's mind. It was the Medici family who complained to the Pope about not being able to bribe their way to the basilica contract. And with bribery excluded, perhaps they had resorted to another type of direct action: murder.

12: BORGIA

The rage was palpable. Domenico and Tomasso could feel its presence as they walked up the steps of the grand palace on the Tiber. It was like a heavy, dark liquid oozing down the marble staircases, flooding through the drawing rooms and across the dance floors, tainting everyone it touched with resentment. And the source of this anger was one man: the syphilitic Duke of Valentinois, Cesare Borgia.

As Domenico and Tomasso waited on the upper landing to be granted an audience, they watched the small army of servants dismantling what had once been a formidable seat of power. Paintings were plucked from the walls and taken away in crates; rugs were rolled, tied and carried into the courtyard; six men were struggling to manoeuvre a massive mahogany table from the breakfast room and down the stairs. With every tapestry and piece of silver plate that was removed, the soul of the palace died a little. It was like watching a huge stone tree shedding its leaves in autumn.

"*Testa di cazzo!* Tell them to go to hell!" a voice shouted from behind gilt doors. Someone mumbled a protest in reply, but the voice wasn't listening. "I don't care! I'm not interested in anything those *stronzi* have to say."

Domenico and his deputy exchanged a wary glance. "Nothing like a warm welcome," Tomasso whispered.

The double doors opened, a servant emerged and gave a small bow. "I'm afraid His Grace is in a meeting, so regretfully he is unable to grant you an audience."

"Seriously?" Domenico allowed himself a sardonic smile.

"Perhaps I could take a message, sir?"

"You'll have to do better than that." He pushed the servant to one side and marched towards the doors.

"Excuse me! You can't go in —"

Domenico raised his boot and kicked open the doors. He strode into the ballroom, Tomasso following in his wake, and saw a team of workmen lowering a vast crystal chandelier from the ceiling using pulleys and ropes. They were trying to coax the glass monster into a huge, padded box for shipping, but it was so heavy, some of the wooden slats had split.

"For each broken crystal, you lose a day's pay!"

It was the same voice that had been cursing just moments earlier. Domenico turned to his left and saw a young man lounging on a velvet throne, directing operations. He wore the finest clothes, closely fitted over a tall, athletic body; he had shoulder-length black hair, and the arrogant bearing of a soldier. But on his face he wore a mask to hide the terrible disfigurement from syphilis that had ravaged him for the last six years. This was Cesare Borgia.

Domenico gave a respectful bow. "Your Grace, may we have a few moments of your time?"

Cesare glanced across. "Go screw your mother!"

"We need to ask you some questions."

"The Pope's pimps! Come to chase me from my own palace, no doubt."

"That is not why we're here, Your Grace."

"The Holy Father has exiled me yet does not have the civility to let me leave Rome at my own pace." Cesare stood up and strode towards Domenico and Tomasso. "So he sends his lapdogs to chase me away." He circled them like a predator, so close that Domenico could smell the man's perfume, liberally applied in a futile attempt to mask the foul stench of syphilitic puss.

"Your Grace, we have no interest in your moving schedule. That is between you and the Pope." Just as well, Domenico thought as he glanced over at the chandelier, which was now wedged at a precarious angle, neither in nor out of the crate.

"You should be ashamed of yourself," Cesare said with quiet venom.

"Why is that, Your Grace?"

"You served my father like a lapdog. I remember your face. 'Yes, Holy Father. No, Holy Father. Let me kiss your ring, Holy Father.' Yet now you serve a man who would trample on his reputation."

"A soldier's duty is to the office, not the man, Your Grace."

"And my duty is to my late father, Pope Alexander VI. The greatest pontiff Rome has ever known."

Domenico was trying hard to be patient, but it wasn't easy. "History may judge him less kindly, Your Grace."

Instinctively, Cesare put his hand on his dagger, ready to defend Borgia honour with violence, but Tomasso quickly drew his own sword.

"Would you really exchange exile for imprisonment?" Domenico warned.

Cesare's hand relaxed as he channelled anger into his tongue instead. "At least history will remember the Borgias. Unlike you, one of the little men, a mediocrity who strives for nothing and achieves less."

"I have given loyal service to the Vatican. That is not nothing."

"Pathetic," Cesare scoffed. "My father conversed with God. My family enriched Rome and built the power of the Papal States. We negotiated with kings and emperors. We brought peace to Europe." Cesare looked at the dismounted chandelier with contempt. "And this is our reward: exile." He paced around the denuded ballroom. "Exile!"

Domenico watched the duke stalk the room like a demented animal. Was this the madness of syphilis? Or had Cesare always been so bitter? "I can see Your Grace is upset," Domenico ventured.

"*Stronzo!* Upset doesn't even begin to describe what I feel!"

"Then perhaps murder does."

Cesare stopped pacing and turned to Domenico. "What did you say?"

"A man who feels so aggrieved, Your Grace, would have compelling cause to murder."

Cesare gave a low laugh. He knew that Domenico was trying to goad him into making a mistake. "There have been many murders in my life. Sometimes diplomacy gets a little rough. But whatever I did when in power is immune from prosecution, as I performed my duties on the direct command of the Pope."

"This is not about what you did in power, Your Grace, but what you might have done yesterday." Domenico studied Cesare closely, watching for any hint of guilt.

"Yesterday? You mean Antonio Ricardo? Why would I waste my time on a trivial man like that? Such a murder is beneath me."

"On the contrary, Your Grace, the crime was brilliantly executed, which is why we are here. To consult with a master."

"I don't know whether to be flattered or offended," Cesare mused as he plonked himself back into the velvet chair. "What possible motive could I have, now that I am being exiled and stripped of power?"

"Envy."

"Of a lawyer?" Cesare's face creased with disgust.

"No, Your Grace. Envy of Pope Julius' determination to build a new St Peter's. An achievement that eluded your father."

"And?"

"And now you cannot bear to see anyone else succeed where a Borgia failed," Domenico said calmly.

"You think I would murder for art?" Cesare's voice trembled. "I'll show you what I think of art." He leapt from the chair, strode across the room and plucked a painting of Judas betraying Christ from the wall. "I commissioned this. Four years ago. It was very expensive."

Carefully Cesare laid the painting on the floor, then pointed to one of the servants wrangling the chandelier. "You! Come here!"

The servant hurried over.

"Drop your pants and shit on that painting," Cesare commanded.

Stunned silence in the room.

"I ... I ... I don't understand, sir."

"Which word don't you understand: 'shit' or 'painting'? Or perhaps you are a moron?"

"But —"

"Do it!" Cesare screamed. "NOW!" He pulled the dagger from his belt and pressed it to the poor servant's throat.

"Enough of this!" Domenico turned to leave.

"No! You will watch!" Cesare commanded. "Or I will slit his throat."

Reluctantly Domenico and Tomasso did as they were told.

Cesare smiled at the servant. "Now, think of something nice, and leave your tribute on the painting."

"But it'll ruin the picture, sir."

"Don't think. Just shit."

Reluctantly, the servant dropped his breeches, crouched over the painting and relieved himself.

"Excellent," Cesare said as he looked at the pile of ordure on the face of Judas. "Here. For your troubles." He tossed the servant a ducat.

"And what does that prove?" Domenico said with disgust.

"The Borgia family has brought great art into the world. Paintings, sculptures, palaces, wonderful creations by gifted artists. But its only purpose is, and always was, to glorify the Borgias. To show the world our great wealth and power. As for the art itself…" He shrugged and looked at the ruined painting. "Who gives a shit?" Then he roared with laughter.

No-one else in the room so much as smiled. Everyone sensed the monstrous ignorance of what they had witnessed, but Cesare Borgia was unrepentant.

"So you see, I don't have to sneak around in the middle of the night to destroy art, I can do it in plain sight." He bent down and picked up the painting, then taking care to keep it horizontal, he crossed the room and offered it to Domenico. "Have it as my parting gift."

"No thank you."

"Such ingratitude! Clean the shit off, then sell it somewhere to supplement your meagre wages."

Domenico could feel this creature laughing at him, mocking everything he believed in. "You've made your point."

"Come now, don't be churlish. Even spoiled, this painting is worth more than you get paid in an entire year. What does that say, I wonder?"

Domenico refused to absorb any more insults. "At least, Your Grace, I haven't slept with my own sister." The calmness of his voice made the words more insulting. He watched shock turn to disbelief in Cesare's eyes. "Not that I'm one to listen to rumours," Domenico added.

The muscles in Cesare's neck tightened as he struggled to control his rage. "For the record: I am delighted that Pope Julius has run into bloodshed and scandal so quickly. I hope that his reign is miserable and violent. And I shall pray every night and every morning that his glorious new St Peter's crumbles around his ears. Now get out."

13: UPSTAIRS

There was a warmer welcome at the imposing Medici Palace on Piazza di Spagna.

Cristina had obtained an introduction from Professor De Luca at Sapienza University on the pretext of cataloguing the vast collection of paintings that lined the Medici's fine corridors, yet it hadn't always been so easy to gain access to the head of that family. For two hundred years the Medici had dominated all aspects of Florence's political and social life, whilst simultaneously creating the biggest bank in Europe; they were the epitome of a ruling elite … until 1494, when ambition and overreach led to failure and expulsion. Down on their luck and desperate to rebuild, the Medici were now sheltering in Rome, eager to meet anyone who might help re-establish their network of influence.

Isra looked up at the gleaming five-storey building that stretched the entire length of the piazza. "This is down on their luck?"

"Everything is relative." Cristina smiled.

"I wish I was so unlucky."

"When you've financed Kings and Popes, normal standards no longer apply."

They had a clear plan: while Cristina was being entertained upstairs, Isra would mingle with servants in the kitchens and stables, trying to find out what was *really* going on through household gossip. Between them, the two lines of inquiry might shed light on potential Medici involvement in the murder of the lawyer.

At just twenty-eight, Giovanni di Lorenzo de' Medici was now head of the family, although thanks to his well-fed jowls, he looked ten years older. He was flanked by two extremely attractive young men, although the exact nature of their relationship remained unclear. Giovanni introduced them only as 'Cucciolo e Toro' (Puppy and Bull), nicknames which did not reflect their chiselled faces, preening manner and sulky dispositions. From the way they prowled possessively around Giovanni, it was clear that Cucciolo e Toro were not family, but while refusing to engage in conversation, they also seemed determined not to leave his side.

Giovanni's passion for art was beyond doubt. He delighted in guiding Cristina from salon to salon, explaining the origin of each painting, the philosophy of the artist and the symbolism behind the choice of subject. Yet his generosity had an agenda, for when they reached Giovanni's study, dozens of drawings and sketches had been carefully displayed, all of them by Sangallo, the artist they were sponsoring for the competition.

"My father adored him," Giovanni said as he handed her the architectural plans of Medici Villa on the outskirts of Florence. "Said he had never met a man with more exquisite taste."

Cristina studied the sketches on the long table. "They are certainly striking buildings," she agreed.

"Look at the way he uses classical elements to add grandeur, whilst creating the illusion of simplicity to make the building feel effortless."

"The effect is quite new. An innovation."

"It is, isn't it?" Giovanni enthused. He glanced over to Cucciolo e Toro, wanting them to share in his passion, but the two beautiful men had grown bored of all the art talk, and were now sprawled in leather armchairs on either side of the roaring fire.

Undeterred, Giovanni thrust more drawings at Cristina. "See how well the technique works with his Augustinian monastery. And again at the church of Santa Maria, built to commemorate the famous miracle."

"*If* you believe in miracles," Cristina didn't try to hide her scepticism.

"You don't? Come now. A child saw the vision, an innocent child. Why would they lie? She saw a painting of the Virgin Mary and infant Jesus come to life and bless the village."

"Regardless, the building itself has a strong classical feel. The Greek cross is striking."

"And unusual in Italy. I tell you, Sangallo is the man," Giovanni enthused. "Castles, fortifications, palaces and churches, there is nothing he cannot build. And that is what is needed for a stunning new St Peter's Basilica."

Now they were getting to the heart of the matter; this is why Giovanni had been so attentive. "The decision is in the hands of the Pope now," Cristina said.

"But it's never that simple, is it?" Giovanni poured two glasses of port and ushered Cristina to a seat by the window. "The Holy Father listens, takes advice from those he trusts. People like you, perhaps."

"If you think I can influence his decision, then you are quite wrong," Cristina replied.

"Building is a serious work for serious minds." Giovanni was not going to let her leave until he had said his piece. "St Peter's needs an experienced architect, not a dilettante. It needs someone who understands the mathematics of engineering, not some painter who woke up one morning and decided to try his hand at building."

It was clear who the slight was directed against. "So you fear Visconti?" Cristina replied.

"I fear what will become of any building that charlatan designs. I doubt it would last a year."

"And you do not trust the Holy Father to realise that?"

"He cannot be an expert in everything. Responsibility for the entire Church rests on his shoulders. But this competition…"

"Will surely make it clear to the whole of Rome who is the best artist for the job," Cristina suggested.

"How to explain this?" Giovanni sighed. "There is art, and there is fashion. And the two make uncomfortable bedfellows. I admit Visconti's recent work has shown an impressive power. And yet … there is something about the man that doesn't add up."

"Perhaps your judgement is tinged with envy," Cristina suggested, trying to coax Giovanni from behind his well-polished etiquette.

"The Medici don't envy genius. We admire it. We become its patron. But this man Visconti…" He shook his head, trying to articulate his feeling of unease.

"So you would rather Visconti was not in the competition?"

"Of course!"

"And to what lengths would you resort in order to see him eliminated?"

Giovanni froze and his face flushed. "No, no, no! How could you suggest such a thing?"

"I am merely asking —"

"You are implying! And I am insulted that you would suggest such a thing."

"Forgive me, I did not intend —"

"Antonio Ricardo was a friend of this family. A dear friend who was particularly close to my cousin. We had high hopes … and now we are devastated." He took a handkerchief from his robe and ostentatiously dabbed his eyes.

So that was it. Ricardo was trying to marry his wealth to the prestige of the Medici name, and the Medici wanted to use Ricardo's money to buy their way back to the top table of power. It would have been a perfect match.

"Is that what they really think of us at the University?" Giovanni asked, revealing his insecurity. "That we were involved in the destruction of *Salvator Mundi?*"

"They are baffled by the crime. The whole of Rome is baffled."

"And appalled," Giovanni added. "People kill for many reasons, but art should never be one of them. Art is the very best of humanity, the only thing that justifies our sordid and compromised existence."

Cristina studied Giovanni's face, trying to determine his sincerity.

"To destroy a rival is politics. Or business. But to destroy art is to destroy the whole of humanity."

"Yet someone in Rome is prepared to do exactly that."

"And I can assure you, Signorina Falchoni, that someone is *not* a Medici."

14: DOWNSTAIRS

A quite different story was emerging downstairs.

Isra knew that the quickest way to gain trust was to get her hands dirty. Many servants of visiting dignitaries would lounge in the kitchens demanding food and wine, but Isra made a point of rolling up her sleeves and helping the junior scullery maid scrub a huge pile of red carrots. As the lowest servant in the household, the young maid was used to being either ignored, or beaten when something went wrong, so she was grateful for a friendly face and shared conversation. The more Isra drew the girl out of her shell, the more amazed she was at how little escaped her notice. In a 'great house' run by an army of staff, there really is no such thing as a secret.

When Cristina's audience upstairs was finished, she haughtily demanded the return of her housekeeper, then handed Isra a basket of pomegranates that Giovanni di Lorenzo de' Medici had given her. "Hold it carefully," she instructed. "I do not want them bruised."

"Yes, mistress."

They set off into the wet streets, Isra trailing at a respectful distance, but as soon as they turned into Via Frattina, all pretence of rank was dropped, and the two women started comparing notes. The mysteries of upstairs were soon explained by the gossip from below stairs.

"Cucciolo e Toro are exactly what they appear," Isra said. "A thinly disguised secret that fools no-one."

"I wasn't sure what to make of them," Cristina frowned. "What do you mean?"

"Well, they didn't say anything. They just seemed completely bored. They certainly didn't have anything in common with Giovanni."

Isra tried not to laugh. "Anything in common? Are you serious?"

"Giovanni is passionate about art," Cristina went on. "He has a very lively mind, but Cucciolo e Toro seem completely vacant."

"You were looking in the wrong place, Cristina. Forget their minds, look at their tight-fitting doublets and bulging breeches. They are lovers."

"So why were they lounging around Giovanni?"

"All three of them."

"What?" Cristina stopped in her tracks. "All three are lovers?"

"Yes."

"Simultaneously or consecutively?"

"Would you like me to draw you a diagram?" Isra broke open a pomegranate and handed half to Cristina, whose faced creased in concentration as she ate. "The point is, a few weeks ago the three men had a vicious row."

"Interesting. Go on."

"Cucciolo e Toro discovered that Giovanni had been visiting courtesans at one of the high society brothels, and they became extremely jealous."

"Wait, wait. Society brothels only offer women."

"Exactly."

"But … but … any rumour of sodomy and they would be closed down."

"Correct."

"Yet Giovanni…" Cristina tried to work it all out. Isra waited patiently, chewing on the pomegranate. "Oh … you mean Giovanni likes women as well?" Cristina exclaimed.

"Congratulations. You got there in the end."

"It's certainly confusing."

"Cucciolo e Toro have seen off plenty of male rivals for Giovanni's affections. Few men can compete with them on looks or prowess."

"Prowess?"

"The scullery maid talks to the chamber maid, and she has seen —"

"I'm not sure I need the details."

"The point is, women terrify Cucciolo e Toro. Because they cannot compete with a gorgeous woman."

"So if Giovanni were to decide that he prefers women after all, Cucciolo e Toro will be cast off."

"Hence their fear of high-class courtesans. The men got scared and that made them vicious. There was a bitter argument. Now Cucciolo e Toro have banished Giovanni from their bedchambers until the start of Lent."

Cristina gave a soft whistle. "A lover withdrawing love is a high-risk strategy."

"I can't blame them. They're terrified he might have contracted the French disease. They want to leave enough time for any signs of syphilis to appear."

Cristina finished the pomegranate and licked her fingers. "That all makes sense. But how does it relate to the murder of Ricardo? Because Giovanni was mortified by what happened."

"Two days after the fight, Cucciolo e Toro vandalised a magnificent portrait of Giovanni that hung in the gaming salon."

"Ahh. I wondered why there was an empty space on the wall. It was a big painting."

"They scored the canvas, covering it with syphilis scars and festering wounds, as a warning to Giovanni."

"Vicious."

"Oh, they are. And you know what they used?" Isra took a piece of muslin from her pocket and unfurled it to reveal a glinting scalpel. "Negroli blades."

Cristina picked up the blade and studied it. "Purchased from Padrino Coda, no doubt."

"I couldn't say."

"How did you get this?"

"One of the servants found it on the floor. It had fallen behind a marble urn."

"And they didn't hand it to Giovanni?"

"No-one in the house is supposed to know what has happened. The painting was taken away in the dead of night to spare Giovanni's shame. They hid it in one of the wine cellars."

Cristina scoffed. "They may as well have read a proclamation to all the servants."

"If it was me, I'd have burnt it. Leave no trace."

"Giovanni is not one to destroy a work of art. Not for any reason."

As they entered Piazza Navona there was a rumble of thunder and the rain started to splash down heavily, forcing them to dodge growing puddles as they ran across the cobbles. By the time they reached home, they were wet and the hems of their clothes muddy. Isra hurried into the laundry room and returned with two warm towels.

As Cristina dried her hair, Isra noticed her looking at the vases of beautiful flowers that still covered every surface of the entrance hall. "No sign of them wilting yet," Cristina mused. "Visconti must have spent a fortune."

"Beauty is a fool's trap," Isra said pointedly. "Cucciolo e Toro have proved that."

Cristina put the towel down. "You're not seriously comparing —"

"It's all about show with some men. But look beneath the glittering surface, and it's rotten to the core."

"Isra, you talk as if I'm getting married," Cristina laughed. "A talented artist sent me flowers. That is all."

"I'm just saying. When the time comes, you need to choose a husband carefully. Men lie as easily as they breathe. And you are all about truth."

Cristina folded the towel carefully. "Do you really think I could be so easily fooled?" She wasn't being defensive, it was a genuine question. "Am I weak like that?"

Isra shook her head. "Absolutely not weak. But that is a side of your life that you have blocked out. It's a blind spot. Which makes you vulnerable."

Cristina nodded but didn't say anything.

"Let me brush your hair before it dries." Isra fetched some combs from the dressing room, and quietly got to work.

Both seemed lost in their own thoughts, but just as Isra was finishing, Cristina turned and looked at her.

"I haven't blocked it out. It's just that no-one wants to let me in."

"Men fear intelligent women," Isra replied. "But that's their problem, not yours."

15: SUSPECTS

"So … where does that leave us?" Domenico asked.

Tomasso put his quill back in the ink pot, dusted the paper with sand to soak up any excess, brushed it off then looked at the case notes he had spent the last hour writing. "It's hard to see a breakthrough." He handed the sheet to Cristina, who read back everything the three of them had been discussing.

"I think we can start ruling people out," she said finally. "Like the Sforza family. If they were behind the murder, they wouldn't be fearfully hiding their art in the Vatican's Deep Vaults."

"Agreed," Domenico nodded.

"And the Colonna family wouldn't destroy the work of the very artist they are championing. That doesn't make sense. So we can rule them out as well. As for the Orsini…" Cristina hesitated. "It is unlikely they're involved. They know how temperamental Da Vinci is. If he thought the competition was being rigged to help him win, he would walk away. They don't want to risk that."

"Which leaves the Medici," Tomasso said. "You did brilliant work uncovering some nasty behaviour there, Cristina."

"I'm not convinced they're involved," she replied.

"Violent jealousies? Vandalised artwork? The elements are strikingly similar."

"The Medici have a long history of patronising the arts. They wouldn't destroy a masterpiece. Even if it belonged to a rival."

"They are also desperate to win the competition and recover their fortune," Tomasso insisted. "Who knows how low they would stoop?"

"They understand that rebuilding their *reputation* is the key to rebuilding their wealth. Murder is no way to win friends and influence people."

"Which leaves the House of Borgia." Domenico started pacing the room as he marshalled his thoughts. "It seems to me they are the primary suspects. Cesare Borgia has motive. He has the criminal connections, and the resources to execute such a crime."

"I agree," Tomasso said.

"I don't," Cristina frowned. "There is an element of insanity to the crime ... that's not the Borgia way. Whatever the depths of their corruption, there is always a logic to their actions. But the way Ricardo was butchered ... I think a different type of mind is at work."

"What if rage at their downfall has made Cesare insane?" Domenico suggested.

"You should have heard the venom in his words," Tomasso added. "The pure hatred. Especially of this Pope and what he is trying to achieve."

"But if Cesare Borgia is guilty, he would be doing everything in his power to throw you off the scent, not arouse your suspicion," Cristina countered.

"I still want a covert tail put on Cesare Borgia. Day and night."

"It's already in place, sir," Tomasso confirmed.

"The crucial point is access," Cristina said. "How did the killer get into Ricardo's palace? How could he spend so much time there undisturbed? He dismembered a body, vandalised a painting, then meticulously arranged all the bloodied fragments, yet no doors or windows were forced. Deputato Tomasso has checked that thoroughly."

"Twice," he said pointedly.

"So the logic is telling us…" Cristina left a pause for the other two to finish her sentence, but they just looked at her blankly. "It's telling us that the killer was known to the household. He was welcomed in. Allowed to be on his own. But no-one trusts the Borgia anymore, least of all Cesare. No-one wants to be seen with him. As a man busy climbing the social ladder, Ricardo would have been acutely aware of the importance of keeping far away from the Borgias and anyone in their pay."

The room fell silent as the three of them considered where their investigation should go next. In the barrack rooms outside, Cristina heard the chatter of Apostolic Guards on shift change; through a barred window overlooking the courtyard, she heard a horse sneezing in the damp Roman air.

"Maybe this is not the work of humans at all," Tomasso suggested.

Domenico winced in anticipation, as Cristina's eyes flashed with irritation. "For the last time, there is no room for ghosts and demons in this or any other investigation."

"I was just —"

"God works through reason and knowledge. The Devil's trade is ignorance and superstition. Let's not make his work any easier by pandering to supernatural delusions."

"Apologies." Tomasso picked up the quill and started fiddling with it nervously.

"So where do we look next?" Domenico asked, trying to take the heat off his deputy.

Cristina turned over the piece of paper with their notes, then took the quill from Tomasso, dipped it in the ink pot and wrote the word 'Genius' in large letters. "Artistic genius will build a new St Peter's. But venal politics is trying to corrupt the purity of art. Our job is to prevent that from happening."

"Agreed," Domenico said impatiently, "but how does that translate into a real-world investigation?"

"Right now, the artist everyone fears is Vito Visconti. After years of competent but mediocre work, he has finally been touched with genius. And that genius is now at the centre of a horrific crime. I should pay him a visit. Maybe there is a clue in his own studio."

"I'll come with you," Tomasso said. "We can make it an official search."

"No. The less attention we attract, the better."

"But —"

"I will go alone."

"What do you hope to find?" Domenico asked.

"I'm not sure," Cristina replied, "but I'll know it when I see it." She underscored the word 'genius' with two black lines. "One thing is certain, brilliance always attracts enemies."

PART TWO

16: NEMESIS

When the Contessa del Copertino's husband abandoned her to run off with a young bombardier from a corps of Swiss mercenaries, the aristocrat had to endure a bitter humiliation that would have broken lesser women.

The key to her survival was rage.

Rage nourished Contessa Copertino's soul, it gave her a reason to wake each morning, it directed her thoughts through the long, fevered days, and it soothed her to sleep at night.

The contessa's friends prayed that time would heal her wounds; every day they reminded her that her foolish husband had merely destroyed his own prosperity, for the great family wealth was hers, and when the handsome young bombardier tired of his ageing lover, the count would have to return on his knees, begging for forgiveness.

Yet time healed nothing.

And the count did not return.

Contessa Copertino resolved that catharsis could only come through a public declaration of her hatred, so she turned to Vito Visconti and commissioned *Fountain of Nemesis* to sit at the top of the steps in Piazza di San Marco.

Visconti produced a bold and brilliant sculpture of the winged goddess. Her face was beautiful, yet the heightened sharpness of her features left no-one in any doubt that revenge was in her heart; in her right-hand Nemesis wielded a lethal sword, in her left the scales of justice. It was a terrifying vision of anger transformed into marble.

But that was not enough for Visconti. Striving to go further than any other artist, he engineered a skeleton of copper pipes inside the goddess, so that a curtain of shimmering water flowed from each of her wings. It created the illusion that Nemesis was surging forward, ready to pounce on any sinner who approached.

In this one, brilliant commission, the contessa was declaring to the whole of Rome that if she ever crossed paths with her husband again, she would destroy him.

What cruel irony that it was her own life that was consumed by the beautiful sculpture.

Now Contessa Copertino's body floated face-down in the fountain pool, her skin waxy-white because all her blood had drained from the six-inch gash across her throat, turning the fountain water red.

Two curtains of blood shimmered from the wings of Nemesis and were endlessly recirculated by the ingenious system of paddles that Visconti had engineered.

Yet this was not a desecration of art; the brutal truth was that it elevated the sculpture to a new level of brilliance. The dead aristocrat, the blood-wings, the white marble staining red … the power of this art was undeniable.

If the contessa had not been sacrificed to it, she would have been delighted.

But those who live by rage, die in pain.

17: AESTHETICS

Cristina stood in front of *Nemesis*, studying each morbid detail of the fountain, while everyone else ran around frantically trying to contain the horror and avert panic.

Domenico was busy directing Apostolic Guards to seal off the piazza and prevent ghoulish onlookers from interfering with the murder scene; Tomasso had just arrived, escorting Contessa Copertino's housekeeper, who had the unenviable task of confirming the victim's identity.

"God help her! God help her!" the housekeeper wailed.

"It's all right. Take your time." Tomasso held the woman firmly as her knees buckled under the shock.

"Everyone loved mistress! Everyone!"

"Whoever did this will be punished. I swear," Tomasso said with grim resolve. "But I'm afraid someone has to formally identity the body before we can investigate."

The housekeeper trembled as she watched two guards use wooden poles to drag the floating corpse closer. "It's her," the woman sobbed fearfully. "That's her nightdress."

She turned to go, but Tomasso stopped her. "I'm afraid you need to see her face."

"No! I can't … I can't bear to."

"There's nothing to fear."

"Don't make me!"

"I'm right next to you. Please."

The housekeeper wiped her eyes with her sleeve and tried to control her sobbing.

"That's better," Tomasso reassured. "Shall we try this?"

The housekeeper nodded and clasped the deputy's hand as two Apostolic Guards hauled the body from the pool and laid it with a heavy slap on the stone balustrade that encircled the fountain. One of them swept the wet hair from the Contessa's face and gently closed her eyelids.

"Is this the Contessa del Copertino?" Tomasso asked the housekeeper.

"Yes." She buried her face in the deputy's jacket as sobs overwhelmed her again.

Tomasso looked up at Domenico. "Can she go home now?"

Domenico nodded. "But make sure she stays in the contessa's palazzo until we've interviewed her. We need to find out everyone's movements leading up to this."

"Yes, sir."

"And put a guard on all the doors."

Cristina watched Tomasso lead the weeping woman away, impressed by his patience. A part of her felt guilty that she wasn't as upset as everyone else, but the simple fact was, now that the contessa had been murdered, the body itself was stripped of all emotion; it was just decaying meat. All Cristina's energy should be focussed on catching the monster who had done this.

There was no doubt in her mind that they were dealing with the same killer who had murdered Antonio Ricardo. As with *Salvator Mundi*, a huge amount of thought had gone into the choreography of this killing, and immense care had been taken with its execution. Once again, the killer had cleverly combined human flesh with a work of art. *Fountain of Nemesis* had been turned into a living sculpture of death, built from marble and blood.

Yet one thing still didn't make sense: if someone had this much talent, why were they a killer?

"Let's hope this is the last one," Domenico said as he approached.

"Is that what we're reduced to? Hope?" Cristina replied.

"With good reason. As soon as we were alerted to the murder, we sent guards to arrest Cesare Borgia, but he fled the city last night. Now he's gone, perhaps he's taken his vindictive malice with him."

"I think you might be jumping to conclusions, Domenico."

"Many people believe the contessa was behind the rumours that Cesare Borgia was having an incestuous relationship with his sister."

Cristina looked surprised. "I didn't know that."

"So it makes sense that he would settle an old score before fleeing to Spain, beyond the reach of justice."

"Would he really go to all this effort to kill a gossiping contessa? Especially after she had already been humiliated by her husband's betrayal."

"No-one bears a grudge like a Borgia."

"But there are many people who did far greater damage to the Borgias. People who triggered their fall from power. If Cesare was really settling old scores, there are plenty higher up on the list."

Domenico shook his head. "I still think he's our strongest suspect. I'm going to follow it through, see if I can get enough evidence to prove Cesare's guilt."

"You're wasting your time."

"Who else is there, Cristina? We've ruled out the other dynastic families, and this is clearly not the work of a backstreet assassin."

"Let me speak to Visconti. See what I can find."

"But he's the victim. Again."

Cristina's eyes roamed over the beautifully chiselled marble form of Nemesis. "Don't you think it's strange that both murders have involved works by Visconti?"

"Not really. Right now he is the most popular artist in Rome. His work is everywhere."

"And popularity should lead to wealth and glory. But for Visconti..." Cristina dipped her fingers into the blood-red water of the splash pool. "It is as if a curse has descended on him."

"You of all people shouldn't use language like that," Domenico admonished. "Especially as it may just be a coincidence."

"It's not."

"You don't know that."

Cristina locked eyes with her brother. "Two killings. In both cases, Visconti's art is vandalised, and the patrons who commissioned it brutally murdered. These are warnings to anyone who wants to commission work from Visconti. Hire him, and risk getting butchered."

"So you still think this is about the competition? About trying to frighten the Pope."

"The crucial question to answer is why does death stalk Visconti? If we cannot answer that, we will never catch this killer."

18: BOTTEGA

Just a stone's throw from Piazza del Popolo, the Via Margutta was a narrow street with big ambitions. For over three hundred years, masons and marble cutters, painters and engravers, architects and sculptors had made their homes here, feeding off one another's creativity, each artist inspiring the next in a chaotic maelstrom of activity.

As Cristina picked her way down the alley, she could feel the crackle of energy; it was the sensation you got immediately before a violent thunderstorm, both thrilling and unnerving. Maestro Visconti's workshop had spread along the street, acquiring adjacent houses as the painter's career flourished, until it occupied an entire block of buildings stretching south from Vicolo del Babuino.

"Welcome to the wonderland!" a voice boomed as Cristina ducked to avoid a huge carved crucifix that was being loaded onto a cart. She looked up to see Visconti waiting for her by the gates of his workshop. He was dressed in flamboyant clothes: a vivid black and white striped doublet and hose, with huge sleeves and trailing swags, all covered with a flowing silk cloak; on his head the artist wore a crimson turban.

Visconti noticed the startled look on Cristina's face. "Not like those dull Vatican bureaucrats you're used to, eh?"

"Have you been posing for a painting?" Cristina asked.

"The painting of life." He smiled. "One's talent must be expressed in everything one does. My life is just as much a work of art as the paintings I create. Eat like an artist, die like an artist … *love* like an artist." He took Cristina's hand, bowed low and gently kissed her fingers.

"Well, someone in Rome is murdering like an artist," she replied, withdrawing her hand.

"Ah!" Visconti gave a dramatic cry. "They told me about that. Quite extraordinary. And appalling. Did you see the aftermath?"

"It was a brutal murder of a defenceless woman. It was sickening."

"But the fountain itself is unharmed?"

Cristina hesitated; was Visconti's only concern for his creation, rather than his dead patron? "In a strange way, the fountain was enhanced," she suggested.

"Enhanced?"

"Shouldn't vengeance always be articulated in blood?"

Visconti studied her, trying to work out what kind of a game she was playing. Then a smile creased the corners of his mouth. "Only someone with the soul of a true artist would say such a thing. Perhaps you really do belong in my world, Cristina Falchoni." He ushered her through the doors and began the Grand Tour of his studio-workshop.

The ground floor was where the apprentices toiled, grinding pigments, preparing glues, mixing plaster and paints, preparing canvases. The boys were mainly teenagers, some as young as eleven, and all glanced at Visconti with a mixture of gratitude and fear.

"Wherever I see talent, I extend the hand of patronage," Visconti boasted. "That boy, for example —" he pointed to a dark-skinned lad who was washing blocks of marble, searching for any flaws in the stone — "I found him begging in the Colosseum. He had built the most extraordinary pillars from loose stones to catch the eye, and I immediately knew the boy had a talent."

Visconti guided Cristina to the back wall, where one young lad was cutting boars' hair into precise lengths, while another fixed the tufts to wooden handles. "These two were making a nuisance of themselves by covering buildings with charcoal sketches. It infuriated their neighbours, but the sketches showed promise, and what artist can contain his passion? So I adopted them."

Cristina watched their little hands fashion the paintbrushes. "Do you ever buy brushes, maestro?"

"Occasionally. For special commissions."

"From Padrino Coda, perhaps?"

"He does sell the most exquisite sable brushes. And he has a fine supply of pigments. Shall we?" He guided Cristina to some stairs leading up to the first floor. "A boy who finishes his apprenticeship, if he has been honest and hardworking, will find himself in this studio as one of my junior assistants."

Six young men were positioned in separate areas of the room, all of them drawing with intense concentration. Some were sketching bowls of fruit and small statues draped in cloth, others were copying Visconti's own drawings, the most advanced were working on chiaroscuro and perspective.

Visconti walked over to a young man with a hawk-like face, who was working on a life drawing of an urchin, embellishing her features to turn the street child into a heavenly cherub. The maestro studied the sketch, then gently started rubbing some of the charcoal lines with his finger. "Sfumato. That's the key. Soften the lines, let the cherub emerge from the paper. Always sfumato."

"Yes, maestro." The assistant gave a little bow of gratitude.

"Some never make it beyond the copying stage," Visconti explained as he guided Cristina up the next flight of stairs. "But the talented ones become my senior assistants."

This floor was starting to feel more like an artist's studio than a workshop. Banks of north-facing windows let in a soft light which fell on three huge canvases mounted on easels. They were all in preliminary stages, with assistants hard at work on background elements: some applied layers of colour for the distant landscape, others worked on trees, shrubs and other minor elements of the composition. One assistant was carefully painting the hands of a Madonna who did not yet have a face.

Immediately he caught sight of this painting, Visconti strode over. "Good. But the fingers can be slightly darker."

"How many shades, maestro?"

"I have set the composition to draw the viewer in and guide his eye like this —" Visconti's hands swirled across the painting. "You see? So if the fingers are too light, they interrupt the visual flow."

"I understand, maestro."

"But the texture is good."

Cristina watched as Visconti moved from painting to painting, giving advice, making adjustments, aligning everything to his vision. She realised there was not one detail in this entire studio that escaped his attention; all these assistants and apprentices were just extensions of his own creative will.

The next floor up was a mezzanine level, with a number of small offices crowded into a dark space. "This is the money level," Visconti explained as he ushered Cristina past three clerks who pored over huge ledgers. "Contracts, payments, budgets, credit control. In some ways it is the engine room of the whole operation, but let us not dawdle over filthy lucre!"

Finally, they emerged onto the top floor where only Visconti and his most valued clients were allowed. It was a vast, open space, flooded with light that was diffused through giant white sheets that hung from the ceiling.

"And this is the floor where genius resides," Visconti announced with the solemnity of a priest. "Where *I* create."

A single canvas was positioned in the centre of the space, a huge oil painting of Socrates drinking hemlock as punishment for allegedly corrupting the youth of Athens. The image had been realised with extraordinary power: a single shaft of light fell on the philosopher's face which was torn between stoicism and defiance; his eyes gazed at the viewer, challenging them to intervene and prevent this monstrous injustice.

"It's beautiful," Cristina whispered.

"Yes, it is."

She turned and looked at Visconti, amused by his complete lack of modesty.

"I know I am brilliant," he said, "so why should I pretend otherwise?"

Cristina laughed. "This whole studio is … you can really feel the creativity in every room."

"I like to think of my talent as a waterfall," Visconti explained. "It manifests in this room, from my soul, then cascades down through the floors, inspiring young artists at the beginning of their careers."

Suddenly, a stocky young man emerged from the paint cupboard and was momentarily startled by Visconti and Cristina. Even though he was in his early twenties, he had thinning hair, which he'd tried to compensate for by growing a full beard. In his hands he clutched a brush and palette loaded with six shades of ultramarine. Cristina glanced from the man to the painting and realised that he was working on Socrates' eyes.

"I … I don't understand." Cristina turned to Visconti. "I thought only you worked up here?"

Visconti hesitated, then quickly recovered. "This is my assistant, Lupo."

The young man gave a humble bow. "A pleasure, signorina."

"As a special favour, I have allowed him to watch me finish this commission."

Cristina glanced at the palette and brush in Lupo's hands. Visconti noticed and immediately strode across the room, took the brush from Lupo, dipped it in one of the blue swirls on the palette, then very carefully added three tiny flecks to Socrates' eyes. He stood back and studied the painting. "Better. So much better." Then he dropped the brush and Lupo lunged forward to catch it. "You can take those downstairs and clean up."

"Yes, maestro." Lupo bowed again and hurried away.

"And now for some wine." Visconti pulled back an exotic tapestry that hung across the room to reveal a hidden space beyond. "This is where I entertain my most valued patrons ... and my special friends," he said with a seductive smile. "Shall we?"

19: ENVY

The client lounge was like an Aladdin's cave. A circle of luxurious chairs covered in bearskin throws was surrounded by a phalanx of ornate display cabinets. Each contained a cornucopia of exotica: small lizards preserved in glass jars, miniature carvings from ancient Greece, gemstones from the far east, skeletons of deformed animals, gold nuggets from the New World, tribal curios from the Barbary coast and perfume flasks from Arabia. The treasures were so eclectic, Cristina found it overwhelming.

"Is this where you get your inspiration?" she asked, trying to discern some logic in the collection.

"That ... and this." Visconti held up a bottle of distilled spirit. "Akvavit. From the Baltics. A gift from a Russian fur trader." He poured a glass for each of them. "*Salute*. Down in one."

"*Salute*."

They both slugged back the spirit; when Cristina had finished coughing, Visconti guided her to one of the soft chairs.

"If akvavit is your inspiration, I'm surprised you get anything done," she laughed.

"In all seriousness, the inspiration is not mine, but God's," Visconti said. It was extraordinary how intensely his mind focussed when it turned to art. "There are certain moments in the day when I feel ... it is as if the hand of the Divine is upon me, touching my soul. But *when* that happens ... that cannot be predicted. I could be bathing, or walking along the street, or enjoying one of my mistresses, when suddenly..." His eyes filled with tears as he recalled the deep spirituality of those moments. "Suddenly an image coalesces in my mind. Fully formed. In one instant I glimpse the composition and colour palette, I understand the emotion and drama of the moment I must capture. After that, it is merely a question of marks on canvas." He gave a modest shrug. "That is technique. The moment of creation has already happened."

"But what technique," Cristina said with genuine admiration.

"That is what it means to be a maestro. To put one's formidable technique at the service of the mysterious act of creation. To serve a greater vision."

"If only the rest of Rome could live up to the ideals practised in this studio," Cristina replied.

"That is precisely why we must never give up." He poured some more akvavit. "We must never be dragged back into the Dark Ages. And above all, we must fight off the Ottoman threat from the East."

"Yet whenever I talk about that, people think I am being alarmist."

"Not me, Cristina. I feel your pain here." Visconti touched his heart. "Civilisation is fragile. Like a thin sheet of ice covering a lake. At any moment a crack could appear and we would slip through the surface to be consumed by the darkness beneath. We are the Enlightenment, Cristina. You and I. Remember, Islam forbids the depiction of the human form, so imagine what would happen if the Ottomans overran Europe. There would be a bonfire of all the art we treasure and admire. No more Madonnas or saints, no more portraits of military heroes, no more great leaders immortalised in oil. Artists would be reduced to painting abstract patterns and meaningless shapes. Like infants scribbling in the schoolroom. It would be a tragedy."

Cristina studied Visconti's expression, impressed by the depth and integrity that lay behind the showman's façade.

"Why is someone attacking your work, maestro?" she asked.

Visconti nodded thoughtfully, but said nothing.

"Is it because you are not afraid to speak out?"

"I fear the reason is more prosaic." He looked at Cristina.

"Such as?"

"Can I trust you with my most precious secret?"

"Of course."

"Because only then will you understand why I must endure such hatred."

"You and I want the same thing, maestro, to rid Rome of these appalling acts of barbarity."

Visconti fell to his knees and started to roll up the rug around which the chairs were clustered. Carefully he removed two planks from the floor, reached into the cavity and pulled out a large scroll of paper. "This is my design for the new St Peter's. I believe when the Holy Father sees it, he will understand that it has come not from me, but from God Himself."

Cristina watched as he unfurled the plans … to reveal the most astonishing building she had ever seen. Twelve huge concentric curves rose from the ground as if a single point in the earth had been struck with an enormous force, producing a series of shockwaves. Imagine throwing a stone into a pond, but instead of diminishing, the ripples grow larger as they spread. That was the building in its entirety, a continuous undulation in stone, the new St Peter's.

"It's incredible," Cristina whispered. "But can it be built?"

"A mere technical detail." Visconti shrugged. "More to the point, do you understand it?"

Cristina looked at the plans, mesmerised yet baffled. "No."

"At the centre, here, the point of impact is Jesus Christ. The twelve circles represent the Apostles, and the increasing height of each ripple symbolises the unstoppable rise of Christianity."

"It's brilliant. Revolutionary. And yet so simple."

"This is why I am being persecuted. All the other artists are jealous of my vision and terrified of my innovation. When I was a mediocrity, everyone liked me. But now that I have found my true voice, now that I have matured as an artist, they feel threatened. So they want the world to believe that I am cursed, that to commission Visconti is to condemn oneself to death. But they will not stop me. I swear, these attacks will only strengthen my resolve. What you have seen of my work so far is child's play compared to what is yet to come."

Cristina watched as Visconti rolled the plans up, tied them with a ribbon, and gently placed them back under the floor.

"Who, maestro?" she asked. "Who is capable of mounting this campaign of hatred against you?"

"Who is jealous and powerful and ruthless? There is only one answer: the Medici."

"We have investigated them and found no evidence."

"Because they are too clever."

"They absolutely deny all involvement."

"Of course they do. But the Medici are world-class liars. How else do you think they built a banking empire? They want their man, the plodding Sangallo, to design St Peter's, and through that they intend to claim the one prize that has always eluded them: the Papacy. You must expose the Medici, or these brilliant plans will all come to nothing."

20: CONTESSA

As soon as they entered the central lobby, Domenico and Tomasso realised that Contessa Copertino's housekeeper had recovered her composure sufficiently to transform the palazzo into a house of mourning. All the blinds had been lowered to block out daylight, black silk had been draped over every painting, the harpsichord was shrouded and the clock pendulums stopped. Now the only sound in the house was the sound of weeping.

The contessa's body had been wrapped in a white shroud and laid out on a plinth in the middle of the ballroom. Just seven days earlier, friends and family had danced across this floor, flirting and laughing, making plans for Christmas; now they were gathered in grief, the women's faces hidden behind black veils, the men sitting silently, heads bowed.

The contessa's daughters wept openly and loudly, fingers tearing at their clothing as if trying to let sorrow escape from their bodies. The priest knelt, eyes shut, mumbling through a litany of prayers for the dead.

"Forgive the intrusion," Domenico whispered to the housekeeper as they stepped out into the corridor, "but time is of the essence if we are to catch Contessa Copertino's killer."

"Of course. I'd rather you question me than the family," she replied. "They are numb with grief. And in any case, there is little that happens under this roof that I am not aware of."

The housekeeper followed Domenico into one of the day-salons, where Tomasso made her comfortable in a chair close to the crackling fire.

"We believe the same person who killed Contessa Copertino, also murdered the lawyer Antonio Ricardo," Domenico began.

"She didn't even know the lawyer," the housekeeper frowned.

"But the way the murders were carried out, there are striking elements in common. At the moment, we believe Cesare Borgia may be involved, but we have yet to establish a firm link."

"That scum," the housekeeper sniffed. "I thought he'd been thrown out of the city."

"He has. But he may have killed out of spite and revenge as he left."

"My mistress refused to have anything to do with those Spanish barbarians."

"Let me ask bluntly: was your mistress the source of rumours that Cesare Borgia had an incestuous relationship with his sister?"

The housekeeper looked stunned. "How dare you suggest such a thing?"

"It is just a theory —"

"My mistress never engaged in filthy rumour, and I will not have you smear her name in death."

"I apologise for any offence —"

"Even after her husband abandoned her, and she became the victim of other people's scurrilous gossip, my mistress never retaliated. Never."

Domenico and Tomasso exchanged an anxious glance; their principal motive for this crime seemed to be unravelling.

"Did Cesare Borgia ever visit this house?" Domenico pressed.

"Once. With his father, Pope Alexander."

"Did he ever threaten the contessa?"

"No."

"Did any of his friends make threats against the contessa?"

"No."

"Can you think of any reason why someone would want to take the contessa's life?"

The housekeeper hesitated and looked down at the polished wooden floor that was laid in an ornate pattern. Domenico realised she was holding onto something that could be significant. "Is there anything you can tell us that might help?"

The housekeeper fixed her gaze on Domenico. "I know who I would blame. But I have no evidence. I may be wrong."

"We are not accusing. We are investigating. You should speak your mind."

The housekeeper drew a deep breath. "Three days ago, my mistress's estranged husband returned unexpectedly. It was late at night, to avoid any scandal."

"Did he want money?"

"Of course. He is always broke. But what he really wanted was for the *Fountain of Nemesis* to be dismantled. He felt it was publicly humiliating him. My mistress refused. She said the humiliation was all hers."

"Did he threaten legal action?"

"On what grounds? And with what money? My mistress knew he was weak and started taunting him. Mocking his lover. Questioning his virility. They argued. It became ugly."

"Violent?"

"They were screaming at each other with such hatred. It was terrible to hear."

"How did it end?"

"The count stormed out of the house, threatening her."

"And was that the last time she saw him?"

The housekeeper nodded. "My mistress thought she had won. How wrong she was."

"And yet," Tomasso began, "the killer left the statue of Nemesis unharmed. If the count hated it so much, why didn't he vandalise it himself?"

"He desecrated it with my mistress's body."

"And in so doing, drew the attention of the whole of Rome to a statue he hated?"

"Count Copertino is a stupid man," the housekeeper scoffed. "He has no depth. He married for money, abandoned his wife for sodomy, and achieved nothing in between. That he cannot exact revenge without humiliating himself will surprise no-one. Forget the Borgias. The man you need to hunt down is Count Copertino."

"Do you have any idea where he might have fled?" Domenico asked.

"Like all cockroaches, he will have scurried into the nearest crack."

21: MANHUNT

They had procedures for this.

Criers were dispatched across the city carrying the urgent message that Count Copertino was wanted on suspicion of murdering his wife. Anyone with information of his whereabouts was ordered to report to the authorities immediately. Under no circumstances were individuals to try and apprehend, or even approach the count, who was believed to be armed and dangerous.

Working with the City Watch, Tomasso had all eighteen gates in the Aurelian Walls closed within the hour, then dispatched Apostolic Guards to set up extra document checkpoints at each one.

It triggered chaos.

Farmers, tradesmen, priests and ordinary families soon found themselves caught in huge queues trying to get out of the city. Tempers frayed, fights broke out, the wealthy attempted to bribe their way to special treatment, but the guards held firm; everyone had to have their documents checked and stamped. No exceptions.

Tomasso looked down on the heaving mass of citizens from the walkway that ran for twelve miles along the top of the Aurelian Walls, encircling the city and its seven hills.

Thank God for these walls. Fifty feet high, eleven thick and impossible to scale, they had been keeping Rome safe from gangs of marauding bandits for over a thousand years, but they were just as effective at preventing wanted felons from escaping the city and vanishing into the surrounding forests.

Tomasso studied the faces in the crowd below. What the angry citizens didn't realise was that these long queues weren't a by-product of the extra checks, they were the whole point, for it enabled guards to study the behaviour of the trapped. Who was angry? Who was impatient? Who was acting suspiciously?

"This is a disgrace!" An angry monk caught in the crush had noticed Tomasso on top of the wall and rightly assumed he was responsible for the mess. "Let us go! We're not criminals!"

Others caught on and started hurling abuse at Tomasso.

"Let us go!" "Shame on you!" "*Figlio di puttana!*"

But Tomasso didn't flinch. He had a job to do, and he wasn't going to let a mob get in the way of catching a serial murderer.

With the roads in lockdown, the only other way out of Rome was by river, which is why the Apostolic Guards launched patrols on the water and set up two checkpoints: at Ponte Sublicio in the south, and Ponte Sant'Angelo in the north. Every vessel was stopped and searched, from the smallest boat carrying a young bride and her dowry to her new home, to the enormous grain barges heading downriver to the coast. By noon, the Tiber was gridlocked; at its narrowest points, you could cross the river by leaping from boat to boat without getting your feet wet. At the same time, Domenico was leading surprise raids on known criminal haunts. Count Copertino was a dissolute gambler, addicted to losing his wife's money by betting on dice, cards, dog fighting and just about anything else that could be reduced to a set of odds; on any day of the week, many of the so-called respectable men in these dens of vice could have been arrested for a host of minor offences, but it suited the authorities to turn a blind eye so that when they were desperate for information, these 'worthy men' could be squeezed, and would invariably squeal to protect their honour.

When all that yielded nothing, Domenico and Tomasso started a shakedown of informants … which led them down an alley off Via della Croce, to the house of the notorious snitch Ragno.

As Tomasso kicked open the door, Domenico glimpsed a trapdoor in the kitchen floor slamming shut. "Quick! Before he bolts it!" They surged into the kitchen and managed to lever up the hatch just as Ragno was trying to slide the securing bars across from the inside. Tomasso reached down into the gloom and hauled out a wiry man whose face was heavily covered in pox scars. "Hands off me!"

"And I thought you'd be pleased to see us," Domenico said, bundling Ragno into the corner of the kitchen. "Why were you trying to hide?"

"I thought it was the mother-in-law."

"Of course you did."

"You haven't heard her talk. Goes on and on about nothing."

"Well now *you* can do the talking."

Tomasso peered into the hole: it was the size of a tomb, but Ragno had fitted it out with candles, a skin of wine, two jars of dried fruit and a thin air pipe that went sideways through the wall to the back of the house. "This looks cosy. How long did it take you to dig?"

"It's nothing. Just a bit of fun."

"How do you stop it filling up with water?" Tomasso asked. "Especially with the rain we've been having."

"Lined it with stone, didn't I? Watertight."

"Very nice."

"So," Domenico leaned over the snitch, "why were you hiding?"

"Me? I wasn't. I told you. Why would I hide?"

"Wrong answer." Domenico grabbed a large barrel that was stacked against the wall and hauled it over, sending gallons of water cascading into the hide-hole.

"No!" Ragno screamed. "*Testa di cazzo!*"

"Oops." Tomasso shook his head and peered into the hole that was now a quarter full of water. "That's going to take some scooping out."

"Shall we try again?" Domenico suggested.

"I don't know nothing!"

"Then why do we pay you every month?"

"A ducat a month! You call that pay?"

Tomasso grabbed a second barrel and hauled it onto its side, sending more water flooding into the hide-hole.

"All right! All right!"

"Doesn't like his hole getting wet," Domenico said to Tomasso.

"Plenty more where that came from," Tomasso replied, looking at the remaining barrels.

"The murder's nothing to do with Count Copertino," Ragno said.

"Now we're getting somewhere."

"But it's not what you think."

"Oh? How about this: he held her down while you slit her throat," Domenico replied.

"No! That's not true!"

"The other way round then? You held her, he killed her."

"No!"

"Well, which is it?"

"Neither!"

Crash! Splosh! Another barrel of water went thundering into the hide-hole, which now flooded chest deep. "Stop!"

Ragno yelled. "Please!" He looked in dismay at his flooded hiding place.

"How do you know he's innocent?"

"Because the count wanted to poison his wife. Just make her sick. Really sick, so he could return and take charge of the house. He wanted me to supply the poison."

"That makes you an accomplice."

"No! I didn't do nothing. I told him poison's not my thing."

"But I heard you can supply anything," Tomasso said, his fingers walking along the rim of the final barrel.

"I said I would ask around. Before I had a chance, he arrived here in a panic. Screamed that someone had murdered his wife. He wanted me to hide him."

"In there?" Domenico pointed to the flooded hole.

"I turned him away," Ragno insisted.

"Don't believe you." Tomasso gripped the barrel, ready to tip it over.

"Wait!"

"Talk!"

Crushed, Ragno looked at the ruined hole. "It'll take me forever to empty that out."

"Talk, Ragno."

"I told him to go to the dead."

"He's killed himself?"

"No. The city of the dead. The old catacombs under Rome."

"Why didn't you just say that in the first place?" Tomasso asked, handing Ragno an empty jug to start scooping out the water.

"Because I'm not a snitch."

"Oh no, that's *exactly* what you are. A snitch. It's why we love you."

22: COURTESANS

"How do you know he's not lying?" Isra demanded.

"Why are you so hostile to the man?" Cristina replied.

"I'm just saying, you went to Visconti to uncover threads connecting him to the murders. You spent the morning being charmed —"

"We talked. That was all," Cristina interrupted.

"And drank. And flirted, no doubt."

"What's got into you?"

"And now he has spun you round to reopen a line of investigation that you had already closed down."

"The link is, and always was, that the rival dynasties are trying to put each other out of the running to build St Peter's. Visconti is convinced the Medici are behind the murders."

"So you trust his instinct more than your own?"

"He has close contacts with the powerbrokers. He sees them in a way outsiders cannot."

"You and I got the measure of what is going on in the Medici palazzo."

"But what if we missed something, Isra?"

"And what if Visconti is deliberately trying to throw your investigation off course?"

"Why? What possible motive could he have?"

"Maybe *that's* what we should be investigating."

Cristina drew a deep breath, trying to ease the tension. "Indulge me a moment. Let's assume that the Medici are playing a very dark game, so dark that even the servants know nothing about it. How can we get behind all that polished charm and discover the truth?"

They sat in silence in the library, mulling the problem. The only sound was the steady tick of the verge and foliot clock, marking everyone's time to the grave.

Finally, Isra looked up. "There is another possibility," she said warily.

"Go on."

"Courtesans."

Cristina felt herself tense; that was not a world she felt comfortable with.

"It was Giovanni de' Medici's visit to a courtesan that caused the violent argument with his lovers. That could be our way in."

Cristina shook her head. "Why would a prostitute know more than servants who live with the family day and night?"

"Courtesans," Isra corrected, "not prostitutes."

"Either way, it's irrelevant," Cristina said testily.

Isra studied her, then smiled.

"What?"

"You need to broaden your reading."

"Who writes about courtesans? What on earth is there to say? It's just a physical process. Like … like going to the toilet."

"'If you do away with harlots, the world will be consumed with lust.' Who said that?"

"A brothel owner?"

"St Augustine."

"Really?" Cristina's eyes widened. "*The* St Augustine?"

"And Thomas Aquinas agreed."

"I had no idea."

"What is the population of Rome?" Isra continued.

"About a hundred thousand. Give or take."

"And how many licensed courtesans are there in the city?"

"I don't know. And I don't want to know."

"Six thousand."

"What? No! That's impossible."

"It's true. One courtesan for every eight men."

Cristina's mind pulsed with incredulity. How could she have lived in Rome all her life yet remained oblivious to such a startling fact? She looked at her young housekeeper. "How do you know so much about all this?"

"I know women who have chosen that vocation."

"Vocation?"

"The point is, those six thousand women are like a city-wide information network. And that's what we need to plug into. They know what is really going on in Rome."

"So ... so we need to start cruising dark alleys at night? Talking to bedraggled streetwalkers?"

"No, no, no."

"I can't see how that will shed light on political machinations swirling around the Vatican."

"You've got it all wrong, Cristina." Isra stood up and made her way to the door. "I'll fetch your cloak."

"Where are we going?"

"To broaden your horizons."

It was a chilly winter evening, but the clouds had cleared, and now hard sunlight cast long shadows across the streets around Piazza di Spagna.

"So ... where do we start looking?" Cristina asked.

"We don't. We just walk and keep our eyes open."

Cristina surrendered herself into Isra's hands and let herself be guided through Rome's familiar streets, only now she listened to Isra's running commentary.

It was a revelation.

In upmarket gown shops, the beautiful young women cooing over furs and velvets were accompanied not by their fathers, as Cristina had always assumed, but by old men who were desperately trying to buy back a youth and sexual vigour that had long since abandoned them.

At least a third of the carriages delivering Rome's glitterati to banquets and dances in the palazzos on the banks of the Tiber contained young women who were being paid for love by the hour.

The most fashionable women walking elegantly in the most precarious chopines were not part of Rome's elite, rather they were paid by that elite to deliver the wanton passion that no longer interested well-established wives.

And the young women who were still waiting to be snapped up by rich old men attracted attention by strolling along popular arcades in boisterous groups, sometimes accompanied by lute players who serenaded their beauty, and at other times walking monkeys or other exotic animals on leads.

Now that she could see it, Cristina realised that it was everywhere: beautiful young women being spoiled by rich older men. And the reason she had never really noticed until now, is that it was so blatant; these women weren't the benighted souls of the popular imagination, they were the lifeblood of Roman society.

"Do the heads of the great families really parade themselves so shamelessly?" Cristina asked.

"No. Because there is yet another level, even higher than this," Isra replied. "A place where discretion is absolute."

"And where is that?"

"Behind closed doors. Where the most elite men enjoy the most elite women. And that is the place where men have no secrets."

Cristina frowned. "This doesn't make sense. Why would someone have a clandestine meeting with a stranger, only to reveal family secrets?"

"Because in the arms of courtesans, men say all sorts of things."

"Why? They're only there for sex."

"Quite the opposite," Isra replied. "They think they crave sex, but what most men really want is intimacy. They long to tell their innermost secrets without any repercussions. And that is the one thing that cannot be done in a society marriage."

"So rather tell a stranger than a wife?"

"Is she still a stranger if you see her twice a week, month after month? Surely she is then a lover."

"But without any loyalty."

"The key to the success of a great courtesan is not sexual prowess, but discretion. Absolute discretion," Isra said. "Whatever Giovanni de' Medici's darkest secrets, it's a fair bet that his courtesan knows all about them."

"So how do we find her? This secret lover?"

"In Rome, the most celebrated courtesan of all is Giulia Campana."

"Will she even talk to us? Why would she be interested if we're not clients?"

"I believe I can get us a meeting," Isra said cryptically.

Cristina looked at her friend, wondering what other strange worlds this young woman was privy to.

23: CATACOMBS

Legend had it that there were hundreds of miles of catacombs under Rome containing countless thousands of bodies, but no-one could be sure since many of the tunnels had been sealed up for centuries to prevent looting. Now the only way to enter this city of the dead was through the catacombs of St Sebastian.

Tomasso lit a couple of slow-burn torches and handed one to Domenico. "Have you been into them before?"

"Oh yes. All the time." Domenico glanced at the ominous black mouth of the cave. "Nothing nicer than a family picnic surrounded by an army of the dead."

Tomasso grinned. "Me neither."

Domenico checked his sword and dagger. "Ready?"

Tomasso nodded, and followed Domenico as he picked his way past some fallen boulders and entered the darkness of the catacombs.

The early Christians who lived in Rome didn't agree with the pagan custom of cremating the dead, so they created these vast underground cemeteries instead. As Domenico swept his flaming torch back and forth, he started to get a sense of the true scale of the place.

The primary tunnel was about eight-foot square and had been cut into the solid rock for hundreds of feet. Carved into the walls were thousands of rectangular niches, sometimes stacked ten high, into which the dead were placed. The bodies weren't embalmed, each one was just wrapped in a sheet and laid in a nook, which was then sealed with a gravestone onto which names and prayers were engraved.

"The stench must have been terrible," Tomasso whispered, glancing at the endless walls of skeletons.

"It's bad enough now," Domenico replied. "And that's after a thousand years."

In truth, there wasn't much left to smell; natural decay, looters and a small army of rats had stripped the bodies of everything that could rot, leaving jumbles of bones spilling out of the nooks and strewn across the floor. Yet the deeper they went, the more pungent the musty smell of damp earth became, until it felt as if they were wading through the heavy, frigid air.

Suddenly Domenico stopped and raised his torch: the main tunnel split into three branches. "So … which way did the count go?"

Tomasso thrust his torch into the mouth of each tunnel, but there were no obvious differences between them. "He wouldn't want to risk getting lost down here."

"Then he must have left himself a clue or he'd never get out again."

The two men ran their torches over the walls, searching for any sign that was out of place amongst the carved symbols.

"Here. What about this?" Tomasso pointed to a neat groove that had been cut into the corner of the tunnel wall close to the floor.

Domenico ran his fingers over it. "Looks recent." He unsheathed his sword and rested the blade in the stone scar — it was a perfect fit. "That's how he marked each junction. He hacked it with his sword so that he knows which way to come back."

"So all we have to do is follow the grooves?"

"In theory." Domenico thrust his torch into the chosen tunnel, but the intense darkness immediately swallowed up the light like a starving man devouring morsels of bread.

They waded deeper into the darkness, checking each junction carefully, trusting the stone scars to keep them on the right path. Every now and then, the tunnels would widen out into small underground chapels whose walls were covered in faded frescoes depicting ghoulish moments from the Christian story: Jonah being swallowed by a whale, gladiators feeding martyrs to the lions, Saint Sebastian being executed with arrows fired by his own soldiers.

Further on they came to some steps going down, deeper into the earth, leading to yet more layers of labyrinth; it was a wonder the city above hadn't collapsed in one giant sinkhole.

Still trusting the hacked grooves, Domenico and Tomasso edged down the steep steps, fighting off the sense of dread that threatened to engulf them.

Then suddenly —

The clattering, rolling sound of a rockfall. The very last thing you want to hear when you're deep underground.

Domenico and Tomasso froze, desperately hoping that this was not the start of a chain reaction.

A few more rocks rolled in the darkness.

Then silence. Mercifully.

"That must be him," Domenico whispered. "He's triggered a rockfall."

"Maybe we should turn back, sir."

"Not when we're this close."

"What if he's buried alive? We don't want to go the same way."

"Just don't touch the walls. Don't disturb anything. We'll be okay." Without waiting for a reply, Domenico headed deeper into the tunnel, giving Tomasso little choice but to follow.

Three hundred paces further, they came to it — a huge pile of rocks had fallen from the ceiling completely blocking the tunnel, wisps of dust were still swirling around the debris. On the other side, they could hear the frantic squeak of terrified rats hurrying away.

"You think the count's under there?" Tomasso said, looking at the chaos of rocks.

"We didn't pass him coming back, so he's under it, or trapped beyond it. Either way, he's dead."

"Let's get out before the same thing happens to us," Tomasso urged.

But just as he turned to go, Domenico grabbed his deputy's arm. "Can you feel that?"

Both men strained their senses in the darkness.

"What?"

Domenico tilted his head back. "There's a breeze coming from somewhere."

"But we're four levels down."

"They must have cut ventilation shafts, going all the way up to the surface. Or they would have suffocated down here." Slowly Domenico led the way back up the tunnel, moving his face from side to side, trying to home in on the source of fresh air.

Finally, he stopped under a ragged hole in the tunnel roof and peered up — he could feel the air dropping directly onto his face. "Here. Breathe in."

Tomasso stood next to Domenico, tilted his face up and breathed deeply, enjoying momentary relief from the pungent earth.

And then he felt it — a tiny trickle of dust falling onto his face. Immediately Tomasso thrust his flickering torch up into the shaft, but it barely punctured the gloom.

Another trickle of sand pulsed down. "I think he's up there," Tomasso whispered.

"What?"

"He's climbed up."

Both men held their torches into the shaft...

A scream ripped through the darkness like a howling demon.

Before Domenico could react, a huge black shape dropped down onto him, crushing him under his weight.

The shape lashed out, striking Domenico in the chest and face in a furious frenzy.

Tomasso swooped at the figure with his torch, forcing him to recoil. The creature spun round, lashing out, and for a split second Tomasso saw the face of Count Copertino, pale and angry, his grey eyes filled with spite.

Domenico reached for the dagger in his belt, but the count was faster. He grabbed the blade and hurtled back up the tunnel.

"Are you all right, sir?" Tomasso asked.

"After him!" Domenico scrambled to his feet. "Don't let him escape!"

They lunged forward, chasing the sound of footsteps. Any thoughts of checking the grooves vanished, all they could do was hope the count wasn't leading them deeper into the labyrinth.

Whoomph. Whoomph. Whoomph.

It sounded like a blade chopping the air as it sped towards them.

Instinctively Domenico ducked, just as a human femur spun through the darkness, skimming his head, and thumped into Tomasso's chest.

"Ooof!"

"You okay?"

Tomasso gasped, but before he could recover his breath, more bones were being hurled at them: skulls, collarbones, a pelvis skimmed like a saucer.

Domenico and Tomasso flattened themselves against the floor, pinned down under the fire of human relics. Domenico glanced around, desperate for inspiration, and saw that a gravestone covering one of the niches to their left was half-dislodged. "There! Help me pull it down."

The two men scrambled across the floor, grabbed the stone slab and yanked it away from the niche.

"Hold it up!" Domenico commanded. "Like a shield!"

They grabbed either end and held it in front of them like one of the rectangular shields Roman centurions used in battle. It was clumsy, but effective. As more bones hurtled out of the darkness, they hit the stone shield and splintered, allowing Domenico and Tomasso to make their way up the tunnel without getting knocked unconscious.

As he saw the flickering torch getting closer, Count Copertino realised what was going on. Abandoning his bombardment, he turned and ran.

But Tomasso was quicker. As soon as he heard the count's footsteps, he dropped the shield and hurtled after him, running faster than he could see.

He burst into one of the underground chapels and glimpsed the count hiding behind one of the pillars holding up the roof.

Tomasso leapt into the gloom, arms stretching out, and slammed into the count like a cannonball.

Count Copertino tried to get to his feet, but Tomasso was stronger and younger, and he leapt on the count's back, smothering him. "It's over! Enough!"

Still the count tried to wriggle free, refusing to accept defeat. Until he felt the sharp point of a blade pressed into the side of his head.

"Don't tempt me," Domenico said, pressing the point harder into the count's temple. "Because it would be my absolute pleasure to kill you now."

24: MADAME

The hunting lodge was hidden amongst the vineyards on the gentle slopes of the Pincian Hill, just outside the city walls.

As they approached on horseback, Cristina thought how unassuming it looked; well-appointed yet modest, built with a combination of pastoral charm and classical elegance, it was the sort of place you might expect to find a retired general and his wife living out their twilight years. The only thing that didn't fit were the large number of elegant carriages waiting patiently on the driveway that looped in front of the lodge.

"Is that it?" Cristina turned to Isra. "Rome's most illustrious brothel?"

"What did you expect? Naked women lining the road trying to kidnap punters?"

In truth, Cristina didn't know what to expect; this was not a world that had ever engaged her mind, and she wasn't convinced it would yield any useful results. It was only Isra's insistence that had persuaded her to give it a chance.

As they arrived at the imposing front doors, Cristina looked for a bellpull or knocker, but there was no way of summoning the people inside.

"Don't worry," Isra said. "They already know we're here."

"How?"

"They just know."

Cristina and Isra stood there in silence; after a few moments they noticed movement behind the door's spyhole: someone was looking at them, so why didn't they let them in?

Isra gave a small laugh. "They're confused. We're neither clients nor courtesans."

Suddenly the doors flew open and a glamorous woman in her late thirties reached out and hugged Isra. "I knew you'd change your mind! Eventually!" She planted extravagant kisses on Isra's cheeks.

"You look well," Isra said, disentangling herself. "Thank you for seeing us."

"For you? An open invitation."

"Giulia Campana, this is Cristina Falchoni."

Giulia turned her quick gaze on Cristina, sizing her up. "At last. I've heard so much."

"You have?" Cristina glanced at Isra for an explanation.

"Don't worry," Giulia smiled, "it's all good."

Cristina studied the courtesan who dressed with unabashed allure: plenty of cleavage, fine silk clothes, with three ostrich feathers sticking coquettishly from her coiled blonde hair. There was a sparkle in her eyes that suggested both willingness and rebellion; it was a potent combination.

Giulia Campana put an affectionate arm around Isra. "Are you sure you made the right choice? Signorina Falchoni looks very serious."

"The work is interesting," Isra replied.

"Keeping house?"

"Cristina has an extensive library. She's taught me English and French —"

"Not the French I would have taught you." Giulia gave a confidential laugh that excluded Cristina.

"Am I missing something?" Cristina asked.

"I tried to hire Isra. Twice, in fact. I offered her plenty of money, glamour, the chance to mix with the finest gentlemen in Rome." Giulia gave Isra a playful punch. "And you turned it all down to become a housekeeper."

The way she said it made Cristina feel a twinge of guilt. "I didn't realise. You never said."

Isra looked awkward, caught between these two wilful women. "It was when I first arrived in Rome. I was young."

"It's not too late," Giulia said seductively. "You're still very beautiful. Men do love the exotic. But are you still a virgin?"

"Is that really an appropriate question?" Cristina said testily.

In a flash, Giulia's playfulness vanished, revealing a steely businesswoman. "I'm merely being pragmatic."

"Asking about a woman's purity?"

"Purity?" Giulia smiled as the charming façade returned. "Now that is an interesting word. It tells me much about you, Signorina Falchoni."

"I doubt it," Cristina replied.

"For a start, it tells me that you are a virgin. Which means that for all your book learning, you are still very naïve."

"You don't know anything about me."

"And you don't know anything about me. Or my world. Which is why there is judgement in your eyes."

"That's not true," Cristina said, glancing away.

"Perhaps you are one of those voyeurs who wants to taste forbidden fruit, then hurry back to your respectable life where you can feel morally superior," Giulia said, pacing slowly around Cristina. "But you have misunderstood the nature of my business. Just because no-one here is pure, does not mean that we are all swimming in shit."

"I never jump to conclusions, Signora Campana. That is not my way."

"Perhaps. But let me enlighten you: we are the most honest house in Rome, even though we have to hide in the hills. We explore the boundaries between love and lust, which are more complex than someone like you could imagine. We allow men and women to be who they want to be, without judgement or moralising."

"And that is precisely why we came to see you," Cristina said, scrambling to return to firmer ground. "To find out the truth about a man who presents himself to the world as the epitome of respectability."

"We never betray the confidentiality of clients." Giulia turned to Isra. "You should have known better than to bring her here for that."

"Not even if it is to solve a brutal double murder?" Cristina's words seemed to jolt the courtesan. "I saw Contessa Copertino shortly after she had been murdered," Cristina continued. "Her throat had been slit. The beautiful fountain she had commissioned was running red with her own blood. I need to bring her killer to justice. That is why Isra brought me here. Now, you can help, or we can leave. The choice is yours, Giulia Campana, but I really do not have time to play games. So, which is it to be?"

25: DISCRETION

For a few moments Giulia Campana studied Cristina with a cool, enigmatic gaze. Then she clicked her fingers at a young woman who was replenishing the brandy glass of a man with long grey hair. "Take my guests to the south veranda."

"Yes, madame." The woman hurried over and started to usher them through the lodge.

Cristina tried to appear nonchalant, but her eyes darted in every direction as she soaked in the details of this strange world. The brothel wasn't like anything she had imagined. Musicians played civilised music in every room; elegant hostesses were plying guests with copious amounts of finger food and alcohol; in one salon, a dozen men wearing nothing but bath towels were listening to a young woman dressed as Aphrodite reciting erotic poems by Catullus; in the next, two athletic eunuchs were dancing a pavane. The whole lodge could have been an upmarket Salon of Arts, were it not for the nakedness and wanton flirtation. And yet Cristina was struck by how playful the atmosphere was; rather than being sordid, it felt strangely innocent, like a Garden of Delights without the guilt.

"Apparently, there are cellars," Isra whispered, sensing that she needed to correct the sensual glow of first impressions.

"Cellars? For all the wine?"

"Er … no. For more specialised tastes."

"Oh. You mean —"

"I would leave it there if I were you."

They were shown onto a large veranda that looked south over the city. "Madame will be with you soon." The young woman set down some wine and left.

It was a surprisingly mild evening for December, and the humid air that had ballooned up from the north African coast during the day still had a sweet tang.

"I think Giulia likes you," Isra said, handing Cristina a cup of wine.

"It didn't seem that way."

"Trust me. If she didn't, we'd already be on the road back to the city."

Cristina walked to the balustrade and gazed at the thousands of flickering torches dotted across Rome, illuminating streets and courtyards. What a different world it was down there, where the moral framework of the Church held everyone tightly, while just a mile up into the hills all the rules had been dissolved. Yet the result wasn't anarchy, but pleasure.

"I knew Contessa Copertino. She was a friend."

Cristina spun round and saw Giulia Campana standing by the veranda doors. "Really?"

"Don't sound so surprised."

"How can an aristocratic patron of the arts be friends with a courtesan?"

"There you go judging me again." Giulia crossed the veranda and joined Cristina and Isra at the balustrade. She gazed across the city as if she owned it. "You'd be amazed at my circle of friends."

"For example?" Cristina replied.

"Princes and professors. Cardinals and cavalry officers." Giulia chuckled to herself. "If I wanted to take over the Italian peninsula, I would have little problem. I know so many secrets of the rich and powerful, I could have them dancing in the palm of my hand."

"So why don't you?"

"Because I have no interest. My life is defined by pleasure, not power."

Something about this didn't ring true for Cristina. "I don't believe that princes are so starved of love, they have to come to you."

"Love has nothing to do with it. Love is just a myth peddled by the timid."

"Sex, then," Cristina corrected herself.

Giulia studied Cristina. "Do you know why men come to courtesans? Because they don't have to pretend. They can just be."

"Even cardinals?" Cristina countered. "Men who have taken a vow of chastity?"

Giulia scoffed. "There is no such thing as true purity. Even the purest have a vein of corruption running through them. That is what it means to be human."

"An extremely cynical view."

"Quite the opposite. It's what Christ himself believed; it's why He died on the cross for us. 'Behold the Lamb of God who takes away the sin of the world.' But recognising that we are flawed sinners is not a reason to give up. It's just being honest. And one should always try to see the world with unclouded vision."

"So what does your unclouded gaze see when it falls on Giovanni de' Medici?" Cristina asked.

"I cannot discuss individual clients."

"We have been given very specific information that the Medici family was involved in the murders of Contessa Copertino and Antonio Ricardo," Cristina insisted.

Giulia glanced at Isra. "Is she always this stubborn?"

"I think 'determined' is the word you're looking for," Isra replied.

"My, my. What a loyal housekeeper you've become." Giulia turned back to Cristina. "I'm sorry, but I cannot help. If I betrayed a confidence, it would ruin my business."

"So much for your fondness for the contessa."

"Do not judge me!" Giulia said sharply. "I've already warned you about that."

Cristina could see the courtesan was getting rattled, now was the time to press harder. "You boast of all the secrets you hold, all the people you know, yet when it comes to stopping a killer, you become suddenly mute."

"My knowledge, my choice," Giulia countered.

"What use is knowledge if you refuse to apply it? It becomes a sin, like gluttony, only worse because it is tainted with arrogance and conceit."

"I think it's time you left."

"Perhaps now we are touching on the elaborate fraud you have constructed up here in the hills," Cristina was going in for the kill. "You pretend that your 'lodge' is all about being truly alive through the senses, but when it comes to preserving life, you refuse to lift a finger."

"Enough!" Giulia snapped. "I will not be insulted by a woman who has only ever known the love of a book!"

"Why don't we all take a moment?" Isra stepped between the two women.

"No. I think we're done," Giulia said.

"You know how much I respect you," Isra said to Giulia. "But I also respect Signorina Falchoni. Like you, she's had to fight prejudice at every turn. Like you, it has made her strong and resourceful. The truth is that she is the most intelligent person I have ever met."

Giulia looked from Isra to Cristina. "You're not just the housekeeper, are you?"

"Who knows what problems you may encounter in the future," Isra continued. "But if you help us now, it will put us in your debt. A debt which you can call in without question."

"Are you trying to play me?" Giulia demanded.

"We're just trying to find a way forward," Isra replied.

Giulia went very still, considering the proposal. Then she snapped her fingers and beckoned to one of the young women standing in the doorway. Moments later the two eunuchs strode into the room and stood menacingly in front of Cristina and Isra; it was clear the men were no longer interested in dancing a pavane.

"I suggest you rest awhile in my study," Giulia said. "Try to find some manners. Then perhaps we can resume this conversation."

She strode back into the main building.

"Wait!" Cristina tried to chase after her, but the eunuchs grabbed her and Isra and bundled them away.

26: INTERROGATION

"Only the guilty run."

"Who says I was running?" Count Copertino stared at Domenico with petulant defiance.

They were in the largest interrogation room of the Apostolic Guards' complex at the Vatican. Outside, troops of the night shift were preparing to start their patrols; inside, Tomasso had just put a flaming torch into the wall bracket. As holding cells went, this was luxurious: no rats, dripping water or torture instruments, and a fresh breeze blowing through the barred window. Domenico and the count sat opposite each other on either side of a sturdy oak table.

"What else could you have been doing underground?" Domenico asked.

"Perhaps I chose to spend the night in the catacombs. Perhaps I wanted to get closer to God and pay my respects to the dead, until I was rudely interrupted by two blundering Apostolic Guards."

"Do you always pray by attacking people with human remains?"

"I thought you were grave robbers. It was self-defence."

Domenico and Tomasso exchanged a weary look; they had questioned many suspects over the years, but it was the slippery ones with attitude who always proved the most difficult.

"While we're on the subject of the dead," Domenico pressed, "let's talk about your late wife, Contessa Copertino."

"Talk? Is that all you can do?" Count Copertino mocked. "You should be out there rounding up suspects."

"We have. You're it," Tomasso replied.

Count Copertino gave a snide laugh. "Pathetic."

"We have a sworn witness statement giving a detailed account of the argument you had with your wife shortly before she was murdered," Domenico said firmly.

"All married couples argue."

"But this was a violent argument. You wanted the *Fountain of Nemesis* dismantled. She refused. So you abused her."

"She was trying to humiliate me!" Count Copertino was starting to lose his supercilious calm. "I have led troops into battle. I have survived enemy fire. I should be honoured, not held up to ridicule before the whole of Rome."

Domenico rocked back in his chair. "Clearly you feel strongly about this. Strongly enough to murder, perhaps?"

"My wife was a *puttana*. Leaving her was the best thing I've done." The count's grey eyes glistened with malice. "But I didn't want her dead."

"Why? Because you're a nice man?" Domenico retorted. "You seriously expect us to believe that?"

Tomasso consulted the witness notes. "Quote: they were screaming at each other with such hatred. It was terrible to hear."

"Ah, the words of the blubber-fat housekeeper, no doubt."

"You should hear what she said about you."

"I really couldn't care less."

Unperturbed, Tomasso again read from his notes. "He has no depth. He married for money, abandoned his wife for sodomy, and achieved nothing in between."

"Exactly what I'd expect a dried-up old crone to testify."

"What a stupid thing to say." Domenico leant across the oak table, scrutinising the count. "Do you not understand, the more insulting you become, the more you incriminate yourself."

"On the contrary." Count Copertino shrugged. "It is you who is stupid. It's blatantly obvious I did not murder my wife, because now that she is dead, the source of my money has dried up. What man would sabotage his own income?"

"Yet you tried to poison her."

"The snitch Ragno is hardly a reliable witness."

"It shows motive," Domenico pressed.

"It was a fantasy. A wild dream to make her sick so that I could control her," Count Copertino scoffed. "Who hasn't thought about poisoning their wife at some point? God knows, most of them deserve it."

The interrogation room fell silent, as if the stone walls themselves were shocked by the count's bitterness.

"What on earth does that Swiss bombardier see in you?" Domenico asked. "Because all I see is an angry man, railing against the world."

Count Copertino became strangely subdued. "Don't talk of him in this cell."

"Who? Your young lover?"

"I said quiet!" Count Copertino snapped.

Domenico turned to Tomasso. "I believe we have touched on something."

"He is nothing to do with any of this."

"Then why are you so desperate to protect him?"

"Because…" Count Copertino's voice dropped to a whisper. "Because he is the only reason I have left to live."

Even though Domenico knew what a vicious, foul-mouthed man the count was, this sudden vulnerability was oddly affecting.

"You cannot know what it means to have lived a lie for so long," Count Copertino said. "To have pretended to be something you are not, then to suddenly find a path to freedom…"

"That's not how your wife saw it," Tomasso said.

Count Copertino shook his head. "She was hurt. For a few months she had to endure pain. But I have been living in pain my entire life. I did not know happiness until I accepted who I am. And now I want to live fully. In freedom. Away from the stinking corruption of Rome."

"There are many who pray to live in the gilded cage you complain of," Domenico said.

"Then let their prayers be answered. They are welcome to that corrupted life."

The three men sat for a while, listening to the bird-like fluttering of the torches as they burned in the gloom.

"What about the first murder?" Tomasso said eventually. "The lawyer, Antonio Ricardo — you knew him?"

Count Copertino shrugged. "I knew of him. He got rich quickly and succumbed to the delusion of money."

"A count is hardly in a position to lecture others about the foibles of wealth," Domenico replied.

"How many times? The money was hers. Which is precisely why I can see how corrosive it is. Having money makes people believe they are clever, while the truth is, they are often just lucky. Ricardo got lucky with his New World gamble. He could just as easily have gone bankrupt and ended up starving in a gutter somewhere. But having got rich, he tried to disguise his luck with cultural pretension. In the end, Antonio Ricardo got what he deserved."

"You really do like to incriminate yourself, don't you?" Domenico said with a wry smile.

But Count Copertino locked his gaze on Domenico. "On the night Ricardo was murdered, I was with my old regimental commanders. We enjoyed a banquet in the officers' mess. It lasted all night. Fifty soldiers can vouch for me. Alibis don't get much stronger than that." The count sat back in his chair as if he had just won a game of chess.

"So why run from us?" Tomasso asked. "Why hide in the catacombs?"

Count Copertino hesitated.

"Tell us the truth this time," Domenico advised. "Forget the attitude."

"I ran because I knew what people would assume. They would point accusing fingers at me. Turn the investigation into a witch hunt. What chance would I have of a fair trial?"

"Yet running just makes you look more guilty."

"All I want is to get out of Rome and never return. Finally, I want to know happiness."

"With your Swiss bombardier?" Domenico said.

"With someone who understands me," Count Copertino replied. "So, unless you want to face legal action for wrongful arrest, I suggest you release me immediately."

Despite all the aggressive posturing, Domenico knew that the count was not the murderer. He may be a spiteful and selfish man, but he was not the killer they were hunting. No-one would use fifty officers as an alibi if they were bluffing.

Reluctantly, Tomasso unlocked the leg irons. "You're free to go."

As he strode to the door, the count turned and looked back at Domenico one last time. "I hope I never see you again."

"The feeling is mutual. Believe me."

And that was it — Count Copertino walked away a free man.

Tomasso listened to his footsteps receding. "There goes our best lead."

Once again they were faced with nothing but frustration and dead ends.

"Go home," Domenico said to his deputy. "Get a good night's sleep. Perhaps things will look less bleak in the morning."

"Yes, sir."

"And thank you, for tonight. You did well."

27: SEALS

The two eunuchs bundled the women into Giulia Campana's private study. "Touch nothing," they warned, then slammed the door shut from the outside.

Cristina and Isra listened to the keys turning in the locks. One, two, three locks, each one double bolted.

Immediately, Cristina glanced around the room, searching for another door, or a window or anything that might give them a way out. There was nothing, this was a secure internal room. "That makes it kidnap," Cristina said. "She's going to regret doing this."

But Isra looked at her friend, wide-eyed. "What are you talking about? She's trying to help us."

"By locking us in her study?"

"Exactly." Isra pointed to the door. "One. Two. Three."

A moment as Cristina tried to work it out.

"The most secure room in the building, and she locks us *inside* without any supervision." Immediately, Isra started tapping on each of the wooden wall-panels, trying to find one that sounded different. "We're not being kidnapped, we're being guided. I think."

"Think? But you're not sure?"

"Just search!"

"For what?" Cristina asked as she started tapping the panelling on the opposite side of the room.

"Letters. Hundreds of letters, probably hidden in a strongbox."

Tap, tap, tap.

"Letters to who?"

"Everyone who matters."

Tap, tap, tap.

"Isra, stop speaking in riddles!"

"Elite courtesans are trusted more than servants. You know why? Because servants can be bribed, their loyalties bought, but a courtesan's honour is her discretion. You saw how Giulia reacted when you asked her to betray a secret."

Tap, tap, tap.

Isra moved onto the next wall. "So what better way to send confidential letters than by courtesan?"

"You mean … they're a messenger service?" Cristina was struggling to keep up. "As well as lovers?"

"The best courtesans are in high demand, requested by wealthy clients in all the great cities of the peninsula. They travel between Rome, Florence, Venice, Milan, Urbino, Naples, conveying messages and replies in absolute secrecy."

Tap, tap, tap.

Tap, tap, click.

Cristina stared at the wall-panel as it swung open to reveal a secret compartment stretching back into the brickwork.

Isra hurried over. "That's the one." She reached into the gloom and pulled out a large basket containing hundreds of letters, all sealed and sorted. "The secrets of the rich and powerful."

Cristina ran her fingers over the neat bundles of letters. "How many people know about this network?"

"The heads of the dynastic families. The most powerful cardinals. Ambassadors from all the great courts in Europe. That sort of thing."

"And the system really works?"

"The fact that even you didn't know about it, proves just how effective it is as a web of secret communication." Isra started searching through the documents. "Now ... let's find the Medici section..."

Cristina watched Isra's fingers rifle through the correspondence with swift ease. "Tell me honestly, have I held you back, Isra?"

"What do you mean?"

"Do you have any regrets about not becoming one of Giulia's women?"

Isra shook her head. "If I wasn't happy with you, I'd have left a long time ago." She reached into the hidden compartment, pulled out another basket of letters and plonked it on the table in front of Cristina. "Please, search. We mustn't be caught doing this."

It was a complex filing system; not just alphabetical by sender, but cross-referenced by city, state, and each client's favourite courtesan, but after a quarter of an hour, Cristina pulled out a sealed letter, held it up and read from the back of the document. "This looks promising. 'From Giovanni de' Medici to the Duke of Nemours.' Dated a day after Ricardo was murdered."

Isra took the document and studied it. "Perfect." Then she picked up a knife, cracked the letter's seal in two and started to prize it away from the paper.

"Wait! You can't do that!" Cristina tried to snatch the letter back, but Isra pushed her hand away.

"Isra! They'll know what we've done! We can't leave a trace."

"Look in the secret compartment," Isra instructed as she picked bits of blue sealing wax from the document. "There should be a wooden box in there."

Reluctantly, Cristina stretched her arm deep into the wall panelling and reached around until her fingers touched something wooden. She gripped it and pulled out a large, flat box made of polished teak. "More letters?"

"Look inside," Isra said.

Cristina undid two silver clasps and opened the lid, revealing row upon row of small metal stamps, each with a stubby wooden handle. She picked out one at random and looked at the engraving: it was the seal of the Farnese family. She selected another: the Duke of Burgundy. And another: the Orsini seal. "Dear God…" Her eyes scanned the neat rows — anyone who was anyone had their seal in this box.

"And that is how courtesans like Giulia Campana are so powerful," Isra said.

Cristina worked through the logic: "So these stamps are forgeries?"

"Naturally."

"And Giulia Campana opens all the letters that pass through her network, reads them, then seals them again so that no-one is any the wiser?"

"A perfect system," Isra replied. "She knows without anyone knowing that she knows. Which means she is always one step ahead."

Reality juddered. For a moment Cristina wasn't sure what was true and what was a lie. She looked searchingly at Isra. "Are you really just a housekeeper?"

"What do you mean?"

"Do you secretly work for Giulia Campana?"

"No!" Isra laughed. "Don't be ridiculous. You heard her with your own ears."

"Or was that another lie for my benefit?"

"Are you seriously doubting my loyalty?" Isra looked hurt.

Cristina hesitated, unable to rule anything out. "Why did Giulia Campana suddenly change her mind? Why did she let us into her private study? How do you know so much about all this?"

Isra looked back at Cristina, defiantly refusing to explain. "Isn't that the whole point? That I know things you don't? Isn't that what makes us an effective team?"

"Yes. But … who are you *really* working for?"

"I have saved your life, Cristina. And you have saved mine. Does that not answer your question?"

"But … did you work for Giulia before you came to me?"

"I would never betray your secrets, Cristina. Do not ask me to betray mine." She held up the Medici letter, free of its wax seal it unfolded easily. "Now, shall we find out what Giovanni really thinks?"

Cristina took the letter and started to read, her eyes scanning the neat handwriting, searching for key words.

"So, business … money … more business … ah, here we go … there is much speculation about who could be behind the Ricardo murder … he suspects that it must be someone powerful to pull off such an elaborate crime … he seems pretty upset by the whole thing. Here he says, 'to destroy a masterpiece is crime enough, but to butcher a patron of the arts is to deprive the world of countless masterpieces not yet created. How I fear the barbarity of Rome, and long for the sweet civility of Florence.' It's exactly what Giovanni told me face to face."

Isra started reading over Cristina's shoulder. "There must be something compromising, or it wouldn't be entrusted to the courtesan network."

"There's a list of cardinals who are being secretly bribed … allegations of bestiality against a magistrate, which could be useful for blackmail … and the names of two family members who have just caught syphilis. I can see why the Medici wouldn't want any of that falling into the wrong hands."

Suddenly they heard the rattle of a key in one of the door locks.

"Quick!" Isra hissed. "Put it all back!"

Cristina slammed the seal box shut and pushed it into the gloom of the compartment, while Isra bundled all the correspondence into the filing baskets.

But they weren't quick enough — when the door swung open, Cristina was still clutching the incriminating Medici letter.

Giulia strode imperiously into the room, glanced from Cristina to the open wall panel, and realised that her most treasured secrets had just been violated.

28: DARKNESS

For once, Cristina was speechless. The Medici letter was still in her hands, the door to the secret compartment was open, and a very unhappy Giulia Campana was glaring daggers at her.

"Forgive me. I … I…"

Giulia strode towards Cristina and snatched the letter away. "You wouldn't listen, would you?"

"It's just…"

"You had to see it with your own eyes!" Giulia sat down at her bureau and took out a box that contained dozens of sticks of sealing wax in every colour imaginable. "Thank God I knew nothing of what you were doing."

Isra started to laugh and sat down at the bureau next to Giulia. "You had me worried. Just for a moment."

"It's all in the eyes," Giulia's tone softened. "I can still outglare anyone."

"I really thought those eunuchs were going to inflict some dreadful punishment."

"Oh, they're complete sweethearts," Giulia smiled. "They look terrifying, but they'd be useless in a fight. There's not a woman of mine who couldn't floor them in under a minute."

Cristina looked on, bewildered, as Giulia searched for a stick of wax that perfectly matched the stain on the Medici letter. "Wait, so you're not angry with us?"

"I recognise a wilful woman when I see one. I knew you wouldn't believe me, no matter what I said." Giulia selected some dark blue wax. "This one, I think."

"It was for a just cause," Cristina tried to explain, but Giulia held up her hand impatiently.

"Please, no grovelling. I read all the letters as soon as they're entrusted to me. If the Medici were involved in the murders, I would already have exacted my revenge. Contessa Copertino was a dear friend. She didn't deserve to die like that."

"No-one does," Cristina replied.

"Oh, I'm not so sure about that. I have a list of people I'd be happy to see butchered."

"I'll pretend I didn't hear that," Cristina said.

"But if it's not the Medici family, then who is behind the killings?" Isra asked, as she lifted the teak box from the compartment and put it on the bureau.

"That is the question." Giulia picked up a small wax-cup and held it over the flame of a candle. Patiently she teased the sealing wax until the cup was full of molten blue liquid, then with well-practised ease, she poured the wax onto the back of the letter, forming a neat circle. Isra selected the Medici stamp from the wooden box and handed it to Giulia, who resealed the letter. She blew on it gently until the wax was hard, then held it up to the light for a final inspection. "Perfect. No-one will ever suspect. File it under 'ready to dispatch.'" She handed the letter to Isra, who filed it back in the basket with the other documents.

Cristina looked at the bundles of letters. "It has to be one of the dynastic families. I'm sure of it."

"Why?" Giulia asked.

"They are such bitter rivals. And the stakes are so high. Not just St Peter's, but ultimately the Papacy itself. These power-families play a long-game."

Giulia loaded all the correspondence back into the secret compartment and clicked the panel shut again. "I think you're looking in the wrong place entirely. It's not the patrons, or the dynastic families you should be investigating, but the artists themselves."

"The artists? No, no."

"Why not?"

"It's impossible," Cristina replied. "Artists create, they don't destroy."

Isra interjected. "But you did say the murders looked like works of art."

"A grotesque parody of art," Cristina insisted. "True art captures everything that is noble about humanity and gives it material form. A real artist could never commit a murder of such ugliness. Never."

"I'm afraid nothing could be further from the truth." Giulia plucked a small oil painting from the wall above the bureau and handed it to Cristina. "What do you think of that?"

Cristina studied the painting. It showed the infant Jesus lying in a manger, watched over by an adoring Mary. The whole scene was bathed in a soft light that conveyed not just innocence, but the power of maternal love. "It's beautiful," she said. "Who painted it?"

"A monster," Giulia replied.

Cristina shook her head. "Impossible. A monster would not have the depth of feeling to create a work of such humanity."

"Don't be so naïve. I saw it with my own eyes."

"What did he do that was so terrible?"

A grim look came into Giulia's eyes. "Simeon Bloccare was a man of depraved sexual appetites. I try not to be judgemental about what goes on here at the Hunting Lodge. Everyone has their own predilections. Yet what Bloccare did … it was bestial. Violent. Degrading. And he took pleasure from it. Then in the morning, he would return to his studio and paint astonishing images of beauty and love." She took the painting from Cristina and hung it back on the wall.

"If he was that bad, how can you bear to keep the picture?"

"Because it is beautiful. A minor masterpiece. But that doesn't excuse the artist's behaviour."

"So what happened to him?"

"I banned him from the Lodge. Then he started following my ladies home, threatening them. In the end I had to get him expelled from Rome altogether."

Cristina studied the painting, struggling to reconcile its serenity with the apparent barbarity of its creator. "To be a deviant is one thing, but to commit murder…"

"Who knows what lines an artist will cross," Giulia replied. "Isn't that what makes a great artist? The refusal to conform?"

"But if art is tainted … what is left?" Cristina whispered.

"Oh no, you're confusing two different things. One doesn't taint the other."

"How can you say that?"

"Do you know Michelangelo's *Pietà*?"

"Of course. It's stunning."

"I cross the river to gaze on it once a week," Giulia said. "No matter how many times I see it, I still cannot believe that a block of marble could have been transformed into something so profound. Michelangelo was only twenty-four when he completed the *Pietà*. Just a few years earlier, when he was a struggling artist, he resorted to forgery and fraud to try and earn a living."

Cristina spun round to face Giulia. "Impossible. That is slander."

"I'm afraid it's the truth. He carved a small statue of *Sleeping Cupid*, then treated it to make it look as if it had been buried for centuries. He sold it as a genuine antiquity. A fake. A fraud."

Cristina shook her head. "I've never heard of this. It would have caused a scandal."

"Cardinal Riario hushed it all up because he was so impressed by Michelangelo's talent. But a lesser artist would have gone to jail, for sure."

"I don't believe you," Cristina replied. "I *can't* believe you."

"Then go and ask him yourself. He is in Florence. Talk to him. No-one knows the darkness of an artist's heart like Michelangelo."

Cristina was subdued as she made her way back through the 'playrooms' of the Hunting Lodge. To catch the killer, every theory had to be investigated, yet now she found herself wanting this new line of inquiry to fail.

Just as they were leaving the Bacchanalian Lounge, Isra suddenly stopped. "Oh, no."

"What is it?" Cristina followed Isra's gaze across the room … and saw Tomasso in the arms of a young courtesan with dark hair flowing down her back. She was sitting on his lap, running her fingers delicately over his face, admiring his chiselled features and soft lips.

As if sensing their presence, Tomasso glanced over and caught Cristina's eye.

It was an awkward moment.

Cristina was shocked to see him here, and the deputy seemed suddenly embarrassed. The courtesan looked across, smiled at Cristina then blew her a kiss.

"Let's go." Cristina strode towards the main hallway.

Isra hurried after her. "Jealous?"

"No. Of course not. Don't be absurd."

29: FAKE

Isra was fast asleep, enjoying a dream about baked apples smothered in zabaglione, when someone started shaking her.

"Isra. Wake up."

"Huh?" she mumbled, taking another spoonful.

"Isra!" The shaking got more intense. "Get dressed."

Isra's eyes groaned open and she tried to focus. "What time is it?"

"Time to get going." Cristina was dressed as if she was going for a long ride in the country.

"What's happening?"

"Baldassari del Milanese. He was the art dealer who handled the fake Michelangelo."

"Didn't you get any sleep?"

"Sleep is overrated," Cristina said dismissively. "The point is, I find it hard to believe that an artist of Michelangelo's calibre would stoop so low as to create forgeries." She grabbed Isra's hand and hauled her to her feet. "We need to check the allegations ourselves. And guess what?"

"Er…"

"I've tracked him down to a warehouse in Ostia. On the coast."

Isra frowned. "Ostia is a dump."

"Isn't that precisely where rats hide?"

It took them three hours of brisk riding to reach the coast, and immediately they realised that Isra had not been exaggerating. Dilapidated and derelict warehouses clustered around the mouth of the Tiber like cold sores, litter still lay where it had been dropped years earlier, and a pungent smell of decay hung heavily in the air. Scavenging gulls screeched their despair, but no-one was listening, for decent people had long since walked away from this place.

After wandering through the maze of buildings for a while, Cristina and Isra finally found a ramshackle warehouse whose faded sign declared 'Baldass'; the piece of wood with 'ari' was nowhere to be seen.

Cristina banged on the shutters with her fist. "Hello! Anyone there?"

"You're such an optimist," Isra said, reaching for an iron bar that had been dumped by the side of the path.

"Good manners cost nothing."

"They're free because they don't usually work. Unlike brute force." Isra jammed one end of the iron bar into the woodwork and pushed. *Crack!* The shutters split open.

Cristina scrambled through the window first, closely followed by Isra. As their eyes adjusted to the gloom, they realised that they were in an Aladdin's cave of abandoned art. Paintings were strewn across the floor and stacked high in chaotic piles; some had been crated up for shipping, others just left to collect dust. Six identical sculptures of armless Aphrodite were huddled in a corner, their beautiful faces covered in a white shroud of cobwebs.

"This is quite a collection," Isra said, taking it all in.

Cristina wiped the dust off a striking painting of the Crucifixion on Golgotha. "The quality of the work is incredible."

"Here, look at this."

Cristina crossed the warehouse to a fire grate where Isra had discovered the charred remains of some financial records. She picked up what was left of a ledger: various art works had been listed against different clients, with money divided into 'bought,' 'sold' and 'bribed'.

"This Baldassari has trouble written all over him," Cristina said, dropping the ledger back into the grate.

"LEAVE!" The hoarse scream bellowed from the darkness.

Cristina and Isra spun round and saw a flabby man lumbering towards them like a drunken ogre. He swung at them with what looked like one leg of an artist's easel.

The women dodged backwards out of the way, and the man stumbled into a pile of crates under his own momentum.

"We just want to talk!" Cristina yelled.

"*Vaffanculo!*" The man grabbed a set of onyx nativity figures and started hurling them at Cristina, but he was too drunk to aim properly, and the missiles were easily dodged.

Thwack!

Isra swung the iron bar with swift precision, striking the man across the back of his knees, knocking his legs out from under him. He fell backwards, tried to grab onto a large oil painting of Jonah inside the whale, but ended up dragging a whole pile of canvases down on top of him.

"Please! Calm down." Cristina looked at the man's legs sticking out from under the fallen pictures. "We only want to ask you a few questions."

No reply. Just the heavy breathing of someone struggling to get a grip.

Gingerly, Isra started to pull away the pictures, one by one, until they found themselves looking at the pitiful sight of the once famous art dealer, Baldassari del Milanese. He had puffy, bulging eyes, strands of lank hair plastered across his pale face, and his trousers were covered in dubious brown stains.

"Here." Cristina extended a hand. "Let me help you."

Baldassari stared at her hand, bewildered, then he looked up at Cristina. "Help? Me?"

"You look like you need it."

Baldassari closed his eyes, and his shoulders started to shake as he was racked with sobs.

It took them a while to calm Baldassari down, but finally they were able to help him through the maze of warehoused art to the back of the building, where he had cobbled together a table and chair, as well as a few meagre cooking utensils. He was living like a hermit in his own crumbling fortress of fakes.

Cristina gave him some water from her flask and watched him drink. "Who did you think we were?"

"Enemies."

"Why?"

"Because I don't have any friends."

"Well, we're not from the magistrates, and we're not creditors. We just want to ask you some questions."

Baldassari looked Cristina up and down. "Perhaps I could interest you in a couple of paintings? Fine lady like you?"

"Perhaps."

Baldassari scoffed. "That means no."

"It depends on how you answer our questions."

"Maybe you want to discuss the influence of Byzantine art on the Sienese School? Or Brunelleschi's experiments in perspective?" There was a glint of passion in his eyes. "Or maybe you are interested in the colour palette of Van Eyck and the North Europeans? Roll up, roll up, it's all here in Baldassari's wonderland!" He gave a slightly crazed laugh, then his face dropped again. "Maybe not."

"What happened to you?" Cristina asked.

"Michelangelo. 'The Greatest Artist in Christendom!' That's what happened to me."

"So you did work with him?"

"He begged me to take him on. Begged me. Because I was the go-to man when it came to dealing in art." Baldassari's face softened as he remembered better times. "I was the man. A beautiful wife, a statement home, adoring children … there was not a salon or palazzo in Rome that was closed to me. 'What does Baldassari think?' That was what cultured Rome asked before anyone bought anything. 'Talk to Baldassari. He knows all the answers.'" His face crumpled as he relived his demise. "Now I might as well be dead. They wouldn't even deign to spit on me if I was lying in the gutter." A mournful silence descended on him.

"And Michelangelo?" Cristina prompted. "What happened?"

"He had carved a small *Sleeping Cupid*. And it was good. The craftsmanship exquisite … but he was an unknown, so no-one would pay more than 15 ducats. I explained to him, money follows reputation, not talent. He stormed off in a rage, then a few days later returned with the same statue, only now he had done something to it … treated it with chemicals, for it looked as if it had been buried for centuries. He begged me to sell it as an antiquity. A genuine Greek sculpture. Begged me! I took pity on him, and I wanted to help a talented artist. So I paid him 30 ducats. He was happy. Then I did what I do, I traded and negotiated and found a good buyer." Baldassari looked up at Cristina with an innocent expression. "Was it my fault that Cardinal Riario was prepared to pay 200 ducats for it? No! He wanted to believe it was an antique. In truth, it was better than most antiquities, so I sold it to him. And everyone was happy." Baldassari started scratching the scabs on his arms. "Until someone ratted me out."

"Who?"

Baldassari spat a globule of phlegm into the dirt. "I don't know. It doesn't matter. What matters is the injustice that followed. Michelangelo tried to extort more money from me. I refused. Of course I refused. Making a profit is what art dealers do. But he wouldn't listen. He demanded an audience with Riario and told him everything. And what do you think happened?" He glared at Cristina.

"It got ugly."

"Yes! Ugly. But not for everyone. The cardinal should have arrested Michelangelo for forgery. Thrown him in jail! But oh no, he hired the criminal. Hired him! To carve the *Pietà*! And me … I was made the scapegoat. I was blamed for everything. They hounded me through the courts, they took my money, my reputation, my family…" Tears welled up in Baldassari's eyes. "Even my children turned against me. When times were good, when the money flowed, how they all loved me. Now they treat me like scum." He wiped away the tears with a dirty sleeve. "Such is the justice of this world."

Cristina glanced at Isra, who was clearly moved by the man's plight. Embittered and angry as he was, it was clear that the man was in deep pain.

Isra gazed at the chaos of art all around them. "Why not start again? Sell some of this. Get back on your feet."

Baldassari scoffed, but didn't reply.

"They're all fakes, aren't they?" Cristina said. "I bet there's not a single original in here."

"On the way down, you trade in anything you can get your hands on," Baldassari muttered.

Cristina walked over to a large, dusty painting and pulled off the covering sheet to reveal a depiction of *Lazarus Rising*. Most of the canvas was in darkness, Christ stood, barely illuminated in a narrow shaft of light, while the pale hand of Lazarus reached out towards him. "Some of this work is stunning," she said.

"Of course!" For a brief moment Baldassari was the famous art dealer again. "The most brilliant artists in the Italian peninsula are all here. When they were struggling, they would line up at my door, desperate to paint anything for cash."

Cristina put the shroud back over *Lazarus*. "But to twist their genius into corruption … that is tragic."

"If you think artists are superior beings, you are deluded." There was a dark relish in the way Baldassari wanted to drag everyone down to his sunken state. "They have to put bread in their belly just like everyone else. Artists aren't gods. They are selfish *stronzi*."

30: FALLEN

"What?" Cristina looked searchingly at Domenico, who glanced uneasily at Tomasso. Neither man spoke.

Cristina turned to Isra. "Was it something I said?"

"Perhaps it's too logical for them," Isra suggested.

"Logical is the one thing it isn't," Domenico finally replied. "It makes no sense for an artist to be the killer. There's no motive."

"Professional rivalry," Cristina said.

"In which case it would make sense to *steal* a rival artist's patrons, not murder them."

"Two days ago, I would have agreed with you, but I am starting to learn about artists. And it isn't good." Cristina drew up chairs for her and Isra so that they could sit around the desk. "Immediately we returned from Ostia, I asked around about Michelangelo."

"But he's not even involved in the design competition," Domenico objected.

"He is a great artist. And everyone who has worked with him or knows him tells the same story: he is brilliant, but dangerous. Not just passionate, but potentially violent. He has threatened patrons who tried to compromise his vision. Once he even threatened to kill a rival artist."

"Michelangelo's been away in Florence for the past year," Tomasso frowned. "How is this relevant?"

"Hypothesis: the killer we're hunting is an artist. An artist who has gone mad and devoted all his talent to murder." Cristina ignored the look of consternation on her brother's face. "So, to catch him, we need to get inside his mind, learn how he thinks. And to do that, I need to go to Florence and question Michelangelo. I need to talk to a man who is both a brilliant artist and a low criminal. How does one mind contain such opposites? What kind of corruption is genius truly capable of."

A heavy silence descended on the room, as if all the air had been sucked out; the longer it went on, the stranger Cristina's hypothesis seemed, until Isra rushed into the vacuum to defend her. "What has become of all the leads *you* were following?" she challenged Domenico.

"Well … we have eliminated the contessa's husband. That is progress."

"Elimination is easy," Cristina retorted. "I can eliminate the King of England, but that doesn't get us any closer to catching the killer."

"Aren't you just wasting time by going to Florence?" Domenico asked.

"I won't know until I've tried."

Domenico turned to Tomasso. "What do you think?"

"Well … every other lead has drawn a blank. And I would be happy to accompany your sister on the trip."

"That won't be necessary," Cristina said.

"At least for security. To offer some protection," Tomasso persisted.

"Please. Don't patronise us. Isra and I are more than capable of looking after ourselves."

Tomasso glanced at Isra, hoping for some support, but she wasn't going to break rank. "If you really want to help, you can lend us horses and weapons."

"Very well," Domenico started filling out an equipment warrant. "Take as much as you need. But please, don't take unnecessary risks."

Tomasso accompanied them to the armoury and helped put together a kit that was lightweight yet offered plenty of protection. Some weapons were to be worn openly, others were concealed in the saddles and kitbags.

Finally, when both horses were tacked-up and ready to leave, Tomasso held the reins as Cristina climbed into the saddle. "Perhaps I could apologise?" he ventured.

"For what?" Cristina locked her gaze on him.

"The other night … it was … I don't normally…" He dried under her gaze. "I'm sorry. That's all."

"You really don't owe me anything," Cristina shrugged. "But thank you." She snapped on the reins and rode out of the barracks.

The road connecting Rome to Florence was one of the busiest on the Italian peninsula, which also made it one of the safest. Every day, merchants, bankers, students, priests, diplomats, artists and soldiers made their way back and forth between the two cities. There were plenty of wayside inns to rest in at night, and the road was home to a small army of itinerant hawkers who made a healthy living selling food and drink to travellers. On the third day, as they passed the fork in the road that led off to Siena, Isra raised the subject of Tomasso.

"Why are you so horrible to him, Cristina?"

"I'm not. I'm perfectly civil."

"I don't think so."

"He's just someone who works with my brother."

"Well, that's not how he sees it."

"Isra, you seem to be obsessed with this business of men."

"Not at all."

"First you imagine that Visconti is chasing after me."

"He is."

"I am charming to him, but that's a bad thing."

"Correct."

"Then you imagine that Deputato Tomasso has fallen for me."

"He has."

"But I'm being horrible by just trying to get on with my job. Make up your mind."

They rode in silence for a few moments while Isra tried to work out the correct approach. "Most women sense when a man likes them. But not you."

"I'm not 'most women'."

"Thank God."

"So what is the problem?" Cristina was exasperated.

"Bad men will keep on coming, no matter how many times you turn them away. But good men, they take you at your word even when you don't want them to. And by the time you realise your mistake, it's usually too late."

"My life is never going to revolve around a man."

"Nor should it," Isra agreed. "That's not what I'm saying."

"Then what is this all about?"

"Visconti dazzles you, Deputato Tomasso doesn't. And that worries me."

"Tomasso is nice, but he's dull. Can you imagine him buying a thousand flowers for me?"

"No," Isra replied. "Which is exactly why you should be interested in him."

31: FLORENCE

Cristina gazed up at the inside of the great dome. She had spent countless hours studying the architectural plans for Florence's Basilica Santa Maria, but nothing could have prepared her for actually being inside the space.

Eight huge triangular shells, seamlessly joined along their edges, reached up to the sky and met at an octagonal opening, allowing a solid shaft of sunlight to pierce the dome's skin. At the bottom of each face a circular window with beautiful stained glass flooded the basilica with an ethereal light. The whole structure seemed to hang miraculously in the air, as if supported by nothing but faith.

"Isn't it stunning?" Cristina whispered. "It is higher and wider than any dome ever built."

"It is beautiful. And yet … strangely plain." Isra sounded a little disappointed.

"That's because the dome itself is the work of art," Cristina replied. "An engineering miracle, made entirely from bricks. Four million of them."

"Bricks? How? I don't understand."

"Ah, now that is an interesting question." Cristina walked to one of the huge pillars on which the dome rested, stretched out her arms and looked straight up, as if checking the angles. "When this basilica was first designed two hundred years ago, no-one had any idea how to actually build the dome. But it didn't stop them. They pressed on, confident that when the time came, a solution would be found. I love that ambition."

Isra studied the great leaves of the dome. "Yet how can bricks sustain such a huge weight?"

"The secret is in the herringbone pattern. You can't see it because of the plaster and whitewash, but all the bricks are laid at an angle."

"And the pattern makes them stronger?"

"It's all about how the weight is transferred down to these massive walls." Cristina slapped one of the columns and listened to the echo bounce around the cavernous space. "This basilica will stand for a thousand years."

With her head craned back, Cristina slowly turned in a circle as if she was trying to hypnotise herself with the sunlight. "This is what genius looks like."

Isra was more concerned with the power behind the building. Everywhere she looked, she saw the Medici name shining in gilt letters: plaques commemorating their contribution to this basilica, statues celebrating Medici achievements in life, and great marble tombs keeping Medici bones safe in death. The family *was* Florence, and it seemed inconceivable that they had now been thrown out of the city.

Eventually, they emerged from the spell of the basilica onto the city's streets, which were buzzing with vibrant energy.

Where Rome was all about power and religion, Florence was about art and inspiration. Gone were the dull blacks and browns of priestly cassocks, here the streets were full of vivid colours and eye-catching fashions. Everywhere she looked, Cristina saw artists: purchasing materials, debating with each other outside taverns, trying to impress patrons or seduce models. Every other building seemed to house some kind of studio; through open windows she heard the clinking chorus of chisels on marble, glimpsed apprentices stretching canvases, and caught the scent of oil paints being prepared. Where Rome had solemnity, Florence had laughter, and the playfulness made it seem as if in this city, anything was possible. Florence felt like the centre of the world.

"We should make our way to the magistrates," Cristina said, steering Isra in the direction of the Palazzo Vecchio.

"I thought you wanted to find Michelangelo?"

"They'll know where he lives."

"In this city, I doubt that's a secret." Isra strode to the nearest shop, a bakery.

"You can't just ask people at random," Cristina protested.

But that's exactly what Isra did. The baker listened, nodded, asked a couple of questions, then started giving a detailed set of instructions, gesticulating with his arms where to turn left and right.

Isra returned looking smug. "In Florence, gossip is art."

"He really knew what you were talking about? A baker?"

"Don't be so patronising. He doesn't just know where Michelangelo's workshop is, he told me that he is in the final stages of carving a massive statue of David."

"David who?"

"The king. As in David and Goliath? Everyone is talking about it. They say it's going to be the finest sculpture ever created."

Following the baker's instructions, they crossed the river by the Ponte Vecchio and headed into the Oltrarno quarter. In contrast to the crowds and tangle of narrow streets in the centre, Oltrarno felt rundown, and Cristina was puzzled why such a rising star would choose to work in such shabby surroundings. Immediately they entered Michelangelo's workshop, she understood: a cheaper neighbourhood meant a larger workshop and the statue of *David* was massive, easily the height of a two-storey house. It stood in the centre of the workshop, surrounded by scaffold, but no-one else was here, no artist and no apprentices.

Both women gazed at the creation in stunned silence. Even now, before the polishing and finessing were complete, *David* was astonishing. The balance and poise were so light, it felt as if the giant figure was about to step down from the plinth and stride away. The texture of the muscles and flesh was so perfect, the trace of the veins so delicate, it was impossible to believe that just two years ago, this had been a lifeless lump of rock.

"He's brought David back from the dead," Cristina whispered.

Isra stepped towards the statue, wanting to touch the marble to see if it was warm like human flesh, but just as she reached out her hand, they heard a voice counting.

"Twenty-three, twenty-four, twenty-five…"

Moments later, a young man paced into the room. He had dark curly hair, a bushy beard, and eyes that seemed to rarely blink. He was counting every step he took.

"Thirty, thirty-one, thirty-two…"

Still counting, he circled the statue three times, then abruptly stopped. Closing his eyes, he squatted on his haunches and stretched out his arms, meditating. He held the pose for several minutes, then slowly stood up and relaxed. Not once did he glance at Cristina and Isra, or even seem to notice their presence.

Muttering to himself, the man selected a small, half-round file from a case of tools, and checked the sharpness of the teeth with his thumb.

"Michelangelo Buonarroti?" Cristina inquired.

Finally, the man looked at her. "Go away."

32: CIPHER

Domenico arrived early at the barracks and was astonished to see Tomasso already hard at work: documents and evidence lists were spread across the floor.

"Another sleepless night?" Domenico put a basket of pastries on the desk. "Here. Fresh from the oven."

"I had an idea. Needed to think it through."

"At least have some breakfast." Domenico offered him a pastry. "Still warm."

As they ate, Tomasso explained his line of thinking. "So far we've been looking at the past: who committed the murders. Instead, we should be trying to predict the future. If we can find the right pattern, we can pre-empt the next attack and catch the killer red-handed."

"Maybe," Domenico was impressed by his deputy's diligence, "but not necessarily."

"There is always a pattern. That's what your sister says. You just have to look hard enough."

"So ... now we have to pretend we're Cristina?"

"Look, the first murder involved a Visconti painting, the second a Visconti sculpture. The next one: maybe the same artist but in a different medium?"

"What else has he done?" Domenico's eyes scanned the lists that Tomasso had drawn up.

"He's getting into architecture but hasn't completed a huge amount. One small church, and a theological library for the University. He's also refurbished a palazzo on the Tiber."

"That narrows it down, but..." Domenico frowned. "How do you destroy a building?"

"I know. It doesn't make sense."

"You can't cut it into pieces or do any big changes without anyone seeing."

"So, I've been going down a different route," Tomasso explained. "The content of the art itself. Symbolism."

The word made Domenico feel out of his depth. "We really need Cristina."

"No. We can do this," Tomasso insisted. "The painting in the first murder was *Salvator Mundi*. Christ, saviour of the world. Salvation. The fountain in the second murder was Nemesis. Revenge. So I think the next one will also be linked to some kind of morality."

"Salvation. Revenge … what comes next?" Domenico started pacing the room as he searched for an eternal value, wishing his mind was as sharp as his sister's. "Salvation. Revenge… Salvation. Revenge…"

Tomasso stared intently at the lists of evidence as he worked his way through the pastries, occasionally wiping crumbs off the documents. "Salvation, revenge, repentance?"

"Or salvation, revenge, forgiveness?"

But it wasn't just a question of finding the right moral value, they had to link that to a work of art Visconti had created.

As their minds slowed and the pastries ran out, Domenico suggested another line of thinking. "Let's look at the victims."

"Number one: a male patron of Visconti. Victim two: a female patron."

"Is he alternating? Man, woman, man, woman?"

"Not much of a pattern."

"Or … is it that people who give Visconti money make themselves targets?"

"That's the line Cristina has suspected from the start." Tomasso nodded. "He who gives Visconti money ends up dead. The killer is trying to scare the Pope away from commissioning him to build St Peter's."

"So who else gives Visconti money?" Domenico asked. "Do we have a list of his patrons?"

"No," Tomasso shook his head. "But it will be long. He's a prolific artist."

"Get one of the lieutenants onto it. We should at least warn all his patrons, so they can be on their guard."

"Has he borrowed money?" Tomasso pondered.

"How could we find that out?"

"Wait, wait…" Tomasso hurried over to the archive shelves and pulled out a ledger of tax records; it was the nearest thing they had to a complete record of people living in Rome, and the Apostolic Guards often referred to it. Tomasso rifled through the pages until he came to the entry he was looking for. "So … the palazzo that Visconti refurbished is owned by Antonio Pozzi. A few years back, Pozzi married into the Fugger family. Remember?"

"How could I forget?" Domenico replied. "The celebrations lasted a whole week."

"And the Fuggers are one of the biggest bankers in Europe. So the palazzo Visconti refurbished is owned by a moneylender, built with the profits of usury."

"Salvation, revenge, usury?" Domenico suggested.

"And all linked to Visconti," Tomasso added. "It fits. Pozzi could well be the next victim."

"Let's pay him a visit."

Palazzo Pozzi was less of a home and more of a public proclamation of extreme wealth. It was a huge crescent-shaped building comprising four storeys, each of which got progressively smaller. There were over a hundred windows on the front of the palazzo alone; those on the ground floor were framed by elegant arches, while each of the windows on the floor above had stone balconettes. But what really interested Domenico and Tomasso was the colourful mosaic frieze that ran along the architrave for the entire length of the building.

"That looks like Visconti's work," Domenico said, pointing to the huge mosaic.

"And Pozzi paid him a lot of money for it." Tomasso checked his notes. "Apparently it depicts the Seven Works of Mercy."

Both men studied the frieze which glittered in the winter sun. Working from left to right, it depicted Jesus feeding the hungry, giving drink to the thirsty, clothing the naked, burying the dead, sheltering the traveller, visiting the sick and ransoming the captive.

"Nothing about glorifying the moneylender," Domenico observed.

"Salvation, Revenge, Mercy," Tomasso said. "It fits the pattern."

"This feels to me like the home of a man who is desperate to cleanse his soul."

"Look at those." Tomasso pointed to a couple of flagpoles on the roof, each bearing a large banner fluttering in the cold breeze.

Domenico squinted his eyes to try and make out the images on the flags. "Is it a family crest or something?"

Tomasso shielded his eyes from the glare. "Finally," he smiled.

"What?"

"All those hours in school memorising the gods … finally it comes in useful." He pointed to the flag on the left. "That one is Plutus, the Greek god of money. And the one next to it is Libertas, Roman god of freedom."

"The freedom to make money. That's the religion Pozzi worships."

Suddenly there was a commotion as four livered servants running in front of an ornate carriage turned into the street. The procession stopped outside the palazzo, and while two servants hurried to help their master out of the carriage, the other two unclipped brooms from beneath the coachman's footboard and started sweeping the steps leading up to the palazzo, so that not a speck of dirt should touch their master's shoes.

With enormous effort, Antonio Pozzi swung himself out of his carriage and waddled up the steps, supported by a servant under each arm. But rather than being grateful, Pozzi didn't stop barking orders at them. "Slow down! You're being too rough! Imbecile!"

Finally, he disappeared inside and the servants closed the doors behind him.

"You know what?" Domenico said. "If I was the killer, I think I would have Pozzi on my list."

33: TEMPER

"Are you always so rude or is it because I'm a woman?" Cristina locked eyes with the unblinking Michelangelo.

"Neither," he replied. "It is because I am busy, and you are interrupting."

"Busy creating works of unparalleled beauty? Or busy forging antiquities?"

Now she had his attention.

Michelangelo glanced from Cristina to Isra, trying to work out their intentions. "One does not exclude the other," he said finally. "My fakes were exquisitely made. Finer than the originals. I will not apologise for that."

"Quality is no excuse for fraud."

"But poverty is!" Michelangelo snapped. "Unlike you I have no private income, so I am not in a position to sit in judgement on others."

"Yet you judge me," Cristina retorted.

"Do you know what it means to come from a bankrupt family? To be shunted from pillar to post as a child? Have you ever in your life had to worry about where the next loaf of bread was coming from?"

"There are many types of struggle," Cristina replied. "You want to try being a woman who seeks an education in a world that is utterly controlled by men."

They glared at each other across the workshop. A shaft of hard winter sunlight momentarily flickered through one of the windows, lighting up clouds of tiny stone particles hanging in the air.

Michelangelo sat down at his workbench and tightened a slab of gritstone in the vice. He sprinkled some olive oil onto the stone, then pressed the chisel blade onto the surface and started to slide it back and forth in a well-practiced movement. "If you won't leave, you may as well speak your mind."

Cristina gazed at the statue of *David*. "This is an incredible piece of work."

"Lesser men will be copying it for centuries to come," Michelangelo said as he patiently sharpened the chisels.

"I see you are as modest as you are talented."

"I am my own harshest critic," Michelangelo said. "But *David*'s beauty was created by nature. He has been trapped inside that block of marble since the beginning of time. All I have done is set him free."

"Now you really are being modest."

Michelangelo lifted the chisel off the stone and examined the blade. "Why are you here?" He tested the edge with his finger, then carried on sharpening. "If it's to offer me a commission, you are most welcome. Otherwise, I'm too busy."

"I wanted to meet the genius who can create the *Pietà*, yet is also happy to commit fraud."

"You are hopelessly naïve." Michelangelo flipped the chisel over, held it at a precise angle, then slid it across the gritstone in a circular motion, removing the burrs. "Worship the art, never the artist."

"Yet art does not create itself."

"You have been to San Clemente al Laterano?"

"Of course."

"What is painted on the ceiling?"

Cristina cast her mind back to the last time she visited the church. "A depiction of the heavens … hosts of angels."

"Correct. But every angel in that fresco is the image of a courtesan. By night the women entertained Rome's decadent rich, by day they modelled for artists. All over Europe, Virgin Marys and angelic cherubs are modelled on prostitutes."

"That does not diminish their value," Cristina objected.

"No. But it points to a truth about art. For all its beauty, it has no purity. It is the work of the fallen. Corruption is deep in every brushstroke. Art is made by sinners, paid for by those hoping to assuage their guilt."

"And what about murder?" Cristina studied Michelangelo closely, searching for a reaction.

He took the sharpened chisel and delicately ran it along the back of his arm, shaving off the hairs. "So you still haven't solved those crimes?"

Cristina and Isra exchanged a wary glance. "We have some documents about the case. You might be interested to see them," Isra ventured.

"I already have a job." He thumbed his finger at the huge statue. "In case you hadn't noticed."

"But do you have a theory about the killings?" Cristina asked. "You seem to know all about them."

"Actually, since you ask…" Michelangelo lined up his tools with meticulous precision, ready to be picked up as the statue demanded. "From the accounts I've read, the solution seems obvious." He started to pace around *David*, eyes examining the marble surface intently, hunting down every imperfection.

"So … are you going to enlighten us?" Cristina prompted.

"The fountain murder required not just imagination, but a detailed knowledge of how the fountain pumped water. Artistic flair combined with the knowledge of a craftsman. The first killing: the carnage resolved into a powerful image when viewed from above, but to create the false perspective of hands emerging from the floor required considerable talent. Especially on such a scale and using pieces of a butchered corpse. Conclusion: the killer is an artist."

"We have been working towards the same conclusion," Cristina said, refusing to be impressed by his deductions. "The question is, *which* artist?"

"That too is obvious," Michelangelo scoffed. "It's one of Visconti's own apprentices."

"What? No. That's impossible."

"Look at the facts. Both murders were committed by a man who had access to Visconti's patrons, who was known to them and trusted by them. They got close without ever raising suspicion. An apprentice could have gained access to Ricardo's house on the pretext of touching up the varnish; once inside the house, he was able to hide until the moment he struck. Likewise with Contessa Copertino, a trusted apprentice could have gained an audience on the pretext of delivering sketches for a new work."

Cristina shook her head. "But what possible motive could an apprentice have for destroying his own master?"

Michelangelo studied Cristina with his unblinking eyes. "You really don't understand the true nature of the artist, do you? Jealousy is the motive. Jealousy that eats the soul of every mediocrity."

"But every apprentice wants to work for genius," Cristina said. "That's the whole point. To learn."

"Until the apprentice reaches that moment when he realises that he will never achieve greatness himself. That he will never get further than painting shrubs and skies. When a man reaches that point, it is no longer inspiring to be in the presence of genius, it is agony. Torture."

Cristina closed her eyes and shuffled all the fragments of evidence into this new alignment. The jealous apprentice, resentful of what he can never be, sets out to destroy the world. He sacrifices salvation in the pursuit of revenge. *Salvator Mundi* is destroyed, *Nemesis* is drenched in blood. It made perfect sense.

"Yes," Cristina whispered. "It's clever. Brilliant, even."

"But not as difficult as turning marble into flesh. So if you'll excuse me…" Michelangelo picked up a fine chisel, climbed one of the ladders in front of *David*, and vanished into a different world.

PART THREE

34: HEAD

It took Domenico and Tomasso four days to make Palazzo Pozzi the most secure residence in Rome, and it was an arduous task. Not only did the Apostolic Guards have to work covertly, they also had to battle against Pozzi's obnoxious character.

Inside his residence, the banker had decided that walking was beneath his dignity, so he deployed a team of four servants to carry him from room to room on a platform covered in duck-feather cushions. Resembling a recumbent sedan chair, 'the meat slab' (as the servants called it behind their master's back) was fitted with a small bell that Pozzi used to signal when to stop and when to move, as well as a cane mounted on a gimbal, which he used to prod the carriers indicating whether to turn left or right. Released from the burden of talking to his servants, the banker was free to harangue Domenico every few hours.

"This is an intolerable intrusion on my liberty! Intolerable!"

"We are only trying to save your life, sir," Domenico replied.

"No-one would dare touch me! No-one!"

"This man has already murdered an innocent lawyer and a contessa."

"I am in a different league to them. A different league!"

"With all due respect, sir, we believe the killer has no respect for class or status."

"And I have armed bodyguards. Do you hear? Bodyguards!" Pozzi snorted. "Anyone who dares touch me will be signing their own death warrant."

"This killer is cunning, sir. And determined."

"Mark my words: I will not hesitate to strangle the man with my bare hands if he comes near me. Bare hands!"

Domenico bit his tongue; quite how a man who was too lazy to walk hoped to overpower the most dangerous murderer in Rome was a mystery.

Pozzi rang the bell and his bearers started to move forward. "This is an intrusion on my liberty!" he declared again as he was carried away down the corridor. "Freedom is all a man needs to prosper. Freedom! Not nannying by guards who are frightened of their own pathetic shadows."

Despite the abuse, the Apostolic Guards pressed on with their work. Not wishing to alert the killer that they were closing in, all weapons and security equipment were smuggled into the building and discreetly assembled, so that to the outside world, it looked as if life in Palazzo Pozzi was carrying on as normal … even though 'normal' was hardly a word that sprang to mind when describing the banker.

Domenico didn't consider himself knowledgeable about art, but even he could tell that the palazzo was decorated in appalling taste. Pozzi seemed to have an obsession with pillars, for every corridor was cluttered with them in a zealous attempt to project power and authority. Stuffed bears and wolves had been positioned on either side of doors, and each room had been decorated according to a different theme, with no thought given to the harmony of the building as a whole.

The Oriental Salon had been designed to look like the inside of a Buddhist temple; the walls of the New World Salon were covered in exotic trees, all painted in gold leaf, while the Mediterranean Salon contained a huge sunken pool complete with scale models of Ottoman fighting galleys.

To preserve their own sanity, Domenico had decided that the primary focus of the security cordon would be the grand banqueting hall, where frescoes of the Seven Works of Mercy had been painted on the ceiling, echoing the exterior façade of the palazzo. Although based on the same design, the frescoes had deepened the emotional impact of the images, using fine brushwork to bring out every nuance of the faces, and creating a colour palette that seemed to glow with Divine grace. If the killer was going to strike at another Visconti work, this would surely be it.

So when the Pozzi household went to bed, the Apostolic Guards turned the banqueting hall into a fortress. Tripwires armed the doors, snipers with muskets were positioned in the musicians' galleries, while swordsmen were hidden in each corner of the hall.

Outside, Tomasso had organised a rota of guards who patrolled the perimeter, watching every door and window, and covering every approach. Which is why the moment Cristina got within a hundred yards of the main entrance, she was apprehended.

"What the hell are you doing here?" Tomasso hissed.

"That's not a very warm welcome." She wriggled free of his grip. "Considering the information I'm bringing."

"I'm sorry. I didn't mean … I'm glad you're safe," Tomasso said.

"Why wouldn't I be?" Cristina's gaze darted from shadow to shadow, picking out the armed guards. "It's you who seems to be courting danger."

"I drew up a list of possible targets. We think the killer is going to strike here next."

"Interesting." She nodded. "You found a robust pattern?"

"I think so. We'll see."

"Because I have been approaching the problem from the opposite direction. I know *who* we're looking for. It's not the dynastic families behind the murders, it's an embittered apprentice."

"An apprentice?" Tomasso frowned. "Why would he destroy his own career?"

"Specifically, I think it's one of Visconti's apprentices. So we must set up surveillance on his workshop, day and night."

"But all our men are committed here."

"What if your pattern is wrong? We should cut this off at the source. Trap the killer as he sets out, then it doesn't matter who his target is."

"Let's discuss this with your brother." Tomasso escorted Cristina past the guards watching the coaching gates, then led her into the moonlit courtyard. She glanced around as they hurried across the cobbles, and saw numerous glints of muskets and swords lurking in the shadows.

But as they entered the main building through the orangery doors, a terrible scream ruptured the darkness.

Tomasso and Cristina froze, ears straining. They heard a desperate gasp … then silence.

"God help us … it's begun," Tomasso whispered. "Stay here."

"No. I'm coming with you."

Tomasso edged Cristina behind him, shielding her from whatever was ahead as he moved deeper into the gloom of the palazzo.

Somewhere on the upper landing they heard footsteps. "Hold! Stay put!" Tomasso ordered. The footsteps froze. "Identify yourself!"

Silence.

"Identify yourself!" he demanded again.

No reply. Then they heard a strange wet thud, picking up speed as it went.

"Who's there?" Tomasso yelled.

"Look!" Cristina pointed to a sweeping staircase that was illuminated by a great shaft of cold moonlight.

Thud, thud, thud.

Something was rolling down the steps…

Something round and wet.

Cristina and Tomasso watched as it hit the bottom step, rolled across the marble floor then stopped by the plinth of an indoor fountain that was shaped like a giant fish.

The object had left a trail of strange marks behind it as it went.

Slowly, weapons drawn, eyes searching the shadows, Tomasso and Cristina edged across the open floor until the object was at their feet.

Tomasso nudged it, rolling it over.

But it wasn't a ball.

It was the severed head of the esteemed banker, Antonio Pozzi.

35: TRAP

Domenico cursed under his breath as he heard the alarm whistle echo through the palazzo. Three urgent blasts — it meant Pozzi was down, the very thing he'd tried to prevent.

He fumbled for his own whistle, put it in his mouth and responded with a single, long blast, instructing Tomasso to stay where he was.

"Cluster position!" Domenico ordered as he ran into the middle of the banqueting hall. Immediately the troops who were hidden in the shadows broke cover and hurried towards him, forming a battle phalanx facing in all directions. Moving as one, braced for imminent attack from any quarter, the Apostolic Guards moved towards the main doors, disabled the tripwire, and emerged onto the upper landing.

Eyes darted in all directions, searching for the slightest movement in the shadows that would betray the killer's location.

"Is he alive?" Domenico called into the gloom.

"No," Tomasso replied, his voice echoing up from the entrance hall.

"You sure he can't be saved?"

"He's a corpseless head."

"Shit!"

Domenico edged his squad of soldiers along the landing to the top of the great marble staircase. His gaze followed the dark splashes leading down the white steps and came to rest on Tomasso, who was shielding Cristina; Pozzi's head lay at their feet.

"Where's his body?" Domenico demanded.

"This is all we've got." Tomasso nudged the banker's head with his toe. "But it must be close. How far can a corpse get without a head?"

"It's not over!" Cristina called up to her brother. "The killer's not finished!"

"Stay down there!"

"He won't leave without butchering the body," she replied. "It's all part of the performance. We're still in the middle of this."

"Tomasso! Don't let my sister out of your sight."

"Understood, sir!"

"We're going to sweep through the rooms. Flush the killer out." Then Domenico whispered to his troops, "Hold tight formation. This maniac is cunning."

Wheeling across the space like a giant crab, the phalanx of guards glided from room to room, searching for clues that would betray the killer. But as they swept through the upper gaming room, they heard footsteps running towards them along the landing outside.

"Here he comes!"

The phalanx braced for attack, swords raised and bristling. The doors burst open…

To reveal the House Chamberlain in his night gown. "In God's name, what is happening?" he demanded.

"Get back to your room!"

"But —"

"Now!"

"Where is the master?"

"Dead!" Domenico hissed. "As you will be if you don't do as I say!"

"You were supposed to protect him!" the chamberlain cried.

"Listen to me! Get all the servants back in their rooms, doors locked. No-one moves until I give the all-clear. Understand?" Domenico heard the chamberlain gasp as if he was about to start crying. "Do you understand?"

It jolted the chamberlain to his senses. "Yes … yes. Locked in their rooms."

"Go!"

Domenico listened to the man's footsteps as he hurried back up the stairs to the servants' quarters under the roof. But just as the phalanx was about to continue sweeping through the rooms, they heard a strange sound echo in the darkness.

Ssscrrreeaaaaowwwww!

It was like fingernails being scraped along violin strings.

"What the hell…?" Domenico whispered.

Hands tightened their grip on swords as the phalanx wheeled along the landing, drawn towards the eerie sound.

Ssscrrreeaaaaowwwww!

"Where are the music rooms?" Domenico demanded.

But before anyone could answer —

BANG! BANG!

A door slammed open and shut, open and shut, with a manic energy. The guards froze. But this new sound was coming from the *opposite* side of the palazzo.

"How many killers are there?" one of the guards whispered fearfully.

BANG-BANG! BANG-BANG!

"Which way do we go, sir?"

Domenico listened to the competing sounds from opposite ends of the building.

"Both. We can't risk being surrounded."

Like a cell dividing, the phalanx split in half and reformed as two smaller units.

"And let's up the pace. Take the fight to them."

Immediately the two groups swooped in opposite directions, like predators hunting in the night.

As if sensing danger, the screeching sound from the music room halted abruptly, and by the time Domenico's phalanx stormed through the doors, the room was empty.

But there was a clue…

Blood.

Huge bloody tracks smeared across the floor, as if from a headless corpse.

"We're close. Brace!" Domenico warned.

They followed the blood-smears out through a side door that led from the music room to one of the service corridors.

It was too narrow to hold formation, so the guards regrouped into single file, Domenico in the lead, the last man walking backwards to guard the rear.

They surged along the bare corridor, following the blood-smears that wavered from side to side as the dragged corpse had bounced off the walls … heading towards a small door that led up to the roof.

As the guards clustered around it, Domenico saw that the handle was covered in blood. "He's up there."

Slowly, silently they turned the handle and swung open the door. As the corpse had been dragged up the steps, it didn't just leave blood-smears — pieces of flesh had been torn off, like bits of meat discarded on a butcher's floor.

Domenico led his men up the creaking steps … and onto the roof.

"Why did he come up here?" one of the guards whispered. "He's trapped himself."

But Domenico was starting to wonder if they were the ones who had been led into a trap.

A gust of chilly air billowed up the Tiber and across the roof. Domenico heard the flags fluttering and instinctively turned towards them.

And that was when he saw the atrocity.

Antonio Pozzi's headless corpse had been slung between the two flagpoles, tied with ropes, arms and legs outstretched in grotesque mockery of a crucifixion. Two crows pecked at his ragged neck wounds.

The decapitated moneylender had died as he had lived, suspended between the gods of freedom and money.

36: HANDPRINTS

Cristina gazed at the ghastly tableau, studying the trickles of blood that ran down the corpse and dripped onto the roof. It wasn't death in itself that was horrific, it was the combination of murder and symbolism, calculated to instil fear. There was no doubt in her mind this was the work of the killer they'd been hunting all along; the pleasure he took in sadism was chilling.

Domenico had no time to gaze at what remained of Pozzi, he was frantically leading the search for clues. Despite the copious amounts of blood spilled, there were no footprints leading away from the corpse. How had the killer created so much carnage without leaving a trace? How had he remained invisible?

Then, finally, a break.

"Sir! Over here!"

Everyone hurried to the edge of the roof — one of the guards had discovered a homemade Jacob's ladder leading down onto a narrow ledge that formed the upper surface of the Seven Works of Mercy mosaic running along the façade of the building.

"Hold the ladder still," Domenico ordered as he slung his foot onto the top rung.

"Wait!" Cristina called out. "That ledge is too narrow."

But Domenico was waiting for no-one. The banker's body was still warm, the killer couldn't have gone far, and this might be the best chance they would ever get.

He climbed down, trying to keep his body centred so the ladder wouldn't sway too much, but as his feet touched the ledge he was dismayed to realise just how narrow it was, barely a foot's width. At least it was solid, as these panels had been installed when Visconti created the frieze. Leaning his weight in towards the building and resisting the ghoulish urge to look down at the sheer drop to the street three storeys below, Domenico started to edge forwards.

There was no way anyone could do this quickly, which meant the killer must have been making his escape along this ledge while Domenico was just a few feet above him searching the roof.

But where had the killer gone now? And how did he get off this ledge, because it seemed to lead nowhere?

Just as Domenico shuffled past *Jesus Clothing the Naked*, his question was answered: a long rope had been tied off to one of the balconettes and dangled all the way down the front of the building. Hurrying the last few paces, Domenico reached out and grabbed the rope.

It felt sticky.

When he looked closer he realised it was covered in bloody handprints. Part of him recoiled, but there was no time for emotion, they had to catch this monster, and he started to lower himself towards the street.

As he edged down, Domenico glimpsed movement in the shadows below — a figure disappeared into an alley between the two buildings on the opposite side of the street.

"Over there! Quickly!" he yelled.

Domenico heard boots running on cobbles, then saw some small figures hurrying to the bottom of the rope: it was Tomasso and a squad of guards.

"He's running towards Via delle Coppelle!" Domenico called down. "Fan out! Cut him off!"

While Domenico rappelled down the façade of the palazzo, Tomasso and the Apostolic Guards surged through the streets. At each junction, they split into smaller groups so that they could cover all directions. They were lucky the clock was with them, for in the dead of night, Rome's streets were deserted of honest people; if you were roaming the city at this hour, you were fair game to be arrested.

Finally, as Via Agostino opened out onto Piazza delle Cinque Lune, Tomasso saw a young man leaning over a fountain, urgently washing his hands in the splash pool.

"Hold!" Tomasso yelled. "Do not move!"

The man looked up and saw Apostolic Guards surging towards him. He turned to run, but immediately saw troops converging on Cinque Lune from all directions.

Realising that he was surrounded, the man calmly turned back to the fountain and continued bathing his hands. Domenico glanced into the water and saw that it was turning red — the man was rinsing blood from his hands … Pozzi's blood.

By the time Cristina arrived in the piazza, the man's hands and feet had been manacled. He hung his head low, and was refusing to talk, refusing to struggle, refusing to engage in any way.

"Was it you?" Cristina asked.

Silence.

"Answer her," Tomasso ordered.

But he didn't.

"Sulking because you've been caught?" Cristina goaded.

He refused to take the bait.

Tomasso reached out and grabbed the man's bearded chin, lifting his face and forcing him to look at them. Immediately Cristina recognised Lupo, Visconti's most trusted assistant.

"Behold the jealous apprentice," she whispered.

"Said the doting mistress," Lupo sneered.

"Me? I have no interest in Visconti."

"Is that why you drool over him?"

"You are even more bitter than I was expecting," Cristina replied.

"As if I care what you think," Lupo scoffed.

"The jealous apprentice, destroying what he can never be."

"You are an idiot, woman."

"And yet you are the one in chains."

"No, no." Lupo looked at the guards gathered around him. "I am the only one here who is truly free."

Tomasso shook his head. "He's insane."

"Quite the opposite," Lupo corrected. "I have lived my life with clarity. And honesty."

"By murdering innocent people?" Cristina said.

"Innocent? Try finding an innocent person in this city."

"Well *your* guilt is beyond doubt."

Lupo shook his head. "I was unable to sleep, so I came out for a walk. I merely stopped at this fountain to wash my hands."

Exasperated, Tomasso lunged forward and punched Lupo hard in the guts.

"There's no need for that," Cristina warned.

"Maybe not. But it felt good."

Lupo recovered his breath and gave a defiant smile. "There is nothing you can do to hurt me. Not anymore. I have been tortured for years. In here…" He tapped the side of his head, rattling the chains around his wrists. "Physical pain means nothing to me."

"What about execution?" Cristina studied his face.

"Don't be smug," Lupo warned. "You got lucky tonight."

"We would have caught you eventually."

"I doubt that. And I had so many more 'performances' planned. The best was yet to come."

Cristina stepped closer. "That was your mistake, Lupo. You were too predictable."

"I am an original! A true original."

Cristina shrugged. "Michelangelo saw through you in a heartbeat."

"Never heard of the man."

"Now he is a truly great artist."

"Says who?"

"The entire world will be singing his praises soon enough. But by the time his fame breaks, you will be long dead, Lupo. Executed as the embittered killer you are."

37: STONEWALLED

Domenico was determined to keep control of the interrogation. After witnessing first-hand the barbarities of 'Inquisition methodologies', he vowed that he would never let such cruelty be unleashed on any of his suspects again. So Lupo the apprentice was locked in one of the larger cells in the basements under the Vatican; he wasn't manacled or beaten, he was given some food and water, and a physician examined him to declare him fit for questioning.

"He looks a hell of a lot more comfortable than his victims," Tomasso said as he and Cristina studied Lupo through the barred window in the cell door. The prisoner sat quietly on an iron bed frame that was bolted to the wall; he had wrapped himself in a blanket to stave off the December chill.

"That's what it means to hold the moral high ground," Domenico replied. "You never sink to their level."

Tomasso turned and studied his commander, puzzled by his attitude towards a man who was clearly a deranged butcher. "I don't know why we have to bother with interrogation. Why don't we just hand him over for execution?"

"Because we have no evidence that *proves* he is guilty," Cristina insisted.

"We caught him red-handed!" Tomasso exclaimed.

"Did we?"

"You were there. You saw it with your own eyes."

"No, I didn't." Cristina stepped towards the cell door and peered through the small grille. "No-one actually saw him commit a murder or mutilate a body. In fact, no-one saw Lupo

186

touch any of the victims, or even threaten them. The evidence is all circumstantial."

"Common sense says otherwise," Tomasso replied.

"Common sense tells us the world is flat. That kind of careless thinking has no place in a rigorous investigation."

Tomasso frowned. "They still don't know for sure that the earth is round."

"Educated people do."

"So why has no-one sailed all the way round it?"

"That is only a matter of time," Cristina said impatiently.

"Can we please just focus?" Domenico interrupted. "Right now, I don't care what shape the earth is! I just need to secure a confession, freely given, without coercion. We cannot risk executing an innocent man."

"Agreed," Cristina said. "Let's get him talking."

But Lupo had other ideas.

For the first four hours he maintained an absolute silence. Domenico and Cristina sat opposite, patiently setting out the details of each murder, and why they believed he was the killer. They tried sympathy, then hostility, then they warned Lupo that refusal to co-operate would provoke the magistrates to hand him over to the torturers for more robust questioning.

Nothing worked.

Lupo maintained his silence with the discipline of a monk.

Then finally, just as Domenico's patience was close to snapping, Lupo deigned to speak. "I am the victim in all this."

A baffled silence filled the prison cell.

"In what possible sense could that be true?" Cristina asked.

"Grave injustices have been perpetrated against me."

"You mean being arrested? And locked up?"

"I mean that I am more sinned against than sinning."

It was a reply designed to provoke, and Cristina knew better than to take the bait. But Domenico refused to let the man lapse back into silence. He stood up and loomed over the suspect. "We *know* you're the killer. The only question is how long it takes before you confess."

"Presumption is not knowledge," Lupo replied petulantly.

"What about presumption with a theory?" Cristina asked.

Lupo shrugged. "What theory?"

"Try this one: you are a man whose ambition outstrips his talent. Gifted enough to become an apprentice to a leading artist, over time you have come to realise that you will never become a celebrated master like Visconti. Failure has devoured your soul to the point where you can no longer bear to live in a world of genius. So you have set about destroying your master's work and patrons. Your bitterness seeks to destroy that which you long for, but can never become."

The apprentice looked at Cristina and blinked. He tried to reach for the right words, but they eluded him, so instead he threw his head back and roared with laughter. Genuine laughter. And once he'd started, he could not stop. Cristina and Domenico could only stare in bewilderment as tears of mirth streamed down Lupo's face.

Eventually he drew a breath and composed himself. "Forgive me. But laughter is such a tonic for the soul."

"You talk about souls?" Domenico warned. "Well, yours is going to Hell."

"An innocent man has nothing to fear."

"Then you should be terrified! *Testa di cazzo!*" Domenico had tried so hard to remain calm, but this man was asking for it.

"Does your brother have to swear?" Lupo glanced at Cristina and tutted. "I find it really quite offensive."

"Offensive?" Now it was Domenico's turn to laugh.

But Cristina stayed focussed. "Perhaps, Lupo, the only way you can avoid damnation, is by confessing."

"To what? I am innocent."

"Tell us why you killed Antonio Ricardo. Why you slit the contessa's throat. Why you beheaded Pozzi and suspended his body from the flagpoles above his house."

Lupo tried to look down, but Cristina grabbed his chin and forced him to look her in the eye.

"Tell us how you chose each victim, and how you tricked them into trusting you. Tell us what drove you to such butchery and how many more attacks you had planned. Clear your soul and maybe, just maybe, you will find some redemption in the afterlife."

But faced with the onslaught of questions, Lupo sank back into defiant silence. He had closed down again, and Cristina's words glanced off him like rain off a window.

"You do realise," Domenico said darkly, "that silence will only incriminate you further. The innocent never remain silent."

"And an artist never explains his work," Lupo replied. Then he lay back on the thin mattress, pulled the blanket up around his shoulders, and closed his eyes as if settling down for a good night's sleep.

"He's insane!" Domenico hurled the ring of heavy iron keys across his office, relieved to finally vent his frustration on an inanimate object.

"I don't think so," Cristina replied. "And losing your temper helps no-one."

"He's laughing at us!"

"But maybe that's what can give us an edge."

"How? I don't understand?"

"Lupo is far too logical for insanity," Cristina explained. "He clearly has a whole philosophy that's drawn him to these murders."

"But what's the point of a philosophy if you refuse to talk about it?"

"He will tell us. In fact, he is desperate to tell the world. But first he wants to torment us."

"I wish I shared your confidence, Cristina."

"What was the one moment where he really opened his heart?"

"He doesn't have a heart," Domenico slumped into his chair. "He just toyed with us the whole time."

"When he laughed," Cristina said, "that was genuine. No-one can fake tears of laughter. And what provoked him?"

Domenico cast his mind back. "When you told him the jealous apprentice theory?"

"Exactly. Visconti still torments him, even now. Visconti is Lupo's fatal weakness. And that gives us a way in."

38: MAESTRO

His mourning clothes were effortlessly extravagant. As befitted a maestro-artist, Visconti had wrapped himself in a long black cape, wore fine leather gauntlets on his hands, and a lush black bearskin cap on his head.

Cristina paused by the entrance to the Sistine Chapel, silently observing the artist for a few moments. Despite the gravity of the circumstances, Visconti showed no sign of religious deference; he wasn't kneeling in prayer or lighting a votive candle, rather, his head was craned back as he studied the silver starscape painted on the vaulted ceiling. She watched him raise a hand to measure the distance between the arches with his thumb, as if imagining a vast painting covering the entire space. Perhaps that's what it meant to be a great artist, you could never stop creating even in the most desperate of times.

"Thank you for coming, maestro." Cristina's words jolted Visconti from his reverie.

He spun round, saw her striding towards him, then crossed his arms over his heart and sank to his knees. "How can I ever forgive myself?"

"You are not to blame, maestro. You are also a victim in this." She offered a hand to help him up, but Visconti remained slumped in guilt.

"I had no idea Lupo was capable of such evil. None! Unwittingly I have nurtured a monster. And now I must live with recrimination for the rest of my life."

"Come." Cristina took Visconti's arm and helped him to his feet. "The shame is not yours."

"How could I have been so blind?"

"Lupo fooled everyone. He lied to the world. And there is no defence against a determined liar."

Visconti reached out and held Cristina, desperate for consolation. "I keep running over the past in my mind. Over and over. Conversations we had. Things I taught him. There must have been a clue I missed, some indication that his soul was corrupted."

"You forget, maestro, I met the man as well, in your workshop. Yet there was nothing about him to arouse the slightest suspicion. Hiding behind a mask of dullness was Lupo's gift, and he used it to deceive the world."

"You are right, Cristina, but that does not ease the pain I feel here." Visconti pressed her hand to his chest so that she could feel his heart beating. "I weep for my poor patrons. They displayed such generosity and were butchered for it."

"I'm sure their souls weep for you now, and for the terrible destruction wrought on your creations."

"Pah!" Visconti shrugged. "The loss of art is nothing. I can paint another picture, carve another sculpture … but only God can create a human soul. Once a precious life is taken, it can never be replaced."

"Then we must give thanks that Rome is safe from Lupo. At least for now."

"Yes, yes. Come…" Visconti led them to a side altar where they both lit candles and offered silent prayers. "Did you know there was illness in Lupo's family? A sickness?" Visconti said as he watched the candles flicker.

"No. He's barely spoken."

"Perhaps it was a warning sign that I should have heeded."

"What kind of illness?"

"A strange insanity gripped Lupo's father. A kind of mania."

"When was this?"

"Five years ago. Maybe six. There was some suggestion of syphilis, but in the absence of physical symptoms, the family called in the priests. They feared demonic possession."

"And did they find any?"

Visconti drew a long breath. "It was inconclusive. The man recovered after some months. But perhaps … perhaps the evil moved from father to son? Maybe the family has been cursed."

Cristina shook her head. "I think the explanation is more prosaic. But I need your help to find it."

"Whatever I can do, I am at your service. Anything. Name it."

"Shall we walk?" Cristina led the way as they left the Sistine Chapel and crossed the courtyard. "The difficulty is, Lupo claims he is innocent."

"What? But he was caught as he killed Pozzi."

"Not quite. And if we are to get justice for your patrons, we have to *prove* our case. A crucial element of that is getting a confession from Lupo."

Visconti frowned. "I don't understand how the man can plead innocence."

"He insists that he is the victim, and that he has suffered a grievous injustice."

Visconti stopped walking. "What injustice?"

"He will not say."

The artist became strangely pensive; his eyes began to wander as if considering different possibilities. Finally, his gaze settled on Cristina. "Has he spoken of me?"

"Maestro, you have been the defining force in his life, and that is why I hope you can help us resolve this."

"Of course. So you want me to talk to him?"

"We want you to persuade Lupo to confess to the murders, and to offer some explanation, some motive that drove him to such atrocities."

"I see."

"Can you do that?"

"If anyone can, it is surely me," Visconti replied gravely.

Nothing more was said as Cristina accompanied him to the lower floors under the Vatican. She was so accustomed to hearing Visconti fill every moment with extravagant language, the silence felt strangely awkward; the artist seemed to be thinking deeply about what was coming; perhaps he was genuinely fearful of his own apprentice.

When they arrived at the cells, Visconti asked for the interview to be held in private, but Domenico refused. "It's far too dangerous. The man is unstable."

"Then manacle him if it makes you feel better," Visconti replied.

"It's not safe. Lupo cannot be trusted."

"I know my own apprentice. He will not confess while you are there. He's already demonstrated that."

Cristina had to intervene to persuade Domenico to change his mind. Reluctantly he agreed to withdraw the guards on condition that Lupo's arms and legs were chained to the walls. When the prisoner was secured, Visconti was ushered in as everyone else left the cell.

Cristina and Domenico waited patiently in the narrow corridor directly outside, watching the candles smoke and flicker in the gloom. It was impossible to make out what was being said inside the prison cell, all they could hear was the murmur of voices, but the longer the meeting went on, the more hopeful Cristina became; they must have moved beyond denial, but was that enough?

Suddenly they heard the sound of manacles rattling, as if the two men were struggling. Domenico leapt to his feet, but Cristina held him back. "Wait!"

"Something's wrong."

"Give him time."

The chains rattled again, frantically, and a voice cried out, "Help! Help me!"

Domenico rushed to the cell and unlocked the bolts.

"Help! Murder!"

Domenico swung open the door and barged in expecting to save Visconti, but froze in confusion, struggling to understand what he was seeing.

Lupo was collapsed on the floor, Visconti was kneeling on his chest, hands gripped tightly around Lupo's throat as he tried to strangle him.

"Help! Hel…" Lupo's voice collapsed into a gargle as Visconti tightened his grip.

"Leave him!" Domenico screamed, lunging at Visconti, dragging him off the prisoner. Visconti's arms thrashed as he tried to claw his way back to finish the job.

"Stop!" Domenico yelled. But he saw Visconti's eyes burning with fury, and knew the man was beyond reason. "Enough!" He pulled a dagger from his belt and pressed it to the maestro's neck.

The touch of cold steel made Visconti recoil. He blinked, trying to recover his senses, then looked at his own hands in shock. "God help me!" he gasped and fled from the cell.

Domenico chased after him, leaving Cristina alone with Lupo.

"What in God's name just happened?" she demanded.

Lupo coughed his throat back to life and spat a huge globule of phlegm onto the floor.

"What did you say to him?"

But Lupo smiled calmly. "Now you see the real man."

"What are you talking about?"

"This is why I had to act. I saw the truth about Visconti when no-one else would. It was my destiny to stop him."

"Are you saying … *he* is the murderer?" Cristina stared at Lupo in disbelief. "Are you accusing him?"

Lupo gave a small chuckle and took a swig of water from the drinking bowl.

Furious, Cristina lashed out, kicking the bowl from his hands, sending water spattering across the wall. "What are you saying?"

But Lupo had sunk back into silence.

39: DIATRIBE

Visconti's hands were trembling so much, he could barely hold the cup Domenico had given him and ended up spilling as much wine as he drank. "Forgive me … forgive me … I didn't mean…" he mumbled.

By the time Cristina arrived in Domenico's office, the artist had recovered enough to explain himself.

"I can only apologise for abusing the trust you placed in me." He looked at Cristina with eyes full of remorse. "I don't know what came over me, but seeing him there … when my beloved clients were so cruelly taken … faced with such evil, I felt impotent." Visconti gazed at his own hands as if they belonged to someone else. "And the rage … I could not contain my feelings. But that does not excuse my actions. A man of my stature should know better."

Cristina studied Visconti, refusing to get drawn into the glib forgiveness that his words invited. Had she just witnessed a moment of righteous indignation? Or was there something more sinister at work? "We need to search Lupo's rooms," she said.

Visconti was momentarily confused. "Why?"

"Do you know where he lives?"

"Yes … yes. I… He lives just outside the city. On a vineyard."

Cristina and Domenico exchanged a wary look. "That's unusual for an apprentice."

"I wanted to help him," Visconti explained. "He showed some talent, so I let him stay in the summerhouse of my villa. Up on the Borghese vineyards."

"And you have no objection to us carrying out a thorough search?" Domenico pressed.

"Objection? Why would I object?" Visconti said. "I want to do everything in my power to bring Lupo to justice. Everything."

There had been a dusting of snow by the time they reached the hills, giving the massed ranks of vines a sinister feel. Silent and still, they clung to their guide wires like an emaciated army awaiting orders. Visconti's villa was built on a ridge of land overlooking vineyards in all directions, and the summerhouse where Lupo lodged was at the back of the complex near the pressing sheds.

The moment she swung open the doors, Cristina could see that this was a place of intense creative energy. Canvases at various stages of completion were scattered throughout the rooms, many perched on easels that had been squeezed into every possible space. Sheets of paper with sketches had been stuck to the walls, and in one corner a huge pile of empty wine bottles had been neatly stacked.

"What exactly are we looking for?" Domenico asked, sniffing one of the bottles.

"I don't know," Cristina replied. "But whatever it is will be hidden."

"A picture? A letter?"

Cristina shook her head. "Lupo is the sort of person who obsesses about things. And obsessives cannot hold everything in their minds, they have to put it down on paper."

"How would you know something like that?" Domenico teased.

Cristina ignored the jibe. "We're probably looking for a set of notebooks, or diaries. Something small enough to conceal. Maybe he even liked to carry it with him."

Domenico turned to Tomasso. "Well, you know what to do."

And they did. A key part of training to become an Apostolic Guard involved learning to think like a felon and how to behave if you were trying to conceal a guilty secret; so rather than ransacking the summerhouse, Domenico and Tomasso walked back and forth through the space, carefully recreating Lupo's domestic movements, seeing what he would have seen, touching the things that he would have touched. Once they had understood the rooms from Lupo's point of view, they looked for a spot that was readily accessible yet difficult to stumble on by accident.

Less than an hour later, they found it: a tatty, leather-bound journal hidden amongst a tangle of roof trusses in the shadow of the chimney.

Cristina flicked through the pages — they were covered with intense drawings and swirling doodles, interspersed with neat blocks of handwriting that broke up the chaos. Strangely, all the writing had been done in reverse.

"That takes some doing," Cristina said, and rummaged through Lupo's desk, searching for a small mirror. Yet even when she found it and started reading, the meaning of the words remained obscure. In between the bizarre sketches, he had inscribed strange aphorisms:

Art will destroy you. It will ruin you. Yet you keep retuning like a dog to its vomit.

Do not even start, for failure is inevitable.

The curse of poverty turns the true artist into a whore.

Across two pages, he had drawn a pastiche of Moses and the stone tablets containing the Commandments. *The Five Curses of Mediocrity*: "*Too bold. Too dark. Too original. Too challenging. Too much for the eye.*"

Then over the page: *To hell with them all! Let me shit in their eyes!*

Under a cruel and ugly caricature of Visconti, Lupo had written: *The Great Thief. Rome's Dandy. The Bloodsucker. The Fraudulent One.*

Another page contained sketches of Greek statues with the scrawled words: *He rapes my brilliance, but I will yet be the Swan to his Leda.*

Further on, he had started writing in the style of a Medieval illuminated manuscript, with each question mark depicted as a serpent. *Why has God abandoned me? WHY? WHY? WHY? WHY? WHY? Why does He bless mediocrity? Why did You give me talent, only to deny me?*

On the next page, a beautiful painting of a butterfly had been spoiled by the words: *I am a butterfly, crushed on a wheel of lies.*

And on the final pages, the most chilling words of all. *One day they will see me. One day they will know the truth. But one day is not today. So today they must see blood.*

Cristina was relieved to finally close the journal.

"Well? Does it help?" Domenico asked.

She offered him the book. "Judge for yourself."

Tomasso looked over his shoulder as Domenico leafed through the pages. "That is a lot of anger for one man."

"It shows he is desperate to talk," Cristina said. "The trick is to get him started."

Slap! The journal landed on the cell floor next to Lupo's feet.

"Interesting reading." Cristina drew up a wooden stool and sat down. "You are clearly a very jealous man."

"Are you blind, woman?"

Cristina flicked open the journal and picked an entry at random. "'Why does he have everything, yet I am denied even the crumbs?' Sounds like jealousy to me."

"To rage at injustice is not jealousy, it is wisdom," Lupo scowled.

"Oh. I see." Cristina was particularly good at playing dumb. "And these childish names? 'Rome's Dandy, The Bloodsucker.' Who are you talking about?"

Lupo's lips curled. "You're as bad as all the others. Sitting in elegant salons, worshipping art you don't understand. Blah, blah, blah, blah, blah."

"So … so these are the patrons, perhaps? The Bloodsucker is the lawyer, Ricardo, the Fraudulent One is the Contessa del Copertino, the Great Thief is Pozzi?"

"Wrong! Wrong! Wrong!" Lupo yelled. "Utterly and hopelessly wrong!"

"I'm sorry, I just don't understand —"

"Yes, maestro. No, maestro. Let me suck your cock, maestro."

Cristina feigned genuine surprise. "You mean Visconti? All this rage is directed against the man who nurtured you?"

"Go! Leave!" Lupo turned his back on her. "Your stupidity is infuriating."

"Forgive me, I am merely trying to understand."

"How many times do I have to tell you? An artist never explains his work. You will never understand, because I am walking a path that no-one else has ever walked. I am a genuine original."

"But..." Cristina prepared to land the decisive blow. "But the world will never see your brilliance, Lupo. You will only be remembered as a killer."

"No!" He spun round. "My writings will be a matter of record."

"These?" Cristina picked up the journal. "But these make no sense. Not to me."

"Those who matter will understand," Lupo scoffed.

"But those who matter are not in power. They never are."

Lupo started to scratch his arms with a strange agitation.

"You should tell me, Lupo. Tell me, so that I can tell the world. How do you want to be remembered?"

Still scratching, Lupo closed his eyes and started rocking back and forth.

Cristina placed a sheaf of paper on the floor; next to it she put an ink pot and quill.

"How do you want to be remembered, Lupo?" she repeated, then stood up and left the cell.

Lupo stared at the ink pot for a long time ... then finally reached out and picked up the quill.

40: CONFESSION

I was born in a pitiful provincial village where ignorance and mediocrity are kings.

Thousands of such benighted places pockmark the Italian peninsula, pustulating settlements where people think only what their grandparents thought, where bigotry and prejudice are passed down the generations in mothers' milk, where peasants destroy anything and anyone who dares to challenge their primitive beliefs.

No doubt you have seen those pastoral paintings of rural idylls, with their sober shepherds, diligent housewives and ruddy-cheeked children. But I have lived the reality and hear me when I tell you it is nasty, brutish, violent and abusive.

The only thing that prevented me from drowning in that cesspit of provincial ignorance was a love of drawing.

My very earliest memory is of painting a picture in mud on a cowshed floor. Once I was old enough to grasp a piece of charcoal, I would spend hours creating fantastical landscapes on the walls of the barn, full of castles and forests, illuminated by multiple suns and peopled with creatures that were part animal, part human, and part demon. It was the fabulous, unrestrained world of a child's mind.

Was my talent cherished?

Was it nurtured and celebrated?

How different my life could have been had I received the slightest encouragement or the faintest praise. But my fate was to be mocked and derided. My pictures were scrubbed away by idiots who were frightened of their own shadow. I was punished for daring to imagine and beaten for the 'unholy visions' that I allowed into my mind.

Yet in those long, lonely hours of solitude, when they locked me in the cellar to 'correct' my mind ... in that dark place I found strength.

Because God had not abandoned me.

There was no burning bush or ethereal light, there was just a quiet, comforting voice inside my head urging me not to betray the gift that He had given me, not to waste my life watching goats shit on a hillside and dullards drink themselves into a stupor.

And He proved His love for me by sending a Saviour...

When I was twelve years old, Vito Visconti arrived in the village with a retinue of servants and apprentices. He had come to study the local landscape and make sketches of flora and fauna that would eventually find their way into the backgrounds of his grand canvases.

The villagers were hostile. Naturally. He was everything they were not, and he had more culture in his little finger than my village had in its entire history. The only reason they didn't drive him away was because he had silver in his purse, and plenty of it. He distributed his coin liberally, renting rooms for his retinue, buying suckling pigs to roast, and consuming cases of local wine.

The villagers exploited Visconti's naïvety, doubling the cost of everything, yet even as they smiled to his face, they despised everything about him: his clothes, his words, his aesthetic sensibility. This gave me the perfect opportunity, and I offered to act as a go-between, running errands and messages for the maestro and his assistants.

Day by day, I ingratiated myself with the great artist. From carrying messages, I moved on to carrying easels and equipment, then to guiding Visconti along obscure hillside tracks to find the most striking views in the most perfect light.

One afternoon, as the maestro took a post-lunch nap in an olive grove, I seized the moment. Stealthily I slid some paper and two sticks of charcoal from Visconti's bag, then created a series of sketches of the olive trees, including minutely observed details of the leaves and bark.

When he awoke, I showed Visconti my work. He considered the drawings for some time, studying the composition and line work. He was impressed. Very impressed. I could see it in his eyes. But he was also crafty.

"Not bad, Lupo," he sniffed. "Somewhat trite, but they show a glimmer of promise."

I begged him to take me on as an apprentice, but he just laughed. "There is a world of difference between sketching for amusement, and being a professional artist, Lupo. You have no idea of the dedication that entails. Unless you are prepared to sacrifice everything for your art, stay here on the farm and shovel shit."

I did not heed his warnings. I could not. There was only one thing I wanted in life: to paint. And there was only one person who could open that life to me: Vito Visconti.

Determined to prove myself, I set about sketching every afternoon while the maestro slept. Portraits, studies in light, cloudscapes, water rippling in a stream, anything that might prove my usefulness to him.

And it worked. On the day of his departure, Visconti struck a deal with my father.

"It is obvious to me," he declared, "that the boy will be useless to you on the farm. He is a daydreamer. So I am prepared to take him off your hands and offer him an apprenticeship."

My father's eyes narrowed as he tried to think his way through this strange offer, but thinking was not his strong suit. "How much?" he finally mumbled.

"No, no, sir," Visconti chuckled, "I am doing you the favour. I will not pay you a single ducat."

"That's what I meant," my father replied. "How much do you want to take him away?"

Visconti plucked a silk handkerchief from his jacket and dabbed his top lip. He looked at the rundown shack we lived in and the wooden clogs on my father's feet, then declared with great magnanimity, "I will do this as an act of Christian charity. As long as the boy works hard and learns quickly, I will feed and house him, and keep a shirt on his back."

My father's eyes twinkled — he couldn't believe his luck. I was useless to him, and now he could wash his hands of me.

I didn't even pack a bag, for there was nothing of that village I wanted to take with me.

As I rode away on the cart, sitting next to one of Visconti's established apprentices, my heart was full of hope and expectation.

"Don't you want to wave goodbye?" the other boy asked, pointing to the receding rooftops.

I turned around, pointed my arse in the direction of that village of the damned, and farted loudly. The other apprentice collapsed in laughter.

Now my destiny lay in Rome, a city of opportunity where talent was nurtured and art treasured. Greatness lay ahead.

How was I to know that Vito Visconti had other plans for me?

Walking into his studio was like entering Paradise. The whole building was alive with young people, full of energy and ideas, all devoting themselves to art. And the equipment Visconti possessed ... he had every type of brush and pigment imaginable, along with different papers for sketching in charcoal or watercolours; some rooms were full of canvases, others stacked with varnishes and oils. I did not know such a world was possible, yet now I was to be a part of it, and suddenly everything felt possible. Here I could truly become.

On my first morning, Visconti set me a test — a still life drawing of a bowl of fruit, a simple task that would gauge my ability. While he went off to supervise his assistants, I studied the fruit, keenly aware that how I performed now might determine the trajectory of my apprenticeship, and therefore my whole life.

How could I reveal my soul through a simple depiction of fruit?

I started arranging the pieces on a table, experimenting with different compositions, but everything seemed dull and pedestrian ... until I had a bizarre idea. I took some string and suspended each piece of fruit at a different height. First the quince, then the apple, from which I cut a single slice; next came some grapes, and finally a pomegranate, so that the fruit formed a sweeping arc from left to right.

I stood back and looked at the tableau: it was strangely dramatic.

Behind the fruit I draped some black velvet, then shuttered a single shaft of sunlight to fall across the composition.

Instinctively this felt right, and my senses tingled with anticipation as I started to draw. My fingers moved quickly across the paper, as if being guided by some higher force. I worked feverishly, without stopping, almost in a trance ... until the drawing was complete. As I laid the paper down, I saw what I had created: through the miracle of art, these humble objects had been transformed into something quite harrowing, for it looked as if the fruits were felons who had been hanged for heresy.

"Let me see." Visconti's voice startled me.

"Yes, maestro."

He took the paper and studied it in silence. His stern expression made me think I had failed.

"What were you thinking, boy?"

"I'm sorry, maestro. I was just…"

But I could not articulate what I was thinking, I was twelve years old. "Shall I do it again?"

"No."

And then I saw it in his eyes, he was puzzled by the picture, but he was also intrigued.

"Where did you copy this idea from?"

"Nowhere, maestro."

"Hanging the fruit? It's unusual."

I shrugged. "They hang sausages and hams in the barn over winter. In my village. Maybe that's what I was thinking?"

Visconti nodded. "Sausages. Is that so?"

"Do you like it, sir?"

There was an inscrutable expression on his face. "This image … it speaks of fear and mortality. It expresses the longing of the soul on being separated from the Divine."

I didn't know what he was talking about. "But do you like it, sir?"

Visconti studied me. "Yes, Lupo," he whispered. "I do."

Without thinking I flung my arms around him as if he was the loving father I never had. "Thank you, maestro. Thank you."

Yet we both understood that I had to pay my dues and work my seven years as an apprentice. And I was happy to do so, for there was much to learn and I wanted to absorb every secret of the craft.

Visconti plunged me into the frenzy of his workshop, where I became the humblest part of a complex operation that produced a stream of paintings, statues, designs for funeral monuments and religious frescoes. Yet in some ways, I was treated differently. When the other apprentices left the studio at the end of the day, Visconti would often hold me back to give extra tuition, studies in perspective and colour and composition, so that my progress quickly outstripped that of my peers. Sometimes Visconti praised my work, gazing at it as intently as he had done with that first still life; at other times he would fly into a rage and tear my work into pieces. And then he would give me long, rambling lectures about life as an artist.

"It's a tortuous journey, Lupo. Much failure has to be endured before one feels the sweet caress of success. But in that failure, a deep strength is forged. The strength of an artist's vision. And I can give you that resilience, boy. I alone can show you the way. But you must prove your loyalty to me. Your absolute, unquestioning, undying loyalty. Do you understand?"

I nodded, but I didn't really understand, for all I wanted to do was paint.

As the months passed, the other apprentices started to resent my rapid progress. While they were still stretching canvases, I was allowed to paint trees and buildings and other background details; and while they were lodged in various hostels scattered along the Via Margutta, I was given my own space in the summerhouse of Visconti's villa up in the hills above Rome. Separated from the others, with all the facilities of a studio at my disposal night and day, I started to feel like a true artist.

Yet soon enough I learned that Visconti had not put me in the summerhouse for my own benefit, but for his…

There was a frantic hammering on the door in the middle of the night, then one of the servants burst into my room and hauled me out of bed. "The maestro, he needs you."

"At this hour?" I rubbed the sleep from my eyes and reached for a candle.

"Here." The servant threw a gown at me. "Put this on. He's waiting."

Drowsy and confused, I did as I was told. The servant led me into the main house and upstairs to Visconti's private study, a place very few people were privileged to enter.

There must have been a hundred candles flickering in that room, turning night into day. The walls were lined with books, the floor was strewn with balls of discarded paper, and in the middle of it all lay Visconti, sprawled on some cushions. He was drunk.

"All hail the arrival of the Peasant Boy!" he slurred, beckoning me to approach.

But I was scared, for I had never seen him like this. Immaculate presentation and elegant clothes were normally so important to him, yet here was Visconti sprawled in a dirty nightgown stained with wine.

"Come! I command it!"

Cautiously I approached.

"Don't be frightened, boy. This is what artists do. Man to man. Artist to artist. What do you say?" he slurred.

"I don't understand, sir."

"Got an exercise for you." He picked up one of the screwed-up balls of paper and tossed it across the room. "A game. You like games, don't you?"

"Yes, maestro."

"D'you know what the Seven Works of Mercy are, Lupo?"

"Yes, I think so."

"Course you do. God-fearing-goat-fucking peasant that you are." He laughed at his own description and downed some more wine.

"So this is the test. Arrange the Seven Works of Mercy into the perfect composition."

"Right now, sir?"

"Exactly so. But there's a catch. On each of these pieces of paper, I have drawn a composition that is rubbish."

I looked at the dozens of paper balls scattered across the room.

"You, Lupo, you … you … have to create a composition that is different to all the ones that are no good."

I bent down to pick up one of the discarded papers but Visconti threw his wine glass at me. "You can't look! Imbecile! That would be cheating."

"So … how do I know what has already been tried?"

"You don't. That's what makes it fun." He tapped his head with his forefinger. "Just draw from in there, Lupo. Rummage around in that little peasant head of yours, and we'll see what happens."

The servant handed me a sheaf of paper, a drawing board and some charcoal, then hurried from the room.

"What are you waiting for, Lupo?" Visconti wallowed deeper into the cushions and closed his eyes. "You draw. I sleep. And no cheating, mind. I know where each piece of paper has been tossed. I'll know if you peek."

Moments later, he was snoring. I didn't know if this was a drunken joke or if the maestro was in earnest, but I didn't dare do anything that might jeopardise my apprenticeship.

So I started to sketch, experimenting with different images as the candles guttered and one by one burnt themselves out. Finally, as dawn started to filter through the shutters, I found a composition with perfect balance, which guided the eye effortlessly from one image to the next, one that had a delicate poise, but opened a window onto the spirituality of Christ's work.

As a shaft of hard sunlight spilled across Visconti's face, he stirred awake. He blinked, but he was not startled to see me sitting there, for he clearly remembered the events of the night.

"Show me." He reached out a hand.

I did as I was told.

Visconti studied the composition for a long time, he turned the paper upside down, then onto its side. But he said nothing.

Finally, I saw a single tear roll down his cheek and plop onto the paper.

"Leave me," he whispered. "Go."

Antonio Pozzi had barely lowered his enormous girth into a chair in the client lounge, when servants hurried forward to offer him cake and sherry, because if there is one thing Visconti is a master of, it is indulging clients.

The banker had been invited to approve designs for the giant mosaic that would adorn the front of his palazzo. I had been instructed to be present, which was unusual, as apprentices were normally kept far away from such powerful clients. But Visconti wanted to make a point, for when he presented the designs for the Seven Works of Mercy, I saw that he had not changed a thing, he had merely redrawn my compositions on a larger scale and added colour. But to hear him talk about the creative process … that was quite something.

"I wrestled with this piece night and day, Antonio. I was searching for the perfect composition that would harmonise the complex elements into a single, powerful whole through which one could experience the divine. But perfection kept eluding me." Visconti closed his eyes as if reliving the creative struggle. "Finally, in a spiritual fever, I donned a hair shirt and lay on the floor of my studio, appealing directly to God…"

Pozzi stopped eating and stared at the artist. "And? What happened?"

A smile of bliss broke on Visconti's face. "An angel visited me in the dead of night and showed me the way."

"An angel?" Pozzi looked at the sketches in awe. "Seriously?"

"This is a work blessed by God himself."

I knew, and Visconti knew, that the 'angel' was me, visiting a drunk man who had run out of ideas. And that was the whole point. In that moment, Visconti was showing me how things were going to work from now on: I would create, he would take the credit. 'Know your place,' he was telling me. 'Accept this lie as the new reality.'

Of course, Pozzi knew nothing of this, he simply gazed at the composition in silence. "Wonderful," he whispered. "And touched by God."

"It is perfect, isn't it?" Visconti agreed. "Change one line, and the whole is diminished."

"You are a maestro, Visconti. A true maestro. And worth every penny." Pozzi beckoned to one of his retinue who started counting out pieces of gold. "I want this both as a mosaic on the outside of my palazzo, and as a spectacular fresco in the grand banqueting hall. Can you manage that?"

"Your honour me," Visconti said with a humble bow.

A part of me was thrilled to see such praise lavished on my work, but another part bridled at the deception. Was no one going to recognise my talent? Would none of the glory be mine?

So in the silence, as everyone watched the gold being counted, I dared to speak.

"Might I suggest, maestro, that the composition would flow better if we changed the shape of the river in Giving Water to the Thirsty?"

Everyone in the room froze. I didn't realise what I had done was a shocking breach of etiquette, that apprentices never speak in front of clients. Slowly Visconti turned towards me with a look of such malevolence…

But I was lucky. Pozzi, in his ignorance of etiquette, took a shine to the suggestion. "Yes, that's a good idea," he said with a mouthful of cake. "Maybe if it went diagonally, like this. What do you think Visconti?"

Now that the client had spoken, Visconti had to be careful. He looked at the picture and ran his hands over it a few times, as if imagining the alterations, then nodded. "I think I could make that work, if you prefer it that way."

Pozzi smiled. "Yes. Yes, I do." In this small detail, the banker had proved that he was God's equal, for he had 'co-created' this image with the Divine.

Yet the moment Pozzi had left the building, Visconti turned on me with a terrifying rage. "Never speak in front of a patron!" he screamed. "Never! You hear?"

He kicked and punched me.

"I'm sorry, sir!" I begged, trying to dodge his fists. "Forgive me!"

But he would not stop until I had witnessed his rage. "This is *my* workshop! The House of Visconti! I built this with *my* vision and talent. You are nothing to me. Nothing! You are scum!"

I slumped to the floor, curled into a tight ball, trying to shield myself from the blows.

"What are you?" he demanded.

"Scum, sir."

"Dog! Wretched dog!" He grabbed me by the neck and hauled me towards the open window. "After all that I have done for you, how could you be so disloyal? I should throw you out onto the street," he yelled, bundling me onto the window ledge as if he was going to hurl me to my death.

"No! Please, sir! I beg you!"

I teetered on the ledge, desperately clinging to the window frame, when finally Visconti's rage burned itself out and he ordered the servants to drag me down to the cellars where I could reflect on my ingratitude.

Hours later, one of the housemaids came down with water and bandages to tend my wounds.

"Will he give me another chance?" I whimpered.

"Course he will," the maid soothed. "This is how it works. You're not the first, and you certainly won't be the last."

The following day, Visconti's manager came to visit the bottega. 'Manager' is a relatively new profession that only emerged with the explosion of art in Florence some fifty years ago. More than dealers who just buy and sell paintings, managers curate the careers of the artists they represent, cultivating their image, negotiating their fees, singing their praises, and taking twenty per cent of everything.

In many ways, Ludovico Labirinto was the opposite of Visconti, for he never used three words when one would suffice, and he spoke so quietly that people had to lean in to hear what he was saying. In truth, it was all a carefully cultivated game of power to create an air of authority.

Visconti and Labirinto walked through the workshops as they discussed business, and happened to stop close to where I was finessing the storm clouds on an altarpiece. I positioned myself so that I could eavesdrop — they were discussing the Seven Works of Mercy commission…

"The client is delighted," Visconti gushed. "More than delighted."

"Then I shall press him for an uplift in the fee," Labirinto replied.

"But we have already agreed a price."

"He's on the hook. Now he's seen your designs he won't be going elsewhere."

"But —"

"Vito, if we don't ask, he won't respect us. The man's a banker."

Visconti looked anxious. "As long as he doesn't cancel the commission."

"Have more confidence," Labirinto reassured. "This latest work is brilliant. You have moved to a higher plane, and that commands a higher price."

"You are too kind, Ludovico."

"I am just being honest. With the Seven Works of Mercy, a mature artist becomes a maestro. The flow of the composition is perfect. This will be the making of you, Vito, I swear. You have excelled."

Visconti affected a humble expression. "As long as the money flows, all will be well."

For the briefest of moments, Visconti glanced at me. And I understood. There was nothing accidental about this conversation, it was a test. If I spoke up and told the truth, I would be beaten; if I remained silent, I would be rewarded.

What choice does a boy from a poor family really have?

And so the pattern was set.

During the day, I was an apprentice learning my craft. But at night, separated from the others, I worked on private paintings that Visconti and Labirinto would present to select and highly prestigious clients in order to whip up bidding wars. It worked. Brilliantly. As the years passed, Visconti's coffers grew heavy, and his reputation reached new heights as his paintings displayed ever greater talent.

Yet that talent was mine.

In return, he paid me a decent wage, and he looked after my family. When my mother was sick, he even sent his personal physician to cure her, all at his own expense.

By the time the commission for *Salvator Mundi* came in, Visconti didn't even try to contribute to the work, he just handed it straight to me. That painting was to be a turning point in my life; I poured my heart and soul into it. Night after night I worked and reworked the image in a frenzied state, applying everything that I had learnt.

It was my idea to paint the portrait on such a huge scale, my idea to use the muted colours, my brilliance that put the haunted sorrow in Christ's eyes. When I had finished, I knew that it was a masterpiece, I could feel it in my soul. No-one had ever done a work like this before.

Visconti was impressed, he too could see what a powerful painting it was, and he even gave me a bonus. Then he took it to Antonio Ricardo and presented it as entirely his own creation.

But Vito Visconti was starting to overreach himself, for a lie can only grow so big until it collapses under the weight of its own delusion.

Salvator Mundi became the talk of Rome. The lawyer Ricardo was so pleased with his purchase, he put it on display behind the altar of Saint John Lateran; for three days, ordinary people filed past in awe, humbled by the spirituality of the painting, until the whole city was alive with admiration.

Visconti had done everything he could to keep me secluded in his villa and isolated from clients, but even I heard the growing talk of his genius. I would sit in taverns where artists congregated and hear them marvel at the boldness of *Salvator Mundi*. In markets where apprentices bought materials for their masters' workshops, I would hear the envy that Visconti had stirred up. Priests, inspired by its spirituality, waxed lyrical from the pulpit about how God had expressed himself through the genius of the painting.

Visconti. Visconti. Visconti.

The work was mine, yet the adulation was his. Do you have any idea how that made me feel? I was elated and crushed at the same time, celebrated yet ignored. It is the sort of unbearable tension that can tear a man apart.

Every day, new clients flocked to Visconti's workshop, all of them wanting their own piece of his brilliance. Beautiful women flung themselves at him, powerful men showed him grovelling deference … it was painful to watch because it should have been *me* they were adoring. Me. Visconti had not put a single brushstroke on the canvas, it was all my work, yet he was the one being lauded.

As the weeks passed, I realised that I had cheated myself. I had entered into a pact with the Devil, and for the sake of my sanity I knew that I must extricate myself. I was twenty years old, it was time to make my move.

So I went to see Ludovico Labirinto, the manager extraordinaire. I explained how Visconti's studio really worked, and the enormous contribution that I had made over the years. I was expecting him to shake my hand and sign me up with immediate effect, but when I finished he just rocked back in his chair and studied me through narrowed eyes.

"What is your game, Lupo?"

"Game? I have no game. I just want to break free, establish my own studio."

Labirinto frowned. "Yet you've barely finished your apprenticeship."

"You've seen my work, you know I have the talent."

"Do I? The paintings you talk about all bear Visconti's signature."

"But I created them."

"So you say." The manager gave a sceptical shrug.

I could sense I was losing him. "Look, I understand it's a risk taking on an unknown artist, but to make it worth your while, I will offer you forty per cent of every sale if you will represent me."

"Lupo, Lupo, Lupo," the manager replied with a sigh. "You have misunderstood the situation entirely. Take a step back and see the way things really are. Everyone is making money now. Wealthy clients are queueing up to stuff gold into Visconti's pockets; he gets paid, I get paid, you get paid, everyone benefits. Do you have any idea how difficult it is to achieve that kind of celebrity? Why would I do anything to disrupt such a harmonious arrangement?"

"Because it is a lie. Because I created the paintings that everyone loves so much."

"That is not how I remember it," Labirinto replied. "All apprentices contribute to the major works of a studio, but it is under the tutelage of the maestro. That is how the system works. Be content that you are in a prosperous workshop, learning from a great man. You are still young, there is plenty of time to satisfy your own ambitions later."

"Tutelage?" I looked at the manager in disbelief. "He is the one learning from me!"

"A very presumptuous thing to say."

"Ask him yourself!"

"Did Visconti not teach you about colour and tone?"

"Yes."

"Did he not teach you about balance and perspective?"

"Yes, but —"

"Did he not guide you through the craft of working and reworking a composition?"

"That is not the point!"

"Oh, it very much is the point, Lupo. For without Visconti, you would still be rotting in a mountain shack."

"But now I have outgrown him!"

"Be patient."

"Why should genius wait?" I threw back the chair and started pacing the room in frustration.

Labirinto eyed me with his cool gaze. "You are very arrogant."

"Only because I am very good! I didn't just assist with *Salvator Mundi*, I created it. In its entirety. Visconti did not touch the canvas until it was finished. He did not contribute in any way. Not a single idea. He is a man of average talent, with nothing to say. That is the truth."

"But he is a dazzling man."

I couldn't hide my bewilderment. "What does that have to do with anything?"

"When Visconti walks into a room, everyone feels more alive. He has charisma, charm, wit. But you…" He looked me up and down. "You are plain and dull. You carry too much weight and have thinning hair. You speak with a strange, provincial accent that makes people snigger. You just don't look the part."

"It is the work that counts!" I slammed my fist on his desk. "Only the work! It should all be about the work."

"Should," Labirinto smiled. "Ah, what the world 'should' be. But I deal in facts, not hypotheticals. And your face simply does not fit. It's a thing. Get used to it."

Nausea overwhelmed me. "You would allow this travesty of justice to continue? This charade?"

"It's not business, Lupo. It's personal. It's you. No-one wants to buy a masterpiece from someone like you."

I took the largest flagon of linseed oil I could find in the storeroom and crept through the corridors of the darkened villa. By now, I knew every creaking floorboard and groaning hinge of that place, so I was able to make my way to Visconti's bedroom without waking any of the servants.

He was in a deep sleep, the sleep of the innocent. It would make my work easier. Gently I undid the stopper and trickled the thick yellow oil over the bedsheets, back and forth until the flagon was empty. As the liquid soaked through to Visconti's body, he stirred and scratched, his mind absorbing the feeling of wetness into his dreams, then he rolled over and started to snore again.

"Farewell, maestro," I whispered, then struck a tinderbox and watched the cloud of sparks sprinkle onto the oil-soaked sheets.

In an instant the bed ballooned into a ball of fire.

Visconti lurched awake, sitting up in shock, trying to understand what was happening.

He looked left and right, then through the flames he saw me … and he knew.

"Forgive me!" he screamed in a voice so full of terror it split the air. "FORGIVE ME!"

And I laughed. With joy. With elation. With a sense that finally justice had been done.

And then I awoke.

Now it was me who looked around in the darkness, confused and disorientated, trying to understand what had happened. As I realised that my revenge had been nothing more than a dream, my heart felt heavy again. I should have been relieved to discover I was not a murderer, but all I felt was crushing disappointment, like a prisoner who dreams of freedom only to wake in his fetid cell.

Yet now I understood that this dream must be a sign from God. He was surely telling me that if I continued along this path of bitterness and frustration, I would be damned. Older generations are supposed to nurture younger generations, not steal their energy and ideas, but the Establishment of Rome would not lift a finger to protect me. If I was to break free from Visconti's suffocating grasp, I would have to act on my own.

And that was when the dark thoughts started.

Dark as the Devil's heart…

So dark they terrified me … and stayed my hand.

Too frightened to commit, I seized upon one last chance to make peace with Visconti: St Peter's Basilica. When my design was selected to be among the final four, Visconti found himself competing with true masters; perhaps the daunting scale of the task would awake his humility.

As I showed him the sketches I had prepared to win the final stage of the competition, I plucked up the courage to speak. "Building the new St Peter's will be a huge project, maestro."

"Indeed." His eyes fluttered over the drawings. "It will change the face of Rome forever."

"And the sheer amount of time it will take, the detailed drawings and designs, year after year … it could be overwhelming."

Visconti put down the sketches and studied me. "Are you hustling for a pay rise, Lupo?"

"No, no. I just … it's not just about money, maestro."

"Oh?"

"Surely, it would not be inappropriate for my creative contribution to this great project to be recognised in some other way as well?"

"Recognised how?"

"Perhaps we could share the credit, maestro. You and I. Visconti and Lupo, joint designers of the brilliant new St Peter's."

Not a flicker of reaction on his face.

"I would pour my heart and soul into it," I continued. "It would occupy my thoughts night and day. I would abstain from all personal pleasures and dedicate my life to this one work. After everything I have done for you, maestro, is this really too much to ask?"

He gave a long, heavy sigh. "Why are you so determined to humiliate me, Lupo?"

"Humiliate? No. Never. That is not —"

"His Holiness the Pope granted me a private audience specifically to discuss my design."

"*My* design."

"It says Visconti on the drawings! It was Visconti who the Holy Father graced with a meeting! The design has only made it onto the shortlist because it is backed by the weight of my workshop." He stood up and selected a silver-topped walking cane from the rack. "And now you want me to say, 'Actually, Your Holiness, I lied. This design that you love so much was somebody else's work.'"

"No. We would share the credit."

"Oh, how generous of you, Lupo." He tested the weight of the cane in his hands. "How damned generous! *Cornuto!*" He raised the cane and swung it with full force at my torso, forcing me to dodge backwards.

"Stop! Please! I didn't mean —"

"I know exactly what you meant." He paced towards me, wielding the cane like a club. "But I thought we had resolved all this years ago."

He swung the cane low across my legs, knocking them out from under me.

"You work, I provide for you."

I tried to slither away, but he kept looming forward.

Another blow landed on my ribs.

"Everything you know, you have learnt from me." He raised the cane, ready to strike again. "Sadly, the one thing you refuse to learn is humility."

He swung down violently, aiming for my head. Instinctively I reached out and grabbed the cane, inches from my skull, and held it there.

For the first time, I felt his weakness. I was no longer a twelve-year-old boy, I was a man, and I was strong.

I roared with anger and pushed the cane away, forcing him to stumble backwards. I could see the shock in his eyes.

Slowly I got to me feet and advanced on him.

"Stay away from me!" He tried to prod me with the cane but I snatched it from his grasp. Now it was my turn to feel the weight of the weapon in my hands, to swing it nonchalantly in the air.

"Don't you dare touch me, Lupo! I can destroy you in a moment."

"Is that so?" I banged the walking cane on the floor.

"It never ends well for people like you."

"Wrong, Maestro Visconti," I replied, pacing towards him. "You will not drive me to suicide or madness. I will not end up in the Hospital for the Incurables, like apprentices before me. No, I will get what is rightly mine."

"You will get nothing!" he sputtered through his rage. "You are fired! Immediately! Get out of my workshop!"

"You want me to beg forgiveness?"

"It's too late! You no longer have a place here!"

I just laughed. "You really are a man with a small brain."

"Get out!"

"If I go, *maestro*, who will create all the masterpieces that have made you famous?"

"Rome is full of apprentices!"

"Not like me. And you know it."

"Don't flatter yourself." By now he was backed against the wall.

"If I leave this workshop, the whole world will see that Visconti has lost his touch, that he is just a mediocrity after all."

Suddenly he snatched the cane from my hands and pushed me away. "It is you who has the small brain, Lupo. For if you leave this workshop, your life is as good as finished."

"Your threats don't scare me."

"Rome is my city. I own it. One word from me, and not a single art dealer will touch your work. No patron or manager will grant you an audience. No supplier will extend you any credit. I will make sure of that."

"When they see what I can create —"

"No-one cares! *Stronzo!*" he smirked. "I thought Labirinto had made that clear."

I felt myself go weak — he knew. He had been spying on me, following my every move, cutting off every escape route I had been planning.

"And if Rome rejects you," he pressed, "then Florence will reject you too. And once you're dead in Italy, you're dead to the world. So either you paint for me, or you crawl back to the mountains."

I had created the art; it was mine to destroy.

There was no turning back now; evil had to be confronted and vanquished. The new St Peter's will stand for a thousand years, but I knew that if I didn't act, I would be forgotten while the fraudulent Visconti would be praised for all eternity.

My first thought was to murder him, yet on reflection I realised that would only cement Visconti's fame. History would remember him as 'A great artist mysteriously killed at the height of his powers.' Genius cut down in its prime is always an alluring narrative.

That could not happen, for my aim was to destroy the man's life and reputation, not secure it. However, by targeting his patrons, I saw how I could put a curse on the man, so that everyone who owned a Visconti would start to fear for their lives.

Very quickly, clients would abandon him, and Visconti would then be forced to witness his own demise; having known fame, he would have to endure the painful ignominy of obscurity.

I soon realised that going after the patrons made my task considerably easier, for they suspected nothing, and viewed artists' apprentices as trusted craftsmen. No-one questioned my presence in Ricardo's house to adjust the hanging wires on *Salvator Mundi*, and retouch the varnish. Once inside, I was left unsupervised, and free to hide in the cellars until the household went to bed.

Contessa Copertino never for a moment doubted that I was escorting her to a secret meeting with Visconti. I explained that he wanted to take her on a clandestine tour of Rome so that together they could search out a site for her next sculpture. She thought it was thrilling and glamorous, and respected the need for absolute discretion.

Pozzi was only interested in counting money, everything else he delegated to his servants, and they had no interest in art: I could have told them I needed to add an Eighth Work of Mercy and they would have believed me.

One by one I lured Visconti's patrons into my trap, and I would have kept on destroying them until the whole of Rome understood that to commission a Visconti was to condemn yourself to death. But you cut my plans short.

I do not deny my crimes.

I have no fear of punishment.

Justice had to be done.

I had to choose between murder and madness. Naturally, I chose murder.

But mark my words: once I am executed, there will be no more Visconti masterpieces. His 'talent' will inexplicably evaporate. He will find some excuse, perhaps he will fake blindness or relocate to another country, perhaps he will experience a 'mystical revelation' and join a monastery. Whatever story he fabricates, it will prevent the world from seeing him as the imposter he truly is.

I may be a murderer, but at least I have not murdered truth.

Here ends my confession.

Signed, the Artist formerly known as Lupo the Apprentice.

41: FLAWED

Cristina read the final words of the confession then slowly put the papers down on the table. She spent a few moments tapping them straight with her fingers, trying to buy time for her mind to wrestle the shocking revelations into submission.

Finally, she looked into Lupo's watery eyes. "How do I know this isn't a pack of lies?"

"Because you're an intelligent woman."

"And you think that makes me gullible?"

Lupo pressed a dirty forefinger onto the pages. "This makes sense of everything. The crimes. The motivation. Visconti's behaviour. His sudden burst of genius. If you choose not to believe it … then you are as bad as them." He turned his back on Cristina and retreated into the shadows of the prison cell. "I have spoken the truth. Do what you will."

Suddenly overwhelmed, Cristina hurried from the cell, bolted up the stone steps and burst into the Vatican courtyard like a swimmer gasping for air.

The new St Peter's Basilica was supposed to be a shining beacon of faith and truth, a physical embodiment of Christian values, a manifestation in stone of idealism and hope; yet now it seemed that a fraud would win the competition. If she did nothing, corruption and deceit would be built into the very fabric of St Peter's, yet to prevent that, Cristina would have to side with a brutal murderer. There seemed no way forward that was not hopelessly compromised.

Through Domenico's influence, Cristina was able to secure a brief audience with Pope Julius II, squeezed in between two prior appointments with ambassadors from the Hanseatic League. With little time to make her case fully, she appealed to the pontiff to simply disqualify Visconti from the competition.

"On what grounds?" Impatience was etched on Pope Julius's face.

"Lupo has made serious allegations about the man's integrity."

"You mean the murderer is trying to talk his way out of justice?"

"Lupo's guilt is not in doubt, Your Holiness, but now I am trying to protect the integrity of St Peter's."

"Have you seen the design that Visconti submitted?" Pope Julius demanded.

"Yes, Holy Father."

"Then you will know that his vision is brilliant and bold. The world has never seen architecture like it. With this one creation, the Church will make a statement of unparalleled leadership and confidence that will echo across Christendom."

"But Visconti did not design it, Your Holiness. He stole the idea."

"You would really take the word of a self-confessed murderer over that of a brilliant artist?" Pope Julius was incredulous.

"I appreciate how this must sound —"

"Ludicrous! It sounds ludicrous because it is an absurd idea! Misguided, wrong-headed, and slanderous."

"Christ was also condemned as a criminal, Holy Father."

The Pope's face tensed with rage. "How dare you presume to lecture me on Scripture!"

"Forgive me," Cristina lowered her head. "I didn't mean it like that."

"No! I will not forgive you!" His anger echoed round the chamber.

"I am only trying to protect the Church."

"Do not interfere with what you do not understand. I forbid it."

"Yes, Holy Father."

"You should learn to respect the institution you claim to love. Obedience is the foundation of the Church's strength."

"Yet there is nothing stronger than truth. Somehow it always finds a way to survive, and when the truth about Visconti's basilica is finally known, I fear it will tarnish St Peter's for ever."

But Pope Julius had heard enough. "No-one cares what you think." He beckoned to one of his attendants who hurriedly escorted Cristina from the audience chamber.

"You're lucky you're a woman," the attendant whispered. "I've known him punch men to the ground for less impertinence than that."

But Cristina's ordeal was not yet over. As she walked down the long corridor towards the Belvedere Courtyard, she saw Vito Visconti walking towards her. Escorted by another of Julius' assistants, he was clearly coming for an audience with the Pope and had dressed for the occasion in a billowing black cloak to give him the gravitas of an academic.

As they got close, Visconti whipped off his cap and bowed. "What a delightful chance encounter. I trust you were updating His Holiness about the schedule for Lupo's execution?" He reached out to kiss her hand, but Cristina flinched. Visconti was surprised. "Or perhaps not."

"If you'll excuse me." She tried to hurry past, but Visconti reached out and grabbed her arm.

"Why the hurry?" He smiled.

Cristina glanced at the papal assistant, hoping he would intervene, but Visconti whispered to the man, "Would you allow me a few moments in private?" He pressed a coin into his palm. "You know how it is?"

The assistant gave a knowing smile. "I'll wait for you by the Great Clock, maestro," and he hurried deeper into the Vatican.

Cristina tried to wriggle her arm free, but Visconti tightened his grip. "I trust you haven't been duped by Lupo the Liar's tall tales?"

"The investigation is not yet concluded."

"Oh, I think you're very much mistaken there."

"Let go of me!"

But Visconti pulled her towards him, so close she could smell the akvavit on his breath. "The wheels are already in motion, Cristina. If you step in the way, you will be crushed."

There was a dread coldness to his words; for the first time Cristina sensed the darkness that was at the heart of this man. She pulled her arm free. "You have just condemned yourself."

"Me?" Visconti gave an innocent smile. "I am a simple artist looking for a commission to keep bread on the table."

"Only the guilty threaten," Cristina replied.

"I don't want to see you make a terrible mistake," Visconti sighed. "I, too, was deceived by Lupo, and my patrons paid a heavy price for my foolishness. God help me, I shall never forgive myself. That man is a danger precisely because he is so compelling, Cristina. If you allow yourself to be fooled, he will destroy your reputation as a woman of unshakeable integrity and fierce intelligence."

"The interesting thing about liars," Cristina observed, "is that they always say too much."

"Yet on this occasion it is Lupo who has spun the fantastical yarn."

"There is a crucial difference." Cristina started to circle Visconti, forcing him to keep turning to hold her gaze. "I had to persuade Lupo to speak. He would have preferred silence. But you … you always speak first and loudest. For that is how you control people, control the conversation. If you have nothing to hide, why do you need to exercise so much control?"

Visconti chuckled at her deduction. "You have misunderstood my intentions, Signorina Falchoni. Forgive me."

He flourished another bow, then turned and strode away.

Cristina watched him pace confidently towards his audience with the Pope. Whatever doubts she may have harboured vanished; now she was convinced that Lupo was telling the truth.

So why wasn't Visconti more worried?

42: ESTABLISHMENT

"This is one fight we can't win." Isra put a steaming bowl of ribollita on the kitchen table. "Now eat."

Cristina pushed it away. "You should know me better."

"I'm not discussing anything until you eat." Isra put a chunk of bread next to the bowl. "You look like a ghost."

"Because it's the middle of winter."

"And if you want to see spring, eat."

Reluctantly, Cristina picked up the spoon and did as she was told. Immediately the soup hit her palate, she remembered how good Isra's ribollita tasted, and made a mental note to stop skipping meals in future.

"Easier to concentrate when you're not hungry, isn't it?"

"I worked it out on the way home," Cristina said, tearing off a chunk of bread. "That private audience between Visconti and the Pope? He's already won the competition."

"But a decision's not due for another two weeks."

"That's the announcement. The decision's been made, I'd stake my life on it. Which gives us just two weeks to expose Visconti."

Isra poured herself a bowl of soup and sat down next to Cristina. "Look, the crimes we were investigating were Lupo's murders, not Visconti's integrity. We've done as much as we can."

"But the job is only half-finished. How can it be right to build deceit and injustice into the fabric of what should be the greatest church in the world?"

Isra shrugged. "If you're looking for purity, I think you're in the wrong city."

"A very defeatist attitude."

"But pragmatic. Think about it. Everyone who has bought a Visconti has a personal stake in suppressing the truth. They don't want to admit they were fooled."

"So everyone willingly believes a lie simply to save face?"

"And to protect their investments; if Visconti is exposed as a fraud, all his paintings will plummet in value."

"Huh." Cristina took her bowl over to the stove and served herself another portion. "So we're fighting money, vanity and pride."

"Like I said, it's a battle we cannot win."

"Unless…" Cristina's eyes darted excitedly around the room.

"Oh no." Isra braced herself for a dangerous idea.

"Unless we involve the rival dynasties. I'm sure the Medici and the Sforza will be delighted to help expose Visconti's fraud."

"That is a dangerous game, Cristina."

"What do they care if a couple of their paintings drop in value? They can afford it, and the prize would be to destroy a rival … yes, this could work."

"But it will set you at war with the Pope, your brother will most likely lose his job, and the minute they have what they want, the Medici will turn on you. They cannot be trusted any more than the Borgias can be trusted."

Without warning, a thunderous pounding on the front door echoed through the building. Isra and Cristina hurried from the kitchen, but as they crossed the hall they heard voices shouting.

"Open up! By order of the Watch!"

"What on earth do they want?" Cristina whispered.

"I don't think we should open the door."

"Well, I don't want them to smash it down."

"I'll go out the back, get a message to your brother."

"It's all right, Isra. We've done nothing wrong." Cristina slid the heavy bolts and turned the handle, but as soon she started to swing the door back, fists pushed from the other side, slamming the door wide open. Six guards of the City Watch stormed into the hallway, barging Cristina and Isra aside.

"The library!" the sergeant bellowed. "Where is it?"

"That's none of your business!" Cristina replied indignantly.

"Wrong!" The sergeant thrust a warrant into her face. "Where's your library?"

Without waiting for an answer, three of the guards surged up the stairs and started kicking open doors.

"Sergente! Up here!"

"This is a private house!" Cristina protested. "You have no right to be here!"

"Wrong again," the sergeant gloated, and led the rest of his men up the stairs.

Cristina and Isra chased after them, but by the time they arrived in the library guards were already hauling books from the shelves and dumping them into sacks.

"Leave them alone!" Cristina yelled.

"Stop screaming, woman," the sergeant scowled. "Read the warrant. We have reason to believe you are in possession of illegal and seditious books."

"What? No!"

"By order of the city authorities, we are confiscating them pending further investigation."

"No, you're not!" Cristina grabbed one of the walking canes in the rack by the door. "Not without a fight!"

"Don't!" Isra rushed over and blocked her way. "There's no point."

Cristina looked at the armed guards and their smug sergeant — there was nothing they would have taken more delight in than arresting her for attacking the Watch. Reluctantly she lowered the walking cane.

"You're making a huge mistake."

"That's up to the magistrates." The sergeant plucked a volume at random from one of the shelves and read the cover. "*Le Morte d'Arthur*. Foreign text. Probably seditious."

"It's a work of literature," Cristina protested.

"In French?"

"About English knights."

"Even worse." The sergeant tossed the book into a sack and selected another one. "*The Imitation of Christ*."

"It's a devotional text of spiritual instruction," Cristina declared.

"No priest lives here. Why do you need it?"

"To study."

"This isn't a university. And you're not a scholar." He tossed the book into the sack. "You shouldn't be in possession of it."

"Do you enjoy being so ignorant?" Cristina glared at him. "Because you're very good at it."

The sergeant replied by plucking another book from the shelves. "*Malleus Maleficarum*. Oh dear. What is a difficult woman like you doing with a book about witchcraft?"

"Studying demonology. Perhaps so I can deal with dark forces like the City Watch."

"Sounds like a confession to me." The sergeant tossed the book into the sack. "Conjuring evil spirits."

"Who has ordered this?" Cristina brandished the warrant. "Who has leant on the magistrates to issue this nonsense?"

"I'm just following orders," the sergeant replied. "*The Trial of Joan of Arc*?" He took the book down and opened the front cover. "Why would anyone want to read about a troublemaker, and a woman at that?"

Cristina felt her grip tighten on the walking cane, but before she could do anything, Isra grabbed her shoulders and steered her out of the library. "That won't help."

As Cristina was led down the stairs, the pattern of what was happening came into focus. "This is how they'll come for me, isn't it? Visconti will mobilise Rome's Establishment."

"If we're going to fight back, we're going to need a bigger walking cane." Isra guided Cristina into the calm of the kitchen. "Much bigger."

43: BARRED

Now it was a race against time.

Cristina knew that if she didn't get her beloved books back within the next few days, they would disappear into the obscurity of Rome's secret vaults. Worse still, some corrupt official might see an opportunity for personal enrichment and sell them on the black market, then her library would be lost forever.

She threw on her boots and raced through the streets to Sapienza University, the beacon of enlightenment that would surely save her. Professor De Luca had the connections and authority to sort this mess out, he could vouch for her and explain to the magistrates the necessity of her private library. But as Cristina strode through the main gates towards the courtyard, two porters hurried from the lodge to intercept her. "Woah! Woah!"

"I have to see Professor De Luca."

"You can't come in here," the head porter was emphatic. "Members only."

"But I've been here a thousand times! You know me!"

The head porter shook his head. "Not anymore. They're sticking to the rules now."

"They? Who is 'they'?" Cristina demanded.

"I'm afraid there's no more turning a blind eye."

"Rubbish!" She tried to push past him.

"Out!" The porters grabbed her and bundled her back onto the street, but she kicked and struggled and protested so furiously they were forced to send word to Professor De Luca.

They needn't have bothered. The professor who bustled through the gates wasn't the lively-minded, perpetually curious man that Cristina so admired; this man was sheepish and apologetic, and seemed embarrassed even to look her in the eye.

"What's going on?" Cristina demanded.

"I'm afraid it's all got very complicated," De Luca said anxiously. "Best to wait awhile and let things calm down."

"They stole my library!"

"And perhaps you should heed the warning."

Cristina couldn't believe what she was hearing. "If you value academic freedom, you need to fight for me, Professor. Right now!"

De Luca shuffled uneasily. "This will all blow over. We just need to be patient. In the meantime, try not to upset anyone else."

"Upset? Do you know how long it took me to build that collection?"

"You still have your liberty, Cristina. You should be grateful for that."

"Grateful?" Suddenly, Professor De Luca seemed like a small, nervous man. "They've got to you as well, haven't they?"

De Luca shook his head. "Now you're jumping to conclusions."

"Are you going to help me or not?"

"If only it were that simple."

"It is! It really is! Are you with me, or against me?"

The professor looked down at the cobblestones. "I cannot teach you until the current situation is resolved. The University authorities have forbidden me. I'm not even supposed to talk to you. I'm sorry."

He might as well have plunged a knife into Cristina's guts; the hurt drowned out her anger. "So much for integrity." She turned her back on him and walked away.

Hour by hour the city was closing down for Cristina. She went straight from the University to the artists' district. Her plan was to approach rival art dealers who might relish the prospect of damaging Labirinto's reputation; once they vouched for her account of Visconti's fraud, the momentum to expose him would be unstoppable.

Yet she couldn't even get beyond their front doors; to a man they refused to see her. Assistants made excuses ("He's in a meeting all morning," "Perhaps try calling back next week?") but it was clear they were lying. The word was out: Cristina was now toxic and no-one wanted to be associated with her. Dazzled by Visconti's reputation and sweetened by his deep pockets, Rome's Establishment had closed ranks against her.

In desperation, Cristina turned to Cardinal Riario, who agreed to see her but not in his offices; instead, they met at Michelangelo's *Pietà*, in the circular Chapel of Santa Petronilla.

Cristina told him everything and the cardinal listened patiently, without interrupting. But when she had finished, Riario did not seem particularly outraged.

"Your work tracking down the killer has been exemplary. Lupo will be tried and executed, and he will have to account for his actions to God." The cardinal hesitated, searching for the right words. "As for the other matter…"

"You mean Visconti's fraud? His destruction of another man? His wilful deception of Rome?"

"Art is a complex business," Riario sighed.

"Which is why I have turned to you, Your Eminence." Cristina looked at the *Pietà*. "You have worked with

241

Michelangelo. You understand that genius can be difficult. But to appropriate another man's work … that is not complex. That is theft. And the Bible tells us clearly, *Thou shalt not steal.*"

"It also tells us, *Thou shalt not murder.* Why should Lupo enjoy the protection of one Commandment while ignoring the others?"

"Visconti and Lupo are both sinners. Both men should face justice. That's all I am asking."

Riario studied her closely. "Have you considered the ninth commandment? Thou shalt not bear false witness?"

"You think Lupo is lying?"

"It's a possibility."

Cristina shook her head. "I have studied every word of his account and referenced it against details of the cases. All lies contain contradictions, but there is nothing in Lupo's confession to suggest he is trying to deceive. Every word has the ring of truth."

"And yet, who can unravel the complex relationship between a master and his apprentice?" Cardinal Riario countered.

"It should be about nurturing and teaching."

"A rather simplistic view, Cristina. Ideas grow by being shared." He turned to the *Pietà*. "Did I create this incredible statue? No. Michelangelo carved it. But did I offer him advice about the composition, the expression on Mary's face, the depiction of the stigmata? Of course I did. That does not make me an artist. Perhaps this is a subtlety that Lupo failed to understand as he worked with Visconti."

Cristina could feel her jaw clenching at the polite rejection. "Perhaps I could show Your Eminence Lupo's actual confession? If you read it, I feel certain you would be convinced of its sincerity."

But the cardinal raised his hands. "No, no. That would only complicate the situation. As things stand, there was a series of terrible murders, thanks to you the killer was caught, he has confessed and will be punished. That is all we need to know."

"And what of the integrity of the new basilica?"

"The end result is all that will matter. How it was achieved, who sacrificed what, which compromises were made … that will disappear in the mists of time."

And that was it. The last door had been closed in Cristina's face.

44: CONFRONT

Now that he had won, Visconti was all charm.

He was reclining on an explosion of oversized cushions as Cristina was shown into the client lounge on the top floor of the workshop. Immediately she noticed he was wearing a loose cotton smock, open to his navel and showing off a chest covered in curly hair. Did he think this was somehow alluring? That she would be seduced by the grizzled-bear look? Cristina checked herself; she was here to manipulate, not fight.

"Can we be friends, Signorina Falchoni?" he said, opening his arms in an expansive gesture.

"I hope so," she replied.

Visconti leapt to his feet and poured two glasses of wine. "You understand that I had to act to protect my reputation?" He placed one of the drinks in her hand. "*Alla nostra salute.*"

"*Salute.*"

"What do you think? From my own vineyard."

"Very smooth." Cristina took another mouthful of wine.

"You need to look at it from my perspective, Signorina. I was being defamed by a madman. A deranged killer who I had once trusted and nurtured. And to discover that you were taking sides with him…" Visconti gave a mournful sigh. "It was hurtful. Especially as I have always been so fond of you." He leant forward and brushed a curl of hair from her face.

Cristina's instinct was to recoil, but she stood her ground. What did Visconti think he was doing? Taming her so that she could become part of his harem?

Well, she too could play that game. "If I have wronged you, maestro, then I apologise."

"Vito, please. Call me Vito."

"Perhaps I was too eager to believe Lupo's confession."

"I admit, he does have a strangely compelling manner," Visconti said magnanimously.

"And women can so easily be swayed by the 'moody artist'. It is one of our weaknesses," Cristina replied.

"Not my style. Though I appreciate your candour. Please…" Visconti guided her to a richly upholstered chaise longue. "Make yourself comfortable."

Cristina did as she was told and savoured another taste of wine. "I awoke early this morning. Too early. With all that's being going on, sleep has been difficult."

"And yet you look so radiant."

"You know, as I watched the sky slowly lighten, I realised there is a very simple way to resolve all this."

A flicker of doubt passed over Visconti's face. "Surely everything is already resolved?"

"Indeed. But for my peace of mind, it would be a great comfort to see proof that Lupo is indeed a deluded liar." She watched his reactions closely.

But Visconti gave an easy smile. "Murdering three wealthy patrons isn't deluded?"

"I wonder, Vito, perhaps you could create a picture for me? Right now?"

"What?"

Cristina opened her leather satchel and took out some sheets of paper and a set of charcoal sticks. "Draw a picture. Of me. Let me be your model."

"Don't be absurd." Visconti laughed.

"Perhaps this isn't the right look. Let me see…" Cristina took off her jacket and let her hair fall around her shoulders. "Something more like this?"

Visconti looked her up and down.

"Or how about this?" She loosened her blouse then lay back on the chaise longue, draping one arm above her head and letting the other trail on the floor. "Imagine me as Aphrodite, awaiting one of her many lovers."

A lascivious smile crept across Visconti's face. "Now this is a game I like." He slugged back his wine and moved towards her, but as he tried to lower himself onto the couch, Cristina raised her boot to his chest and held him back.

"Now it is *you* who has misunderstood," she said.

"But I thought…"

"I am only here to be your life model." Her tone was uncompromising. "Draw, Vito Visconti. Draw for me."

"Is this all part of some coquettish game?" he asked.

"Pick up the charcoal and draw my portrait. Imbue it with that unique Visconti genius that has mesmerised Rome. Prove to me that you can do it."

For a moment, Visconti was thrown. But only for a moment, then his trademark laugh rescued him. "Don't be naïve. That is not how art works, Cristina. It is not some parlour trick."

"Drawing a simple portrait?" Cristina replied. "Isn't that what every apprentice does, day in, day out?"

"My genius is not a tap that can be turned on and off at will." Visconti was starting to lose patience.

"How disappointing," she sighed. "Unless … why don't we go to the prison cells under the Vatican and ask Lupo to draw me?"

"This is childish!" Visconti snapped. "I do not have to prove anything to you! I am Vito Visconti, the toast of Rome."

"And there we have it." Cristina stood up, shed all her coyness and pulled her jacket back on. "When it comes to actually putting charcoal on paper, you run and hide. Just as Lupo said."

Humiliation metastasized into anger. "You are a witch!"

"And you are a thief and an abuser," Cristina replied.

"I will not be insulted in my own workshop!" Visconti boomed. "And by a woman! Who knows nothing of art! Who is championing the cause of a murderer!"

Hearing raised voices, one of his assistants hurried up the stairs and burst into the room. "Is everything all right, maestro?"

"No! As a matter of fact, it isn't."

"Is this woman disturbing you?"

Visconti took a silk handkerchief from the sleeve of his robe and dabbed his face. "After all the emotional upheaval of the past days … she has come here with the sole intention of tormenting me."

The indignant assistant strode towards Cristina. "You need to leave."

"We haven't finished our conversation." The assistant tried to grab Cristina, but she pulled away. "Do not touch me."

Suddenly there was a groan and Visconti slumped to the floor in a faint.

"Maestro! Maestro!" The assistant rushed to his aid, cradling his head. "Some help here!" he yelled.

Moments later two more apprentices rushed in.

"Call the Watch!" the man holding Visconti ordered.

"He's faking it!" Cristina exclaimed. "Can't you see?"

"Call the Watch and put her under arrest!"

The apprentices grabbed Cristina's arms.

"Don't be absurd!"

Visconti groaned theatrically and his legs began to tremble. "Help … help me…"

"It's all right, maestro, I'm here," the assistant soothed. "Be calm."

"That woman…" Visconti raised a finger and pointed at Cristina. "She … she tried to kill me."

45: MAGISTRATES

As she was bundled into the courtroom, Cristina felt completely overwhelmed. The wood-panelled chamber was a chaos of activity as magistrates, clerks, notaries and summoners went about their business. Sprawling desks were covered in legal papers and scrolls, while huge leather volumes of city statutes were piled high on bookshelves. Everyone seemed to have a different uniform, some men were dressed in red robes, some in black, and many sported collars and caps that denoted different ranks and qualifications. They all knew what they were doing … except Cristina, who stood in the middle of the maelstrom, momentarily dazed.

"Over here!" Cristina glanced across the courtroom and saw Isra beckoning to her. Thank God, a friendly face.

Cristina hurried over. "How did you find me? They wouldn't even let me send you a message. The Watch hauled me from Visconti's straight to the cells."

"Stay calm."

"This is a nightmare!"

"Just stay calm." Isra gripped her shoulders. "They want to scare you with all this ritual."

"And it's working!" Cristina saw one of the magistrates staring darkly at her while his clerk briefed him. "I need to find a lawyer," Cristina whispered.

"That might make things worse."

"I need advice, Isra! I've never studied the law."

"Trust me. I know how this works."

"When were you in court?"

Isra gave a half-smile. "I was born the wrong side of the law, remember? This stuff is in my blood. Just listen to what the charges are. Be humble. Don't answer back. Then we'll work out what to do."

"Cristina Falchoni!" one of the officials boomed, and immediately hands pushed Cristina towards the bench. The scribe dipped his quill into the ink pot ready to start transcribing.

The magistrate looked her up and down, then referred to his papers. "There is a long list of accusations against you, from many different parties."

"Who? Because I know all this has come from Visconti. He is the one trying to silence me."

The magistrate scowled at her. "You will not speak until you are questioned."

"I have a right to know who my accusers are."

"This is *my* courtroom. You will do as I say."

"But the law —"

"If you wish to go straight back to the cells, then carry on the way you are going!"

Isra caught Cristina's eye and silently urged her to shut up.

Cristina gave a small bow to the bench. "Yes, Your Honour."

"Better." The magistrate continued reading his documents. "You have been seen consorting with courtesans and other undesirables."

Cristina couldn't hold back. "How is that a crime? Half of Giulia Campana's clients are lawyers."

The magistrate silenced her with another savage glare. "You have also been found in possession of numerous banned books, including volumes on witchcraft, and a vernacular Bible, both of which are proscribed."

"You Honour, I have repeatedly explained this to the city authorities. Those books are for study."

"Which brings me to the next accusation: illegal use of University resources. As a woman —"

"I'm not allowed to read? Is that it?"

"Signorina Falchoni!" The magistrate banged his fist on the bench. "Every time you open your mouth you damage your prospects further!"

Cristina looked down in a superficial show of humility, but couldn't bring herself to apologise.

"By far the most serious charges against you," the magistrate went on, "relate to the harassment of the painter and architect, Vito Visconti, who has proof that you have been circulating slanderous rumours about him."

"The truth is not slander!" Cristina blurted out.

"I did not ask your opinion!"

"Visconti is the one who should be standing in this court facing charges! He is a liar, a cheat, and a fraud. His actions drove Lupo to madness, and then to murder."

Isra clasped her head in her hands in despair.

The magistrate put down his papers with a dreadful finality. "You have just proved your own guilt, Signorina Falchoni. And you will now feel the full weight of the law. In passing sentence —"

"Wait! A moment, Your Honour!"

All eyes turned to the main doors, where Tomasso was pushing his way through a bustle of lawyers. "If I could approach the bench, Your Honour?"

The magistrate clearly knew Tomasso. "Always a pleasure to see you in court, Deputato. Once I have finished dealing with this troublesome woman, you will have my full attention."

"Actually, Your Honour, it concerns this troublesome woman."

"It does?" The magistrate gave a sceptical grimace. "Why would the Apostolic Guard have any interest in such a person?"

"She has been helpful in our work, Your Honour. She was involved in solving the recent spate of murders."

Reluctantly, the magistrate beckoned for Tomasso to approach.

Cristina watched them talk in subdued voices. They seemed remarkably familiar, there was much gesticulating and even some joking; Cristina felt angry that she was so powerless — these two men were deciding her fate and she had no say in it.

Finally, the magistrate turned his attention back to Cristina. "Having heard an extenuating plea, and taking into consideration the festive time of year, I have decided to postpone consideration of this case for three weeks. You are summoned to appear back in this court on Wednesday the tenth of January 1504, to answer further questions." He glared at Cristina with his dark eyes. "I would strongly advise you to have a quiet Christmas and avoid getting into any further trouble."

They hurried down the steps and away from the courtroom.

"Thank you, Deputato Tomasso," Cristina said as they pushed through the crowds that were making their way home for supper. "Did my brother send you?"

"He certainly did."

"Then he has come round to my way of thinking?"

Tomasso stopped and turned to Cristina. "He told me to warn you: stop meddling in things you do not understand. The job is done, the murderer is caught. Leave this case alone."

"Can you not see what they're doing?" she replied indignantly. "They are trying to silence me!"

"Because you keep interfering."

"This is a cover-up! Everyone is closing ranks to protect Visconti. Meanwhile, my life is being stolen! Are you going to let him get away with this?"

"Cristina, I don't control Rome!"

"Nor will you ever control anything if you're happy just to follow orders!" Cristina snapped. "Why can't you take the initiative? Stand up for what you believe in?"

"I just saved you from jail, didn't I?"

"That is not the point."

"You are impossible, Cristina! Utterly impossible." Tomasso shook his head and walked away before he said something he would regret.

"Wait!" Cristina called after him, but it was no use; in a few moments he had vanished into the evening crowds.

"You could have shown a little more appreciation," Isra chided.

"I didn't mean it to sound that way."

"You never do. But that doesn't help. And right now, Cristina, you're running out of friends."

46: ALONE

It was Christmas Eve, and the whole of Rome was preparing to celebrate. Excited chatter filled the streets as everyone hurried home to their families, so that after church they could feast and celebrate with the people they loved.

It made Cristina feel very alone.

Her only family in the city was her brother, but with all the tensions running between them, she really couldn't face three days of Domenico's disapproval.

Instead, she resolved to spend Christmas here in the house, so Isra set about preparing a goose while Cristina decorated the rooms with dried oranges and lemons, a Florentine tradition that her parents had taught her when she was a child.

Yet the harder she worked at creating a festive atmosphere, the lonelier Cristina felt. Her mind drifted across Rome to the households of Antonio Ricardo, the contessa, and even Pozzi the banker — how would they be celebrating Christmas in the shadow of murder? Would they find charity and compassion in their grieving hearts? Perhaps instead of praying, they would focus their thoughts on fuelling a hatred of Lupo, the man who had blighted their lives. Yet in his own way, Lupo was also a victim, exploited and driven to desperate measures by Visconti.

Vito Visconti, the man who was the epicentre of all this, yet a man who would no doubt be enjoying a splendid Christmas, full of laughter and feasting.

How could that be? How could the least worthy enjoy the most happiness? If the world was so perverse and illogical, it should have self-destructed thousands of years ago.

Cristina loaded a fresh log onto the sitting room fire and studied the way the flames licked the new arrival before devouring it. Yet as her thoughts became lost in the glowing wood, she remembered something Lupo had written in his confession…

"I will not end up in the Hospital for the Incurables, like apprentices before me … I will get what is rightly mine."

How many more Lupos had there been over the years?

Suddenly Cristina felt the tingle of an idea. Were there others who could corroborate Lupo's story? Did some apprentices descend into madness rather than murder? If she could prove that this was about much more than one man, that the abuse was systemic and widespread, perhaps there was still a chance for truth to prevail.

Christmas Eve or not, she had to follow this lead. Isra would be busy in the kitchen for a few more hours, Cristina could get there and back with plenty of time to spare.

There was not much festive cheer at the Hospital for the Incurables; perhaps the clue was in the name.

Most of the wards were dedicated to victims of syphilis and cancer, but there was one ward at the back, overlooking Via Leonina, that was kept for cases of acute melancholia. Immediately she entered, Cristina realised there was little practical nursing going on here, the patients were being contained rather than healed. Those who were prone to violence had been chained to the walls in cells they never left, but many were free to wander around the locked ward, where two guards armed with sturdy batons ensured the peace was maintained.

Nearly all the patients here had disappeared into the mysterious landscapes of their own inner worlds, muttering with great passion sentences which made no sense to anyone but themselves, ranting and reciting monologues of nonsense.

Some rocked back and forth to a rhythm only they could hear, while others lay on the floor in a catatonic state. One man combed his hair with meticulous precision, only to plunge it into a bucket of water, returning it to chaos so that he could start all over again.

Had any of these men been Visconti's apprentices?

To question them, she would have to find a way of piercing the protective layers they had wrapped around their hurt minds.

In one of the alcoves that lined the north wall, Cristina came across a man with grey, frizzled hair who had carved dozens of miniature wooden figures depicting the Crucifixion on Golgotha. Even though each figure was no more than an inch tall, the detail was stunning: the expression of Divine Grace on Christ's face, the conflicted Centurion, Mary Magdalene's grief.

Cristina watched as the man finished carving a Roman soldier who was crouched over some pebbles, casting lots for Jesus' garments. The man worked with astonishing focus as he turned wood into living flesh.

Had this talent ever found expression in the rational world? Was this haggard man once a brilliant young apprentice?

Cristina knelt down next to the table and watched as the man positioned each of the figures with meticulous care, recreating the exact moment of Christ's death in a dramatic miniature tableau.

"What is your name?" she asked when he had finished.

The man didn't even look at her. "My name is forgotten. I am nobody."

"These are beautiful figures."

"The more beautiful the creature, the crueller the world."

"What do you mean?"

The man closed his eyes. "Why hast thou forsaken me?"

"I haven't," Cristina said. "I'm here, next to you."

"Why hast thou forsaken *me*?" he cried out, his voice becoming agitated.

"I'm sorry. I didn't mean —"

"Why hast thou forsaken me!" With a violent jerk he swept his arms across the table, sending the carved figures skittering across the floor. "Why? *Why? Why?*"

Cristina was momentarily stunned.

"Don't worry. He does it every day."

She looked up and saw one of the guards standing over her. "I didn't mean to upset him."

The guard shrugged. "Now he can start all over again."

"He doesn't mind?"

"He does it twice a day, every day."

They watched as the frizzled man dropped to his knees and started picking up the wooden carvings, tenderly wrapping each one in a small piece of cloth.

"Have you tried to help him?" Cristina asked.

"He's happy in his own way," the guard replied. "Why should we interfere?"

As she watched the grey-frizzled man place the figures into a beautifully crafted wooden box, she felt a disturbing kinship with him. Was she really so different to this man? Cristina spent her life obsessively discovering connections and building patterns in her mind that nobody else seemed to care about.

Suddenly panicked, she hurried from the ward and burst out through some doors leading to a small courtyard. The rain was tumbling down, so cold it was almost sleet, forcing Cristina to shelter under the canopy of a huge umbrella pine.

Doubt overwhelmed her.

Was there any human activity that wasn't hopelessly compromised? She had poured all her energies into the dream of a new St Peter's, a basilica that would become the beacon of civilisation, but all she had discovered en route was corruption, deceit and death. She had raised the alarm, but no-one was listening; people were as indifferent to her as they were to the man with his miniatures of Golgotha.

Maybe she too should be locked up in here. Maybe this was the best place for her. Maybe her mind held no traction in the world beyond the walls of the Hospital for the Incurables.

Cristina slumped onto her haunches as her whole life threatened to unravel in regret.

Right now, she could be running a wealthy household, preparing for Christmas with excited children and an adoring, prosperous merchant husband. She had made different choices: building a magnificent private library, devoting herself to a life of study and the University, yet those choices had led to this lonely dead end.

Her library was gone. The University was closed to her.

She had sacrificed the chance of a normal life, yet had nothing to show for it.

Cristina covered her face with her hands, overwhelmed with shame and regret, fighting back tears, when suddenly she heard a familiar voice.

"That doesn't look like the woman who has solved a string of terrible murders."

Cristina looked up and saw the courtesan Giulia Campana standing next to her. Gone were the alluring clothes and coquettish peacock feathers, replaced by a sombre black robe with a hood to keep out the Roman winter; despite the display of sobriety, Giulia still had a rebellious glint in her eye.

"How did you find me?"

"It's a quiet time of year for courtesans," Giulia said. "The ladies are visiting their families, the punters are at home with their wives making extravagant displays of piety. Why don't you and Isra come and have Christmas with me at the Hunting Lodge?"

47: TOGETHER

It was strange to see the Lodge out of hours. Cristina had expected the rambling building to feel tawdry and a bit squalid in the cold light of day, but she couldn't have been more wrong.

Giulia Campana retained a small army of cleaners and maids who had done an incredible job, and the mansion now felt more like a serene country retreat than a debauched Garden of Earthly Delights. Fires burned in all the hearths, the rooms had been dressed with fresh winter flowers, and banks of candelabras illuminated a series of pastoral frescoes on the walls, which were of a surprisingly high quality.

"Just the three of us?" Isra asked. "For the whole of Christmas?"

"Make yourselves at home," Giulia removed her cape and shook off the rain. "There's plenty of bedrooms to choose from. Naturally."

But Isra's immediate concern was food; she had brought the half-prepared goose with them, but would need plenty more courses to lay on a decent festive celebration, so Giulia took her downstairs and showed her round the labyrinth of kitchens and pantries.

"This is perfect." Isra smiled, peering into the cheese larder. "We can eat for Italy."

"I accept the challenge," Giulia laughed, and left Isra to it.

She went back upstairs and found Cristina in the salon where the eunuchs normally danced, warming her hands by the fire. "I think we're in for a treat tonight," Giulia said. "Isra's in her element."

"Is that the real reason you invited us for Christmas? Isra's cooking?"

"No. But it's a bonus." She ladled some winter punch into a cup and handed it to Cristina. "Bilberry and pomegranate. It'll warm you from the inside."

The women savoured the sweet-scented aroma for a few moments, then clinked cups and drank in silence, gazing at the fire.

"Cristina, you do know that unless you change course, this will end very badly for you?"

The clinical analysis jolted Cristina from her reverie. "I thought you were offering me sanctuary, not a lecture."

"You have pitted yourself against the city Establishment, but they will win. This is how women end up being locked away in convents, or hospitals for the insane."

The image filled Cristina with cold dread. For a woman who defined herself by her intellect, being deprived of access to learning was worse than death. "But what can I do to defend myself?" she asked.

"When I was a girl, my head was full of fantasies about love and romance," Giulia began. "Of course, my first contact with an abusive man shattered all those illusions."

"Yet you ended up as a powerful courtesan, rather than a nun hidden away behind walls?"

"Just because love is a fantasy, wrapped in the confection of romance, doesn't mean there is no value in sexual relations. It's just not the fairy tale we are taught."

"That's exactly the sort of thing Isra would say." Cristina nodded.

"Isra would have made a great courtesan. She understands that love between people comes in many different forms."

Cristina took both their cups and ladled some more steaming punch into them. "So how does that apply to me? How can I get my life back without abandoning the truth?"

"Certainly not by going to war with Visconti," Giulia warned. "The Establishment are dazzled by the man, convinced he is going to be a 'Master of the Age'. So they fawn over him, they all want to be his friend. No-one will take sides with you. And yet there is a way forward, because if Lupo is executed, then unless Visconti can find another brilliant apprentice, he will be forced to retire."

"Then you do believe me!" Cristina interrupted. "You know that Visconti is dried up!"

"I've known it all along. He is a client, after all." Giulia shrugged.

"What?"

"I've known the man for years. A flamboyant mediocrity."

Cristina was stunned. "And you never told me? What else do you know?"

"Calm down."

"No! I won't be calm!" Cristina sprang to her feet. "All this time you could've helped me, and you just watched me get deeper into trouble!"

"A courtesan never betrays a client's secrets. It is the golden rule. I told you that on the very first occasion we met, Cristina. I made it quite clear."

"But —"

"I'm trying to help you now, aren't I? If you will only sit down and listen."

Cristina slugged back her punch. "I can't believe you withheld the truth from me."

"Forget the truth. I'm giving you a solution."

"Which is?"

"If Visconti is forced to retire, it will deprive wealthy Rome of its favourite artist, and none of those who have invested in him want that. Of course, Lupo must be executed for the murders, justice demands it. The dilemma is clear: how can the Establishment keep Visconti's art flowing, whilst also punishing Lupo?"

"There is no way of squaring that circle."

"What if I found a mechanism to keep Lupo painting from *beyond* the grave?"

Cristina's brow furrowed. "I don't understand. That makes no sense."

"It would have to be a closely guarded secret."

"But how would it work?"

"Let me worry about the details. Just indulge me a little further."

"Go on."

"The crucial part of the arrangement would be that Visconti must call off his attack dogs that have turned their anger on you. So Visconti's paintings would keep flowing, Lupo would be punished, and you would be free to return to your studies. Everyone moves forward."

"How corrupt is this plan? It sounds like a conspiracy of deceit."

"It is. But Rome has a corrupt heart. You've seen it yourself. This city doesn't really care about truth when lies work so well."

Cristina tried to think through the implications of what Giulia was saying. "Would it mean I have to set all my principles aside?"

"Your idealism has robbed you of the life you love. I'm offering you the chance to get it back." Giulia studied Cristina. "So … what do you say?"

48: COMPROMISE

Even though the Hunting Lodge had dozens of bedrooms, Cristina and Isra ended up sharing the same one. Perhaps because it was Christmas, or perhaps because all the uncertainty was pressing heavily on them, both women felt the need to be close.

While Isra put the final logs on the fire to keep it glowing through the coldest part of the night, Cristina plumped up the pillows and turned back the bed covers. As she ran her hands over the sheets, she was struck by the superior quality of the cotton. "This feels like it's Egyptian. So smooth."

"When you charge Giulia's prices, everything has to be perfect."

Cristina looked at the two beds. "It's strange to think what these have witnessed over the years."

"I really wouldn't dwell on that if I were you." Isra stoked the fire one last time, then hurried round the room snuffing out the candles, and dived into her bed. "Oooh ... that feels so good."

Cristina sank into her own bed and pulled the covers up high, but her mind couldn't stop wrestling with the strange offer Giulia had made.

"Sleep on it," Isra whispered. "See how you feel in the morning."

"What will have changed in the morning? Nothing."

"Yet everything seems better after a good night's sleep."

"Not in my world. The problem will remain unchanged. How can I put all my trust in a woman who is a master of deceit?"

"It's the best offer you're going to get. And in any case, Giulia is the only person who's actually offered to help, so you don't really have a choice. If you want to see St Peter's built, if you want to get your life back, you're going to have to start compromising."

Compromise. Cristina hated the word. It meant abandoning the quest for perfection and accepting something that you knew was wrong. None of the great thinkers had compromised, Socrates drank hemlock rather than betray his ideals. Shouldn't she be taking her lead from those philosophers?

A loud guttural snore echoed through the bedroom. "Already?" Cristina looked over and saw that Isra was fast asleep. It was infuriating how she could do that so quickly; she could just turn the world off in an instant. Maybe there was a technique Cristina could learn to help still her own mind. Yes, some form of meditation. She would have to reread *The Travels of Marco Polo* to see if he had encountered such a technique in the Orient. But to do that, she would need to get her library back.

Cristina sighed. All roads seemed to lead to the same point: compromise.

"Christmas present for you!" the guard called to Lupo from the corridor outside.

"Go away. Stop tormenting me."

The guard turned an iron key in the lock and Cristina entered the prison cell.

Lupo rubbed the sleep from his eyes and sat up. "What are you doing here?"

"It turns out you and I are not so different." Cristina glanced at a small stool perched in the corner. "May I?"

Lupo shrugged.

Cristina sat down and studied Lupo's tormented face. "Aristotle wrote, he who is unable to live in society is either a god, or a monster."

"Do you really have nothing better to do on Christmas morning? Go home to your family."

"In our own ways, Lupo, neither of us fit in."

"You seem to be doing all right," he scoffed. "I'm the one in a shit-stinking prison."

"What is the single most important thing to you, Lupo?" Cristina pressed. "Is it the art itself? Or is it the fame and wealth that a successful artist enjoys?"

"It doesn't matter anymore." He looked down at the tangle of straw on the floor. "I'm a dead man walking."

"Not necessarily."

"Who would defend a killer?"

"Answer my question, and perhaps you will find out."

Lupo thought about it for a few moments. "I've never known wealth or success. All I've ever had is the art."

"And is it enough? Because if you can forget the vanities of reputation, and live for your art and *only* for your art, then there might be a way to save you."

Lupo glanced up at Cristina. "Is this just another way of tormenting me? Fool the condemned man into false hope?"

"It is the only way to make sure justice is done."

"For a confessed killer, justice means execution."

"If you were born a monster, then yes." Cristina cocked her head to one side. "But I think you were born a god. And that is what destroyed you."

PART FOUR

49: EXECUTION

The executioner was surprisingly chipper.

Many people would have resented getting up before dawn in the middle of the holiday season to kill a man, but Christmas was an expensive time of year, and the executioner had been offered a bonus payment for the inconvenience, which made it all worthwhile.

Why had the authorities decided to bring this punishment forward from its scheduled slot in the first week of January? The executioner had no idea, and to be honest, he didn't care. The 'authorities' were always changing their mind about something, and you could drive yourself mad trying to make sense of it. Best just to keep your head down, take the money, and do the job.

He hurried across the cobbles, breath billowing, boots clattering on the cold stones, and did a careful inspection of the wooden scaffold, testing each of the struts with his hands to make sure nothing had worked loose with the weather.

A bucket and shovel dangled from two iron hooks under the platform (essential tools used for emergency clean-ups when clients loosened their bowels in their dying moments), but now the executioner used the shovel to scrape a thick layer of hoar frost from the scaffold steps. After all, he didn't want any accidents as the condemned man climbed up to the platform, as a slip or stumble would ruin the solemnity of the occasion. It was this kind of attention to detail that had made the executioner such a trusted part of the prison system.

When the platform was thoroughly clear, he spent several minutes testing and lubricating the trapdoor mechanism which had a nasty habit of jamming when the timbers swelled in the winter damp. Once he was happy that everything was in perfect working order, the executioner made his way to the condemned man's prison cell, where the magistrate was already waiting with four guards and a priest.

Only when he arrived at the cell did the executioner realise who this morning's client was: the notorious Lupo, embittered apprentice turned serial killer, the man who had terrorised Rome's elite. Suddenly everything started to make sense — the execution had been brought forward so that the whole sordid business could be resolved before a new set of magistrates took up their posts in January, and the early morning timing meant that no angry mobs would have a chance to gather outside the prison gates and cause trouble. This way Rome would wake up to the news that Lupo was already dead and gone to Hell, so the city could move on from his appalling crimes. A nice clean start for the New Year.

"Is the scaffold ready?" the magistrate asked.

"It is, sir, yes," the executioner replied.

"Then you can go in and do your final checks."

"Very good, sir."

One of the guards unlocked the cell door and the executioner entered. He was surprised to see that a cloth sack had been placed over Lupo's head and tied around his neck. This was most unusual, and a bit off-putting. The executioner always liked to exchange a few words with his clients, perhaps a comment about the weather, or a light-hearted quip to put them at ease, but it was impossible to do that when you couldn't look a man in the eye.

"It was the prisoner's last request," the magistrate explained, sensing his unease. "To hide his shame in the final moments."

"Oh. I see." In truth, it didn't make much sense to the executioner, but he had known all manner of bizarre last requests in his time, from the counterfeiter who had insisted on eating a plate of deep-fried artichokes, to the heretic who walked to the scaffold on his knees. It didn't much matter, for the real purpose of these final checks was to assess the condemned man's size and weight to make sure the correct gauge of rope was used, and that the drop height didn't need adjusting. The executioner walked once around his client, noted that his hands had already been tied, and that he was of average build, then he left the cell and reported to the magistrate. "Everything in order, sir."

"Very good. You may proceed."

While the guards prepared to escort the condemned man, the executioner hurried back to his scaffold. Sometimes he accompanied the grim procession across the courtyard, at other times he preferred to be already in position, it depended on his mood; this morning he wanted to keep moving as briskly as possible.

When the guards emerged from the prison block and started to march Lupo across the courtyard, the cold was already starting to nip at the executioner's fingers, and by the time the priest had finished reading the prayers and asking for God's mercy, the executioner's teeth were chattering. It was a relief to swing into action, and he wasted no time putting the noose around his client's neck and pulling the trapdoor lever open, sending Lupo to the hereafter.

Unfortunately, they had to wait a good few minutes for the body spasms to subside, and only then was the magistrate able to remove the sack and examine the victim's face. His head had been shaved, and his face was twisted in the usual contortions of strangulation: the bulging eyes, the tongue hanging out and the red blotches made him almost unrecognisable, but that didn't prevent the magistrate from performing a close inspection and declaring that Lupo the apprentice had been duly executed, according to the law.

While the guards dumped the body on a small cart, the executioner busied himself tidying up the scaffold, neatly coiling the rope, and planning how he would use the bonus payment to give his two daughters a Christmas treat.

50: CONTRACTS

As that grim funeral procession made its way towards the cemetery, Domenico and Tomasso led another group, furtive and clandestine, out through the north gates of the same prison. They accompanied a carriage in which a man sat, his hands and legs manacled, a cloth hood covering his face, while outriders at the front and back made sure that no prying eyes were watching.

And the reason for all this secrecy? To stop anyone realising that the man inside the carriage was, in fact, Lupo the apprentice, and that the executed criminal was Hamza bin Abbas, an Ottoman spy who had been caught stealing military secrets from the Papal armies. Abbas' execution had been delayed by some weeks as negotiators tried in vain to secure a prisoner exchange; when those talks broke down, Abbas became the obvious candidate to substitute for Lupo, given that the Ottoman had no-one in Rome to mourn for him. Abbas was beyond saving, they were merely bringing his death forward and ending his tortuous wait for the inevitable.

With eyes cautiously scanning the streets and surrounding buildings, Domenico and Tomasso led the carriage across Rome … towards the workshop of Vito Visconti.

Visconti stood by the arched windows in the client lounge of his workshop, studying the contract. "I do wish you would take a seat. Or a drink. Or something," he said without turning round. "Your agitation is most unsettling."

"I really don't care," Cristina replied. "Just read." She stood in the middle of the space, determined not to be charmed or flirted with; now there was only one thing she wanted — resolution.

But the more Visconti read, the more dismissive he became. "You've all gone mad!" he laughed. "This is nonsense. Utter nonsense!"

"You don't fool me anymore," Cristina replied. "I know the truth. And unless you want the entire world to know it too, you will sign that contract."

"Tell you what," Visconti put the papers down and poured himself a brandy. "I'll think about it over the holiday and give you my answer in the New Year."

"No, you won't. This will be resolved now, or not at all. So pick up the contract and finish reading."

Visconti slugged back some brandy. "You could do with one of these. Might take that frown off your face. It makes you look quite ugly, Cristina."

"What would you prefer? An inane smile? Like the one you see when you look in the mirror?"

"Charm never was your strong point, was it?"

"I prefer truth. Now read."

Visconti picked up the contract with a dramatic gesture and scanned his eyes over the clauses. "In consideration of the discharged representations … I indemnify the disbursements … the aforesaid of the after-mentioned … blah, blah, blah. What frauds these lawyers are, hiding behind their jargon."

"Well, you should know, as a fellow fraudster."

Visconti shrugged. "Look, if this is what it takes for you all to stop hounding me, then I'll sign the damned thing."

"Read the appendix."

"What?"

"The final page."

Visconti gave a weary sigh and did as he was told. "But this is irrelevant," he complained. "This is about you. Why would I care about you?"

"I want my life back, Visconti. And that compels you to call off your attack dogs."

Visconti chuckled. "You really do have delusions of grandeur, Signorina Falchoni. I see the hysteria of the spinster already has you in its shrivelled grip."

"Do you agree to the terms?"

"Whatever." He tossed the contract onto the desk. "In the grand scheme of things, it is really quite trivial. People will be admiring my paintings for centuries to come. That is all that counts."

They heard the rattle of wheels in the street below. Visconti peered from the window and saw the prison carriage pull up outside his workshop. The guards formed a secure cordon, and while Tomasso swung open the loading bay doors, Domenico unlocked the carriage and pulled out the manacled Lupo.

"And lo! He that was dead came forth, bound hand and foot," Visconti declared. "Lupo is the new Lazarus!"

But Cristina didn't share Visconti's joke. "You really find it amusing to destroy other people's lives, don't you?"

"It has a piquant appeal."

"Only for those who have no talent."

"Said the woman who has achieved nothing in her life. Nor ever will."

They listened to the clatter of footsteps ascending the workshop stairs.

"Politicking is not an achievement," Cristina said. "It is the last refuge of the talentless. Which is perhaps why you are so good at it, *maestro*."

The double doors pushed open and Domenico and Tomasso bundled Lupo into the client lounge.

"Well, look what the Apostolic Guard dragged in," Visconti quipped.

Yet Cristina could see that behind the glib façade, Visconti was nervous. He and Lupo stared at each other across the cavernous room like two lovers encountering each other after a betrayal; there was a rawness in the silence that seemed to galvanise the air.

"Has he read the contract?" Domenico asked Cristina.

"I am present," Visconti interrupted. "You can address me in person."

"Then let me spell it out clearly." Domenico looked from Visconti to the apprentice. "Officially, Lupo, you are dead. But in truth, you will be secretly exiled to a monastery in the hills outside Rome, where you will live out the rest of your life in complete anonymity. You will never leave the confines of the building. While there you will work to Visconti's orders, painting one picture each month. Materials and equipment will be supplied. You will have no contact with the outside world, and no claim on the work you produce."

"So life imprisonment and forced labour," Lupo said darkly.

"At least it is life, not the gallows," Cristina replied. "And it's more than your victims have."

Domenico turned to Visconti. "For your part, you will be free to sell the paintings and claim full credit for their creation. In return, you must withdraw all the allegations you have made against Cristina Falchoni, and offer an unreserved apology. You will offer full assistance in restoring her library and her freedom to pursue academic studies. Do you both understand?"

Visconti and Lupo both nodded grimly.

"Any breach of the terms of this contract, by either party, will result in the execution of Lupo, and the arrest of Visconti for fraud. Once signed, the contract will be stored securely in the Vatican vaults. Are you both prepared to sign this agreement?"

Cristina placed the legal document in the middle of the desk. Next to it she positioned an inkwell and quill. "Lupo?"

The apprentice looked down at his manacles. "If this is to be my new life, then I cannot honour the contract in chains. My hands must be free to paint."

Domenico nodded to one of the guards who bent down and unlocked the manacles. Once free, Lupo rubbed his wrists, then stepped towards the desk, picked up the quill, carefully dipped it into the ink, then signed with a confident flourish.

Cristina took the quill and offered it to Visconti. "Now you."

Visconti did as he was asked, ensuring that the flourish of his signature was even more flamboyant than Lupo's. Then he turned to face his apprentice.

They stared at each other for a few moments in silence, each man knowing too much about the other to fully trust him.

"Do you both swear to honour this contract?" Domenico said.

"I don't have a choice," Lupo replied.

Sensing that he had won the day, Visconti allowed himself a smile. "Of course I will honour it." He extended his hand, offering it to Lupo. "For it confirms what I have always believed, that apprentices should be seen and not heard."

It was a quip too far.

Cristina saw Lupo's mind snap.

"You bastard!" He grabbed Visconti's hand and yanked him off balance, sending him stumbling to the floor.

"No!" Cristina yelled.

Domenico rushed forward.

But it was too late.

In an instant, Lupo jammed his knee into the back of Visconti's head, then grabbed a palette knife from the easel and pressed it hard into his neck.

51: SIEGE

"No!" Cristina yelled. "Don't do it!" But she could see that Lupo was pumped up, ready to kill.

"Get him off me!" Visconti screamed, struggling to break free. "Get him off!"

Domenico hesitated. He knew the look in Lupo's eyes, he had seen it on the battlefield a thousand times; the apprentice was a heartbeat away from plunging the palette knife into Visconti's jugular.

"Wait, Lupo!" Cristina urged. "You have much to live for."

"It's all finished!" Lupo snarled. "My life is over!"

"But your art is not! You told me yourself, in that prison cell. If you had to strip away everything else, you would still have art. You told me that!"

Lupo screwed his eyes shut, caught between life and death, between art and murder. His fingers tightened on the palette knife.

"Lupo, listen to me," Cristina urged. "You can still have the life of an artist. The purest artist, cloistered like a monk, living only for your work. Is that not enough?"

"Get out!" Lupo yelled. "All of you!

"Don't leave me with him," Visconti begged.

"Get. Out." There was dread determination in Lupo's voice.

Domenico nodded to Tomasso and Cristina; retreat was now the only way forward. "It's all right, Lupo. We're leaving you now."

"No!" Visconti howled.

"Stay calm," Cristina urged as she followed the others towards the door. "There is still a way out of this. For everyone."

Immediately they were back on the street, Domenico repositioned the Apostolic Guards to cover all the exits from the workshop, while Tomasso rode urgently to the Vatican barracks to gather reinforcements. By the time the church clocks struck eight, summoning people for early mass, Via Margutta had been cordoned off from Babuino all the way down to Orto di Napoli. For once, the Christmas festivities helped, as many of the workshops were closed for the whole week, but Domenico wasn't taking any chances — the last thing he needed were curious onlookers.

"No-one is to get past the cordon," Domenico instructed. "Not under any circumstances. Lupo is desperate and dangerous. Who knows how he might react."

He returned to the makeshift base that had been established on the opposite side of the street, where he found Cristina watching Visconti's workshop closely, trying to work out what was happening inside. "Any change?"

Cristina shook her head. "Noises. Some banging and thumping. Sounds as if he's making something."

"Lupo!" Domenico called out. "Can you hear me?"

No reply.

"Lupo! We have to resolve this!"

A few moments later one of the shutters on the first floor opened a crack and Lupo peered out. He glanced up and down the street, and saw marksmen armed with crossbows positioned on the rooftops and balconies. "Tell them to move back!" he called down.

"I can't do that," Domenico replied.

"Tell them!"

"Let's talk about how this is going to end."

"Move them back or I slash his throat!"

Cristina leant over to her brother and whispered urgently, "He means it. Best do as he says."

Domenico looked up at the marksmen and reluctantly beckoned them to withdraw.

"We've done that," Cristina called out. "What will you give us in return?"

"I don't owe you anything. The world owes me!" Lupo's voice cracked with passion.

"This isn't about the world," Cristina tried to sound calm. "This is about you and me, Lupo. We've done what you asked, help us out a little."

Silence.

Then in a quieter voice he asked, "What do you want?"

"Show us that Visconti is still alive."

"Oh, he's alive," Lupo scoffed. "Cockroaches are impossible to kill."

"Then show us."

"All in good time. You want to end this, send in food."

"We can do that," Cristina replied. "What sort of food would you like?"

"Anything's better than the shit they serve in prison." Lupo slammed the shutter closed.

"Better get them something nice," Cristina said. "And some wine. Maybe it'll ease the tensions."

Tomasso made sure there was plenty of food for everyone, troops as well as captives, for it was going to be a long day in the cold December drizzle. It seemed to have the desired effect — an hour after the food went in, the shutters opened, Lupo appeared and carefully checked the rooftops and balconies again.

"It's all right," Domenico reassured him. "The marksmen have gone."

"I'm going to show you Visconti's still alive," Lupo called down. "Don't double-cross me."

"You have my word."

Methodically, Lupo worked his way along the windows, opening all the shutters until the entire first floor was visible from the street.

Visconti had been strapped into a large, throne-like chair, his limbs securely tied. His head had been shaved, and a gag had been tied around his mouth to stop him from crying out. White sheets had been carefully draped around his body as if Visconti was a model posing for a painting of God seated on his celestial throne. Twelve striking portraits on easels had been placed around him like disciples.

"Behold!" Lupo declared. "The Lord and his host of angels!"

Cristina stared up at the tableau in stunned silence; the bizarreness of the spectacle was tempered by the brilliance of the paintings.

"They're yours, aren't they, Lupo?" she said. "All the paintings are yours."

"The Lord giveth, and the Lord taketh away," he replied. Then he took a large flagon of linseed oil and started dousing the paintings in the flammable liquid.

"Don't do that!" Domenico warned.

But Lupo wasn't listening.

"There's no need for threats," Cristina called up. "We're talking, aren't we? We can find a way out of this."

When the paintings were glistening with oil, Lupo picked up another flagon and poured it over Visconti, who struggled and writhed in terror.

"One twitch of my thumb, and it's all over," Lupo announced as he took a tinderbox from his pocked and held it up in the air for everyone to see. "One twitch!"

"What do you want, Lupo? Tell us!" Cristina desperately tried to sound calm.

"I want to be recognised!" Lupo shouted across the street. "I want the world to know everything that I have created! I want the Holy Father himself to acknowledge me, to know that the design for the new St Peter's in mine!"

"You can't make demands of a Pope," Domenico replied. "That's not how this works."

Lupo stepped forward and flicked his thumb across the tinderbox, sending a shower of sparks gushing over the balcony.

"Wait! Wait!" Cristina yelled. She turned to Domenico. "We have to get the Pope involved."

"He won't do it."

"It's the only way out of this."

"You can't give ultimatums to the Holy Father. Especially not this one."

"If you ask him personally, Domenico, maybe he will understand. He trusts you, perhaps he will listen. We have to try."

Domenico looked up to the studio. "Keep him talking. And make sure he doesn't do anything stupid."

From the balcony, Lupo watched Domenico hurry away with two guards and duck under the cordons. "Don't deceive me," he called down. "No tricks."

"He's going to get a message to the Holy Father. Just as you asked."

Lupo started to close the window shutters.

"Wait!" Cristina called out. "Let's keep negotiating."

"I have nothing to say to you."

"Please, Lupo! At least put down the tinderbox."

"One hour," he warned. "You have one hour."

"It's not that easy to see the Pope. We need more time!"

But Lupo closed the last shutter, locking out the world again.

Tomasso turned to Cristina. "What do you think?"

"All I know is, the Holy Father is our only hope for a peaceful solution."

Tomasso shrugged. "There's a reason they call him the warrior Pope. And it's not good."

52: BURN

What came back from the Vatican wasn't just a message from the Pope, but Cardinal Riario to deliver it in person.

As Domenico ushered him through the security cordon, Cristina could see that the cardinal was in a foul mood, not just because of the interruption to his holiday, but because this whole situation was spiralling out of control.

"Where is he?" Riario demanded as he reached the command post.

"Lupo!" Domenico called across to the workshop. "Show yourself! There's a message from the Vatican."

They heard a latch on the shutters click, then moments later Lupo appeared on the first-floor balcony. When he looked down and saw Cardinal Riario standing in the December drizzle, Lupo's eyes flickered a smile.

Riario reached into his pocket and pulled out a letter. "This is from His Holiness Pope Julius II. Sealed with his official ring." With a dramatic flourish, Riario broke the seal and read the letter.

"*With immediate effect, the submission made by Vito Visconti to design the new St Peter's Basilica is disqualified from competition. We do not care who created the strikingly original design. Whether it was Visconti or his apprentices is of little import. What matters is that their submission is now so mired in controversy and tainted with scandal, it would be blasphemy to transform the design into stone. Another artist will be chosen. This is my final word on the matter.*"

Riario held the letter up, offering it to Lupo. "You can read it if you want. Your design is dead."

Lupo didn't move. It was as if he had been turned to stone, as if all the life had been sucked out of him. His face bore an expression of utter defeat.

"There you have it," Domenico said. "The Pope has spoken."

"I demand —" Lupo stuttered.

"You demand nothing!" The cardinal's anger boiled over. "Because you are already a dead man!" He turned his back on the apprentice and walked away.

In the terrible silence that followed, Cristina watched the last vestiges of hope drain from Lupo's face. "We still have an agreement," she called out. "That doesn't have to change."

Lupo gazed at the Apostolic Guards who cordoned off both ends of the street. "Too many people know."

"These troops are sworn to secrecy. We can contain this."

Suddenly Lupo tensed as the fight returned one last time. "Ask the Pope again," he demanded.

"That won't work."

Lupo fumbled in his pocket and held up the tinderbox. "Tell the Holy Father I will do it! I will destroy his favourite artist and all these creations! I will do it!"

"It's over, Lupo! Accept it."

"I will destroy everything! I swear!"

Cristina looked up at him, tinderbox raised above his head, eyes restless with bitterness and disappointment.

One flick of his fingers and all the brilliant art in the workshop would be destroyed. Paintings that could touch the human soul would vanish forever.

And yet…

The flames would also destroy the hopeless tangle of deception that had trapped them all. Genius would be destroyed, but so would fraud and theft and exploitation. Perhaps this was the real pain of compromise.

"Then do it," Cristina said in a clear voice. "Destroy everything. Put an end to this."

Lupo's eyes filled with tears. He turned and walked back into the room, closing the shutters behind him.

No-one moved. Silence filled Via Margutta.

Then the most terrible howl of pain erupted from inside the workshop. It was the sound of a man's soul breaking apart.

WHUMPHF!

A huge explosion billowed out of the building, blowing off the shutters. Everyone dived for cover.

WHUMPHF! WHUMPHF! WHUMPHF! More flagons of oil ignited.

Within seconds the entire building was a roaring inferno. Flames licked from the windows, driving back any hope of rescue. Cristina could only watch as paintings that would have changed the course of art blistered in the heat and were devoured by fire.

As the flames ate the building's timbers and joists, the floors collapsed onto each other like a deck of cards, sending great plumes of sparks sideways until the entire block was ablaze.

Urgently, Tomasso organised his troops into human chains to haul water from the river and douse the neighbouring buildings, for containing the fire was now the best they could hope for; it was clear to everyone that Visconti's workshop could not be saved, it would have to burn itself out.

When the building was finally just a smouldering ruin, Cristina and Domenico picked their way through the hot tangle of charred debris. The paintings were ash, the statues that were being so lovingly carved had shattered in the intense heat; props and pigments and altar panels had all been incinerated.

"What a waste," Domenico whispered.

"Corruption is a cancer that wraps itself around art," Cristina replied, turning over a charred easel with the toe of her boot. "Sometimes the only way to kill the disease is to sacrifice the patient as well."

In the far corner, they came across a pile of debris that had fallen from the first floor. "Maybe they're under there," Domenico said as he started to heave scorched joists aside.

Cristina gazed at the terrible destruction, awed by the power of fire to obliterate everything men held most dear. "Had he lived, Visconti would have been remembered as one of the masters. Now his name will be forgotten entirely."

Domenico swung aside another beam, then stopped.

"What is it?" Cristina picked her way over and looked down.

The burned bodies of Lupo and Visconti were locked together in a tangle. Their flesh had been scorched away, but their skeletons remained intact; it looked as if they had been fighting with each other as they drew their final breaths.

Cristina tilted her head.

Strangely, in the quiet of the burnt-out workshop, you could almost believe that these two mortal enemies were actually lovers, embracing each other as they died.

53: ST PETER'S

The dust took a long time to settle.

Cardinals and lawyers and members of the great dynastic families met in dimly lit rooms to find a way of moving on from the violence and brutality of that winter. Wounded pride had to heal, flawed histories had to be erased, tarnished reputations had to be salvaged. Finally, over a year later, Rome's great and good were once again gathered in the Sistine Chapel to hear the formal announcement of the winning design for St Peter's.

Cristina stood amongst the guests on the south side of the chapel so that she could study the reactions of Rome's powerbrokers. They were all here in a great display of solidarity with the Pope, yet in one way or another they had all been bought off, many with secret promises of lucrative contracts in the great construction project that was about to commence. The Vatican had dipped deep into its coffers to calm the waters after the Visconti scandal, and it had worked — Rome appeared united again.

As expected, the announcement ceremony was impeccably choreographed by Vatican bureaucrats. They certainly were masters of manipulation, using procession and music and the massed ranks of priestly robes to create gravitas and awe. There was a time when Cristina would have loved being caught up in moments like this because they felt so important, but nowadays she was more wary. The emotions whipped up by aesthetics were compelling and addictive, but that didn't make them truthful. Reason may be a colder mistress, but she was not fickle; you could build solid foundations on Reason without fear of collapse.

At the climax of the ceremony, Pope Julius rose from his throne and with great solemnity announced that Donato Bramante's design had won the competition. "It shows the finest judgement, the best intelligence, and the greatest invention," the Holy Father declared, as Bramante feigned shock and surprise (in truth he had known the result for weeks). As he handed the official charter papers to Bramante, Pope Julius reached for more hyperbole. "This new St Peter's will surpass in beauty, invention, art and design, as well as grandeur, richness and adornment, all the buildings that have been erected in Rome since its inception."

The applause was thunderous, the spontaneity beautifully faked. Cardinal Riario hugged Bramante and laughed as if he was genuinely overwhelmed, even though he had been locked in tough negotiations for many months to secure the commission for his backers, the Sforza dynasty.

Pope Julius led the cardinals from the Sistine, and everyone followed in their wake to a banqueting room where they could celebrate and speculate on the great fountain of gold that was about to be unleashed.

Yet Cristina held back. The contents of the Vatican wine cellars did not interest her nearly so much as the winning design, which had now been unveiled on a series of easels by the east door.

It was certainly a striking design: a symmetrical Greek cross with arms of equal length, and within each of those arms was a smaller cross, and within each of those a smaller cross still, so that the overall impression was of a series of decreasing crosses and circles that was mesmerising. It was as if the perfection of mathematics had been turned into stone, with each shape echoing those around it. The sheer scale of ambition was stunning, for each of the main arms was as big as a conventional church, and at the centre of it all was a cavernous space covered by a vast dome supported by four massive pillars.

In some ways the design was revolutionary. But it was not touched with the genius of Lupo's vision. Twelve concentric waves rising from the ground as if the surface of Rome had been struck by the hand of God … such a building would have changed the world of architecture forever. Bramante's design would dazzle, Lupo's would have stunned.

Yet Bramante's integrity was beyond question. His domed head ringed with curls gave the impression of a craftsman rather than a showman, which was exactly what St Peter's needed. This basilica would be Bramante's masterpiece, the one thing he would be remembered for, and he would surely dedicate the rest of his life to its construction.

Bramante would serve art, rather than art serving his own vanity. Maybe that was the way it should always be, the only way to keep the excesses of the artist in check.

54: RESTORATION

Finally, the last of her books were returned. What had been taken from Cristina in minutes took months to restore, for under Visconti's specific instructions, the collection had been scattered across many different archives and libraries, giving unscrupulous dealers a chance to smuggle some of the more unusual tomes out of the country and into the hands of rich buyers north of the Alps. As a thank you for all Cristina's work, Cardinal Riario personally intervened, sending cajoling letters and financial sweeteners to ensure the return of every volume that had gone astray.

"That bastard Visconti is getting revenge from beyond the grave," Isra observed as she opened the crates containing the final consignment of books. She had taken it on herself to inspect and clean every single title before it was returned to the shelves, as the precise circumstances of their storage and transportation was often unclear, and the slightest trace of mildew could destroy a book if left untreated.

While Isra worked on the books, Cristina set about redesigning her catalogue system to make it easier to find and cross reference different titles, as well as allowing for unlimited expansion of the collection. It was absorbing and deeply satisfying work and there were some weeks when Cristina barely left the house, yet she did make an exception for the University.

Professor De Luca decided to host a private luncheon at Sapienza to announce that Cristina was being made an honorary non-resident member of the faculty, ensuring that she would never again be excluded from the halls of learning.

"And whilst you're here," De Luca said as he polished off the final crumbs of a fig and raison cake, "there is someone I'd like you to meet. He's an artist, doing some research for a new sculpture."

"Why spoil a nice luncheon by inviting an artist?" Cristina quipped.

"Because this one has made quite a stir. Starting to get a formidable reputation."

"Now I'm even less inclined to meet him."

De Luca insisted, and ushered Cristina into one of the studies overlooking the inner courtyard. Immediately Cristina recognised the lean, muscular figure of Michelangelo. "I see *David* has finally let you out of his grasp."

Michelangelo looked up and gave a half-smile. "So, was I right, or was I right?"

De Luca glanced at Cristina. "You two know each other?" But no-one seemed interested in the professor anymore.

"Half-right," Cristina replied.

Michelangelo frowned. "But it *was* Visconti's apprentice. He was the killer."

"Officially, yes. But it is considerably more complicated."

"How?"

"Unfortunately, I am not at liberty to elaborate."

Michelangelo gave a cynical smile. "Spoken like a true Vatican bureaucrat."

"When in Rome, it's best not to insult the Vatican," Cristina advised. "Especially if you're an artist in search of a commission."

"Huh." Michelangelo's gaze returned to his work. "You call someone like Bramante an artist?"

"He will be creating the greatest building in Christendom."

"Because he plays the greatest game of politics. That's the only way such a minor artist could have won St Peter's."

"You sound envious."

"Not at all. I have my commission, and it will occupy me for the next three years."

"May I see?"

Michelangelo hesitated.

"Signorina Falchoni is a member of the faculty," De Luca intervened. "Technically she has more right to be here than you."

"In which case…" Michelangelo unfurled one of the master drawings on the table. "It's the tomb for Pope Julius."

"Who is still very much alive."

"He likes to be organised."

Cristina studied the drawings which depicted a colossal structure, like a freestanding temple, adorned with over forty statues on three levels, all centred on a magnificent depiction of Moses. The scale of Michelangelo's ambition was truly astonishing — this would be one of the biggest tombs ever constructed in Europe.

Yet when Cristina glanced up to congratulate him, she saw that Michelangelo was studying the drawings intently, as if seeing them upside down helped him understand them afresh.

"It's astonishing," she said.

"Not yet."

He picked up a quill and started deleting some of the monument's embellishments, simplifying and strengthening the aesthetic through elimination. It was clear this man lived for his art, refusing to hide behind honey-words and showmanship.

"So, despite your gruff manner, you too have mastered Vatican diplomacy," Cristina teased.

"Only as much as is necessary for my art." Michelangelo removed a bank of statues with the deft stroke of a quill and seemed pleased with the cleaner lines left behind. "After all, who but a Pope could afford to transport fifty tons of marble from the mountains? Sometimes art must get into bed with filthy lucre."

Cristina pondered his words for a moment. "Surely the art of compromise is to produce uncompromising art."

"Absolutely!" Michelangelo turned to Professor De Luca. "You should admit more women to your university. They are the future, I swear."

"We got there in the end," Isra clinked Cristina's cup in a toast. "It was brutal and bloody, but the new basilica will be built after all."

"I wish I shared your optimism," Cristina replied.

"Come on, don't be like that. The most difficult part is behind us. The architect has been chosen, the money's been promised, and most important, this Pope is determined."

"And yet we've been close before, but every time we think the path is clear we get pushed back. It's as if God really doesn't want to be glorified by a new St Peter's."

"Two more of these and it'll all look very different," Isra said, picking up the wine jug to refill their cups.

There was a flurry of movement on the far side of the courtyard as the rear gate swung open. Cristina turned and saw Tomasso walking towards the kitchen, clutching a small parcel.

As the Deputato entered, Isra got up and offered her seat. "I was just leaving."

"You were?" Cristina was puzzled.

"I need to get to the market, or there'll be nothing for supper." Without waiting for an answer, Isra left them alone in the kitchen.

Tomasso stood awkwardly by the table for a few moments.

"You should have a drink. As you're here," Cristina said, pouring Tomasso some wine.

"If you insist." He sat down. "Oh, I brought you something." Tomasso offered her the parcel.

"A gift?"

"It was in the wreckage of the fire. I saved it, but thought I'd wait until everything had been sorted out. Didn't realise it would take so long."

"How exciting." Cristina took the parcel and peeled off the paper wrapping, to reveal a beautifully polished obsidian gem in the shape of a large egg. Suspended inside the glass were dozens of white crystal flecks.

"It's called snowflake obsidian," Tomasso explained.

"I remember seeing it on Visconti's shelves."

"It's one of the few things in there that was strong enough to survive the flames. Which is why I thought of you."

Cristina looked up, and for the first time noticed how gentle Tomasso's eyes were; she was so used to seeing him caught up in the maelstrom of work, she had never really taken the time to observe him properly. "Look, I'm sorry if…" Her voice petered out.

"You've nothing to apologise for, Cristina."

"Sometimes I say things too harshly, but I don't mean it. Things just come out the wrong way. It's always been like that."

Tomasso shook his head. "It seems quite the opposite to me. I have never seen anyone remain as composed under pressure as you."

The back of Cristina's neck started to feel warm. She didn't want to blush, but it was no longer under her control. "If this is what you're like before you've drunk wine, goodness knows what will happen after," she laughed.

Tomasso picked up his cup. "Let's find out…"

A NOTE TO THE READER

Writing *Palette of Blood* has been incredibly therapeutic. I completed the first draft during the late summer heatwave of 2022, and while the country flagged as the thermometer climbed, I wrote in an obsessive frenzy. The reason? One of the central themes of the novel is corruption in the arts, something I have experienced all too often.

When I became a full-time writer in my thirties, I assumed that people working in the arts would be brimming with integrity and inspired by higher ideals. How naïve. Although I've been fortunate to have met and worked with some brilliant people, I have also encountered ruthless schemers, shameless thieves and cunning manipulators, people who thought nothing of ruthlessly dispatching me if I was in their way.

A lot of pain has been left in the wake of those encounters, and the best way for me to deal with pain is to write it out. The problem is, telling those stories in a contemporary setting would be a sure-fire way of getting sued for defamation. But … what if I could transpose all those twisted dynamics into Renaissance Italy, with rival factions bidding to win the competition to design St Peter's Basilica? Then I would be able to let rip without fear of any repercussions. That is one of the great gifts of historical fiction, it gives you the freedom to write about the present while sheltering behind the shield of the past.

My research for *Palette of Blood* uncovered horribly familiar dark practices that would not be out of place in the most ruthless of today's Hollywood studios. It was alarming to think that so little had changed … and also strangely comforting.

I really hope you enjoy diving into the dark side of beauty, and please do let me know what you think. Reviews are a vital part of the creative process; the writer sits in their study typing away to an imaginary reader, but it's not until the reader responds with thoughts and observations that the circle is closed. That is how storytellers develop their craft. I would love to hear your thoughts on these novels!

If you have time to post a review on **Amazon** or **Goodreads**, that would be great, or if you'd rather give me feedback through social media, here are the links.

Website: www.RichardKurti.com
Instagram: RichardKurtiWriter
Twitter: @Richard_Kurti

Either way, I hope you'll join Cristina and Domenico on their next thrilling investigation in *Palette of Blood...*

Sapere Books is an exciting new publisher of brilliant fiction and popular history.

To find out more about our latest releases and our monthly bargain books visit our website:
saperebooks.com

Printed in Great Britain
by Amazon

29662168R00165